I0682030

Tropical Depression

Tyler Trafas

A surfer's journey from concrete jungle to empty shores

Cover art & photography by Kyle Trafas

Final copy edit by Abigail McArthy

Special acknowledgments to my mother for 33 years of love and support, my father for instilling a lasting admiration of history, Amanda for her love, support and head massages during this writing process, my writing coach and working editor James Gray Palmer whom I spent 47 hours on Skype with, all the other supporters who helped with encouragement, backing and the hurtles of bringing a novel to life, the unique people of Bali who share their paradise with the world and finally the energy of waves crashing on perfect shores.

Suksma

Tropical Depression:
A group of thunderstorms in close proximity which collect together to make one major weather system. Under the right atmospheric conditions, this tropical storm can culminate in a severe meteorological event.

Conflict

It's only seven in the morning and the sun is oppressive. Beads of sweat flow till they gather in every crevice of my body. I have never been this skinny. I need a belt to hold up my pants. Last week it was winched to the final notch, this week I had to cut a new hole. The thing chafes into my sides so insistently that blood is starting to seep through my white linen shirt. My feet are raw. Each step is agonizing, causing blisters to grow and multiply. This is not because of the sweat pooled in my boots, but a result of soft feet after years spent barefoot in the gardens of a Buddhist monastery.

Now, deep in the rainforest and far from the coast, the path winds farther from the familiar. The old growth is thick here. Palms and shrubs give way to an ancient canopy. Life is absolutely bursting at every turn of the narrow trail, seemingly unaware of our meddling. Blissfully ignorant. Animals both recognizable and mysterious, fauna massive to microscopic. As cool raindrops trickle to the ground they are quickly heated to steam and sent back to the sky.

The air is so thick I want to cut it with a fork and knife, savoring every bite.

This is where the water source is. Truly fresh, rich in earthen minerals: pure H2O. All the other water on this devastated island is salty, brackish and undrinkable, even at the peak of rainy season.

We begin to dig.

There is no relief from the heat today.

I am about as far from home as the curve of the world allows. Even the most powerful ocean swells rarely travel this far. Weeks of staring at the Indian Ocean in front of our camp. Smooth breaking waves over sharp reef, no one surfing. Instead we trample though this inland path to dig. We are here to help, not surf. The people need water. It is remarkable that something so basic and taken for granted back home is fought over so fiercely here.

Perhaps it is really about the smell. Back there the retch of humans cramped into refugee camps overwhelms the strongest perfumes of prayer services. Not here. Scents are subtle and delightful. Flowers are vivid and aromatic. Tropical fruits ripe on the trees. There is no organization to it, no planting, no human intervention. Mangosteens fall next to mangos, snakefruit with jackfruit. The rainforest grows at random but it is fair in its cultivation. The walk is worth it for the smells.

Panic.

The helicopters are close, nearly overhead. There is sporadic gunfire in the background to scare us off and for the most part it is working. The others don't know the difference. People begin to flee. We came here to rebuild and bring hope. In reality we fight bureaucracy, clash with armed carpetbaggers and grind away at a pitiful excuse for a water irrigation system.

It is incredibly hot today. Did I mention the mosquitoes? Those bastards cut through my linens like daggers into a block of cheese.

All the other volunteers have abandoned the project. Not me, not after five weeks of hard labor, chaotic disorganization and a bout with the bonebreaking fever. The guys in the helicopters have the guns but that does not give them the right to the water. I have dealt with scum of the earth before. Every gangster thinks himself more clever or daring than the last one: self righteous bullshit. These Indos are no different. Just a couple more yards of trench and the aqueduct will be complete. The Sweetwater well below my feet will flow. The people need this water and I have worked too damn hard to bring it to them. I will see it done, whatever the cost.

Or--- I will get pistol whipped by the miniature foot soldier behind me, then bound and dragged unconscious out of the jungle.

PART I

According to the architects of the US Constitution, all people are created equal by the hands of God. Wealth, the earthly measurement of success and happiness, is given from this God to those who pursue it though their natural given talents.

Grommet Days

My name is Deon Montgomery. Most people call me Eddie or Big Ed. I am Black mixed Hawaiian, a longboarder for life and nearly six and a half feet tall. That's two meters on the line for those on the metric.

Just about every Hawaiian thinks about getting off the island for a minute. That is how Mom met Dad, on the mainland. The first ten years of my life were split between the Hilo side of Hawaii, working on Mom's macadamia nut farm, with summers spent kicking cans around my dad's hood. When Mom died suddenly, I was forced to relocate to the mainland full-time.

Growing up in South Central Los Angeles in the early 90's was a trip. You might remember the days of Gangster rap though music videos, my stoop was front and center. Except, I was this tall, awkward, half black and half something else surfer kid in a time and place when it was not cool to surf and it was definitely not cool to be mixed.

LA is an alien world. Arlington and Adams is certainly not the same intersection of Coconut and Beach where Kai and Leliani loaned me their boards before skipping off to a day of work in the field. The street urchins here hustled a very different kind of skill and surfboards were not exactly falling out of the sky. I spent my early days of surfing L.A. trying to put together a few broken down pieces of foam into something that floated and turned.

I didn't see Dad much. He labored as a gardener by day and hustled extra cash by night. Guess a green thumb can be genetic.

The coolest memory of my youth was when he helped me plant a garden in the backyard. All kinds of good stuff can grow under the Los Angeles smog.

"Coffee beans make the best fertilizer," explained dad as he poured a week's worth of grinds over the newly potted soil.

"Really, coffee is so nasty."

"Just watch what happens," he told me.

Sure enough, we had sprouts a couple weeks later. Within a year we had Roma tomatoes, Japanese eggplants, cabbage, watermelon, peaches and strawberries of course.

Once it started growing, Dad took a genuine interest in my work. We had to move things around a couple times during a drought, forcing us to rethink our planting technique.

"Nightshades grow well in the damp air below the date palms," he told me.

"Thanks, Dad."

He taught all kinds of garden tricks. He explained proper irrigation and water control on a small scale. He talked about which plants want higher ground and which can thrive lower. He also demonstrated how to nourish and create a better topsoil quality through natural means. Dad was a bucket of knowledge.

"Here Dad, try this," I said as I handed him a fruit one evening after fighting LA traffic.

"What the hell is that, boy?" Dad asks.

"I'm calling it a 'pluat'."

"What are you on about Deon?"

"Try it," I insist and dad reluctantly takes a bite.

"Not bad, son."

"Yeah, I got the plums to knock around with the apricots and these little guys popped out."

It was only a couple hours a week at best we shared, but they were the best times we had together. One day my garden nearly reached the limit of the backyard, forcing me to search for a new place to work on my surfboards. Fiberglass and strawberries don't mix. The repair workshop went to the basement to save the fruit.

Freshman year of high school was the first time I got shot at. It was a drive by intended to kill a gangbanger named Jorge Azul living a couple doors down. He survived the attempt. I called the police and filed a report. Even though I had plates on the car, they did nothing. Later I learned this was a serious mistake as it painted me a target for the next couple of attempts on Azul. Not only was I caught in the crossfire, but this tied my survival to a street thug.

For everyone else in my hood, when someone shoots at you there were two choices: run or shoot back. Business was my solution. At fifteen, while repairing my enormous 1971 Harbour surfboard, I found fresh soil. There was a whole sublevel on the house's foundation with fantastically nutrient-rich soil just screaming for cultivation. The smell of the fiberglass resin covered the smell of the grass. The gangbangers didn't seem to mind the plastic taste of the smoke as long as I had a flush crop. Azul now had a great product at an unbeatable price. His crew went from a few to dozens and they held the entire neighborhood surrounding the Arlington and Adams intersection. I made more than enough cash to clear the exorbitant electricity bill and save some cash for myself. Mostly it went to new longboards that didn't weigh a ton. Eventually the guys responsible for the drive by shootings were caught by Azul's crew and taken care of. I was never harassed in the hood again, never.

I doubt that I would have survived high school without his protection. I did more than survive. I thrived.

From then on, in the summer I took the bus nearly every day to surf Malibu and Topanga. Those mini palm trees at Topanga State Beach are mine. I planted them as a science project. Back then there were no other black surfers, meaning the rich white boys from the valley gave me constant shit for being on their turf. Luckily they were a little more scared of the tall black looking dude than the thugs back in my neighborhood, but that didn't stop the group intimidation in the water or the four against one brawls on the sand. I learned how to stand up for myself at the beach early on.

I still remember the turning point:

This set wave at Topanga comes directly to me. A two paddle drop and an easy bottom turn right into the pocket. Then, Morrison Whiticurr, this slightly mental valley boy who did way too much cocaine in the 80's, deliberately drops in and cuts me off mid wave. I bend down and gently pushed his board away from mine so at the least we can both ride. Apparently not the party wave type, he tries to elbow me in the head, misses and we both end up falling.

When I resurface, Whiticurr lands a quick double punch to my face and shouts, "Don't ever touch my board again you dirty nigger."

He then takes my longboard, snaps a fin off it and starts chasing his own board toward the beach. I remained for a moment stunned and lightheaded - my hand resting on the spot where he nailed me.

That is when Alex, the local lifeguard, paddles out to the spot where I am treading water. Alex was a Russian ex-spy who defected to the US during the cold war. He has been a lifeguard ever since. He was always in perfect shape even at age sixty-six when the State forced him to retire. Alex was always cool to me growing up.

Alex paddles directly to me and says, "Eddie. Hey Big-E. Snap out of it." I must have given him a more alert expression because he went on to say, "Look, I see everything. If you want to handle this, I don't call cops." Then he paddled away for a few waves.

I catch up to Whiticurr bending down to check his board and tell him to stand up. He cranes his neck slowly and with an annoyed look and says, "Go back to the hood, Nigger." It takes one punch to put him down. As the whole beach watches, I turn his face into a basket of fruit.

"You wouldn't last ten seconds where I come from, wonderbread."

After finding a good stopping point, I take his board, snap all three fins off and calmly walk to the street where I catch the number 47 bus home.

That was the last fight I had over waves.

Around the same time, wetsuits were starting to come out in higher quality, it was just hard to find one in my size. That meant surfing the best winter swells in nothing more than trunks. Still there were some epic days. Towards the end of high school classes got out early and my longboard fit nicely out the back of my Jeep Wrangler. Malibu used to flow better than it does now and people actually followed surf etiquette, for the most part. There was this one south swell when 'The Bu' connected from first point to third. The drop in was hairy, sections were fast and hollow, even some tubes for the rippers. It was over two football fields long. I paddled for the wave of the day. No one dropped in or talked shit. It was the most memorable surf moment and the best wave of my youth.

Ghetto Split

Dad never had the same chance to fight back. After slaving all day in the lavish gardens of Beverly Hills, he powered through nights as a ticket scalper. He mostly worked sports games and concerts downtown. This was back when corporations were trying to monopolize scalping for their own capital gains and often encouraged the police to hassle guys trying to hustle an honest buck. One night, this massively fat cop caught up to Dad running from the shake down and decided to beat him half dead. Dad used to shout the name of this cop during nightmares: Sergeant Sean Henry. This cop was so determined that dad's hands now bend backward, a permanent disfigurement from trying to soften the blows to his face.

It was during the second day spent in the hospital with Dad that college letters of acceptance started showing up in the mailbox back home. Several top universities for science and agricultural studies sent offers. Among these, a full-ride scholarship was offered by the University of Hawaii, a part scholarship to San Diego State College and perhaps the tastiest, the University of Santa Cruz accepted me with full academic scholarship and a grant to cover living expenses.

A week later I found a couple hours to visit sanctuary. Even on flat days I went to the beach. If there was nothing to surf, I would take long paddles from Topanga to Sunset or Malibu. Sometimes Alex would join. Other days I would just stare at the water. Anything was better than the hood.

"Pizdets, this tough situation," Alex said in his thick Russian accent as we made it past the break. "Be finally happy or take care of Papa."

"I just can't leave him, man. Dad can't even pick up a fork to feed himself.

"It is good money, Deon. There must be another way, no?"

"You tell me, KGB."

"I know many babushki. Very gentle."

"First of all, I don't got any money. Second of all, what crazy white woman is gonna be popping in and out of my place a couple times a day?" I ask.

"Russians make the craziest white girls," he responds. We both laughed.

"The best thing you can do for your papa, be leave and go have better life."

"Like you left Russia behind?"

"Da."

"Don't you feel bad about that, miss your family and shit?"

"Niet."

I knew he was right but I couldn't just leave Dad behind for college, even as distant as we were. I tried the home nurse idea but since Dad always worked off the books there was no disability claim and it was doubly out of the question because no one of reputation would venture down to my block. In the end I had to decline all these opportunities so I could spoon feed my dad three times a day. I ended up at J/C and a year later UCLA, which has an excellent oceanography program with only a thirty minute drive to Malibu.

I had to give up my first profession during this time as well. Azul understood and out of respect, he carried on his protection of me and the house. I had to take things slow in order to make it all come together. My studies took five years to complete. Around the same time I graduated, Dad also qualified for state MediCal. At twenty three years old, holding a degree in Agricultural sciences with a minor in Oceanography, I finally had a chance to get out of the ghetto.

Unfortunately, my existence was now anchored to school debt. Being forced to turn down those scholarships hurt me financially, almost as much as the hood hurt me emotionally. So, like a cog in the system, the government bought my life. I served two years as a naval engineer in the Marines and then almost two more years in a special forces unit with a focus on surviving extreme conditions. The Panamanian jungle was a tricky place and not something I reminisce about. Shortly after a minor hurricane my commanding officer sent word that my tour was finished early for failing to report several months in a row. I was given a silent discharge and sent home. For time served, the military paid for my college loans plus put savings in the bank. More importantly, it taught me two new skills: How to survive and how to kill.

Back in Los Angeles for the first time since graduating university, there was just one piece of business to wrap up before freedom. I put on my old black gardening gloves and packed a shoulder bag with a red hoodie, an extra pair of sweat pants, a dark beanie and finally the pistol Jorge Azul left me to guard our crops years ago. The serial number on the gun had long since been filed off. I walked to Pasadena. It was a familiar path because I had walked it several times since locating him.

He lived in one of those older wooden beamed houses built at the turn of the century for the Los Angeles industrial elite. The house needed maintenance work that never got done. Waiting in the shadows seemed like an eternity. Sometime after midnight his car pulled up and an ogre of a man walked to the porch. He reached to put his key in the door lock. I fired two shots. The vibrations resonated down my spine. Despite all the training, actually killing a man in cold blood for the first time was debilitating. The emotion of the moment held me mute and unable to muster a sound to him as life faded away. All those things I planned to say to him left as his breath did. It's highly doubtful the cop even knew why he died or that his last thoughts turned to a senseless beating of a ticket scalper a decade before.

Training kicked in. Motion returned. I picked up the shells from the ground and began walking casually despite my throbbing arteries. It was autopilot. On the walk home, all evidence was disposed of by throwing the gun and the extra clothes contaminated by gunpowder residue into the LA River.

Dad never heard exactly why I had to leave the States the next night but I assume he figured it out from the ten o'clock news.

It was my first experience dealing Karma.

Absolute Yen

I bounce around China and Taiwan for a while, but it is way too polluted for my taste. Laos and Cambodia are too quiet for me and there is no surf. Thailand is kind of a scene but eventually the lady boys get to me. I hear about English teaching opportunities in Japan and decide it is my next stop.

Japan has a different pace and an inexplicably mechanical feel to it. Cities, trains, cars, lights, people, talking toilets, it all comes together like a futuristic bee hive. I hear about English teaching work for college graduates and hope to qualify. It turns out to be quite easy finding a teaching job in Osaka, which provides decent money, lots of late nights and a few days off to get wet. I spend a lot of free time exploring the Kansai region, one of the oldest and most traditional places in the Japanese archipelago. The Japanese culture, so different than the one back home, becomes deeply fascinating. Soon, I am spending as much time as possible learning about Japanese tradition and history.

One of my students tells me about a festival in the nearby city of Kobe and then hesitantly invites me to join. Despite breaking regulations against fraternizing with students, I excitedly agree to go. The first weekend of October, Hyogo prefecture hosts the annual Kenka Matsuri, loosely translated to the 'fighting festival.' Now don't get all excited thinking that this consists of Ninjas flying out of the trees to battle Samurai or ancient martial arts experts. In actuality it is more surreal.

The streets are flooded with Japanese spectators. There are about two thousand participants, all wearing diapers known as fundashi, participating in the festival. They are divided into teams of around two hundred men, each with a vital position. There are the flag bearers, the muscle and the motivation. It is the flag bearers' responsibility to distinguish their team from the others with the brilliant colors of their headbands and waving flags. They stay close to the hundred or so men who lift and carry the team's Mikoshi into the central temple arena. This Mikoshi is a portable shrine about the size of a pick-up truck, supported by solid wood beams that the team lifts with their shoulders. Each shrine holds four musically inclined priests who pound out a feverish beat on their giant drums.

The festival begins in the morning. Once all the groups have moved into the large arena by mid-morning, the sound of the dozen or so drum beats starts to come in sync. The teams dance around their shrines and entertain the tens of thousands of spectators who have come to watch the event. Local men and women carrying cauldrons of Nihhonshu, rice wine, move throughout the undulating groups practically forcing the men to drink their brew. So where does the fighting come in? The battle is in three areas: balance, balls and bashing. Around mid-day the teams are sufficiently buzzed and they begin challenging the other teams. One group will perform a stunt or maneuver with their Mikoshi and the opposing teams must match the stunt. If a shrine touches the ground for any reason, including exhaustion or error, the team has to leave the festival. So the stunts get more ballsy as time goes on and the rice wine really starts to flow.

By the late afternoon there are five of the eight original teams and everyone looks trashed. There is now an alcohol-induced ritualistic air in the arena and the Mikoshi really start rocking. Eventually one team decides to take it to the next level, shouting words of warning and then proceeding to ram their massively heavy shrine into another team's. If neither falter, another shout is heard over the drums, followed by the thunderous sound of a four ton metal collision.

By sundown only two groups remain. The audience lights lanterns and fireworks to illuminate the evening sky. In return the competitors continue the voracious spectacle until one shrine falls and one remains levitated in victory. The winning shrine is placed in the prefecture's main temple, where it will remain until next year's fighting festival. Then the victorious team is lifted up on shoulders all around and paraded through the temple grounds. It must be nice after supporting a Mikoshi for 10 hours.

After the festival, I learn that in the previous year a falling Mikoshi crushed a group of participants to death, a somewhat regular incident of Kenka Matsuri. I also learn that it is a great honor for Japanese to die participating in a traditional festival.

Cutting Rugs

During the day, Japan looks like a relentless machine of proper etiquette, sacrifice and 16 hour work shifts. Nights are different. The underground scene is booming. Business suits and work uniforms come off and the party begins. People, young and old, stay out all night to express themselves in one way or another, often clocking off one night from work and partying straight through until they clock back on.

Michael, a 5 foot 11 Kiwi, is the next largest foreigner I have met in Osaka. He teaches with me at the English school and one day catches me between classes.

"Say, Deon, you ever heard of a DJ named Carl Cox?"

"Can't say I have."

"Well he is kinda a big name in the music world. Plus he is probably the second largest aboriginal currently residing on the island." Mike gives me a moment to let his comment sink in. He loves to remind me that I'm the biggest black guy in Japan. "Well, he is playing in Umeda Thursday night. Wanna go?"

"Yeah, I'm down."

"Party favors?"

"What?" I ask.

"You know, a pill, brain candy?"
"You mean Ecstasy?"

Japan is also the first time I tried real drugs. I am on the train heading north to the show when Mike calls. He tells me that he has a nasty case of curry hot-bum and won't be leaving the can any time soon.

"What about the pills?" I ask.

"You gotta pick 'em up," he says matter-of-factly. "No worries, I'll pay you back for mine."

"He is your guy, how will I know him?"

"Oh, he will find you, Deon, no probs."

Being that it is a really poor idea to tell a Japanese drug dealer, "no," I buy the three pills he hands me. Reckoning Mike was gonna take two, and I am about double his size, I pop all three.

Coming directly from a Russian chemist lab across the strait, Ecstasy here is known for being pure and powerful. The beats pulse and the room reverberates. Everything feels amazing. I meet this beautiful girl and she starts to play with my hair. Amazing. I make eye contact with another across the room and we just know. In one fluid motion I cross the dance floor and lift her above my head like lifting a ballerina. We giggle and spin. Spinning is Amazing. Everyone is Amazing. I smile at the DJ and he smiles back at me. Someone has a feather, Amazing. There is some ice in a glass, Amazing. I kiss the ballerina, Amazing. We dance and dance. AMAZING.

We dance the entire night. We dance away the show and then the after party in Shinsaibashi and then the after after party at Cinquecento.

Then it is gone. The sun has been in the sky for an hour and the effects of the drug have disappeared, entirely. It feels like I have just been run over by a bus. Every muscle and ligament from the waist down throbs. Dehydration is an understatement. No matter how much water I drink nothing quenches this thirst. There is a five fingered scratch running the course of my chest. No idea how that got there. Oh and the headache, no words can describe this.

I try and sleep for an hour on a park bench without luck. I rush home for a cold shower. It is really cold.

I am met with a serious dilemma. In Japan, there are no sick days. Missing a day at work is not only missing good income, but also loosing face. It's not necessarily about the quality of your work, but simply the fact that you are there. When people see all those surgical face-masks being worn on the street, our first reaction is to think the Japanese are paranoid about getting sick. In most cases it is the opposite. The sick person is going about a day like normal, and as a Good Samaritan, does not wish to spread diseases. The face-mask is a preventative while said person saves face. The Japanese go to work, sick or near death.

I arrive at school just past 9am. There is a daily schedule posted in the break room. Mike is already there.

"Looks like it was a good show."

"Ygar," is the only semi-word I can muster.

My first class is with two little kids. Totally doable. We will bounce a ball around and tell Gokiburi jokes. The second is with Naomi and Juko, two middle aged ladies who can talk forever as long as it is about baseball. Third there is a free period and then lunch. That means two hours free. I can sleep.

It goes by almost as planned. The kids throw balls at me and I chase them around the room, pretending to be a giant cockroach. Then I learn all about last year's World Series. It's a struggle to watch baseball in the first place, but hearing about it really brings on the yawn. However, we power through the fifty minute class with little more than an apology here and there for being tired. That nap is just within grasp.

"Check schedule board, Deon–San," the school operator calls to tell me just at the moment my head leans against the wall for some Zzzz's.

My blood freezes. Mike laughs.

"Dude, they gave me Naoki. I will die in there. Please trade classes. She is like a hundred years old and I have to, I need to grab some shut eye."

"Not a chance mate. Staff says she actually requested you today," he informs me. "Plus it will be fun to see you suffer it out."

"Thanks a lot."

It is a full afternoon in the English conversation room and all the teaching cubicles are packed. The room is set up like any office space, except here there are five small teaching areas, separated by short, transparent, dividers to minimize cross-noise. You can see every class but cannot hear the conversation taking place. It looks cheap and compact but it is functional. I walk into booth 3, she is waiting.
"He-wow tea-o-cha," Naoki addresses me.

"He-llo, Naoki," I respond and open the picture dictionary I use when we work together.

"How are you to-day?"

She looks at me with a tilted head, a common Japanese mannerism seen when an individual is totally lost.

"I am good," I say, pointing at my own chest, "Anatawa genki des." I pause and point to her. "How are you?"

"Hmn," she grunts, indicating an understanding but simply saying, "Yes."

"Lets talk about food today." I point to a chapter in the book titled 'food'. "Can you say the word 'food'?"

"Hmn," once again she grunts, indicating an understanding but simply saying, "Yes."

"Oh, brother," I say to myself.

Flipping to an easy one, I point to a picture of a fish.

"Hmn," she grunts, "Sakana."

"Yes, fish." I ask slowly, "Can you say 'fish'?"

"Hai, Fish-e."

"At least we are getting somewhere," I say under my breath.

We get through sushi, fried fish, octopus, cow, beef - ooh, hamburger, McDonalds-su, cheese, Chi–ken, KFC, ho-ney-wah and a few others.

It is rough. My brain hurts. I struggle to stay awake and then I cannot. I hear music. There are flashing lights. People are everywhere, packed shoulder to shoulder. The place vibrates. It feels Amazing. Then I wake up from the dream. Seems I have fallen from my chair and made it to the floor, propped up against the wall separating booths 2 and 3. The room is disheveled. Our learning papers are everywhere. The desk is ajar and my right thigh hurts. I am a little dizzy. There is concerned chatter mixed with laughter. Everyone is looking into our class. Some are standing, some stay seated. They all point and gesture.

"Gomenzasai, Maiko-San. I am so sorry. I fell asleep."

She is standing and glares down at me while packing her things. We still have twenty minutes of class or so left. There is a look in her eyes I do not quite recognize. Some blend of dumbfounded, shock and fear. She backs out of the booth slowly and from a safe distance says, "You no sleep-y. You dance."

Sleep-dancing. That was the last time I rolled down E street. It was also the last day I worked a legitimate job.

A Black Man's Place in a Yellow Country

Being unemployed is not all that bad. Now I have time. I become more and more engulfed in Japan and its quirks. All my English conversations turn to the subject and I take as many days as possible to explore. I begin to learn Japanese and read the news in Romanji. I chat with anyone willing to teach me about this unusual place, my new home. My effort is not encouraged by most Japanese. Because of my dark ethnic appearance, I am constantly treated either as a celebrity or something grotesquely sinister, depending on the Jap.

One time on an early morning commute, I enter a half empty train car. I am wearing a full business suit on my way to an interview and I would say looking quite distinguished. There is a middle aged Japanese woman on the train car. From the time I board the train, her eyes fixate on me. A seat opens just a couple down and across the aisle from her. I take the seat. For three station stops she remains staring. She does not blink. Her eyes bulge. Eventually I say, "Ohayou Gozaimasu," which means, "Good morning," in Japanese.

She shrieks and runs out of the car.

The Japanese word Gaijin means, 'foreigner' or, literally, 'outsider.' However, a more culturally accurate translation would be something like, 'dirty stupid inferior.' Every person on earth who is not Japanese is called Gaijin. So, dating girls in Japan proves to be a challenge. The Japanese are so profoundly, openly and legally xenophobic, the only girls who would ever consider to date me seriously are Korean girls or other Gaijin. I find how deep this racism runs shortly after deciding to move to a more central area of the town, the only place a Gaijin is legally allowed to live. It is familiar to me because my hood at home bordered Koreatown in Los Angeles, just as my current apartment in Osaka borders the Korean Ghetto here. This is not Koreatown as most people from the western world would think of it: an ethnic enclave in which residents choose to live.

Ayumi, my girlfriend for a time in Japan is also considered Gaijin by the Japanese and its government. So, she lives in the Korean Ghetto of Osaka. She lives there because the majority of housing companies and apartment owners rent exclusively to Japanese citizens. Only specific areas of the city will rent apartments to foreigners and they are all within official ghetto borders. This is protected by common law and not considered discrimination. Ayumi does not speak Korean, nor has she ever been to Korea. Both her parents were born in Japan and so were her grandparents. Her great-grandparents came to Japan as laborers before the Second World War.

One night we are having dinner and discuss the fine points of her status in Japan.

"Lemme get this straight, your father is a full Japanese citizen but your mother is not?" I ask her.

"Hai," she responds in the Japanese affirmative.

She goes on to explain that her father, who is fully Japanese, is forced to live in the Korean ghetto as well now because his family, wife, son and daughter remain legally Korean, everyone in the family except himself. The only place Koreans in Japan are allowed to live in is "da ghettos." Ayumi will most likely never attain Japanese citizenship. Even if she does marry a Japanese man and have kids it is doubtful they will be considered Japanese either.

Now you can imagine how I am treated during my time in Nippon.

My interest in Japanese history and culture is not limited to old buildings, loud festivals, and eating. As interesting as these colorful aspects are, I blend better with the darker shades of Japan. Many people have heard of the secret perversions of the Japanese sexual appetite but in fact, most are not so secret and right out in the open. There is a massive industry build around this. At first it is just a whisper to me, then it becomes a siren.

First off, there is no legal age of consent in most areas of Japan. Neither are there legal regulations for arranged sexual transactions. In Japanese, the Term Enjo Kosai means "support sex." The rather new term was coined to explain a growing phenomenon in Japan. Young women, predominantly between fourteen and sixteen years of age, sell their virginity on the open market. Internet sites as well as black market agencies connect affluent men with this one-night golden opportunity. Prices hover between two and five thousand dollars, which for most working Japanese is a couple month's wages in yen. Occasionally agreements are made even higher. Customer and client connect and the transaction takes place. The most common thing girls purchase with Enjo Kosai funds: a Louis Vuitton handbag.

These transactions often take place in the shadowy regions of cities. I start to spend a significant amount of time in bars in these areas, having late night conversations with bartenders, one night stands with hookers and even more ominous characters. One night I am approached by Ken Kaunami, who, amongst other things, organizes discreet arrangements for the ultra-wealthy. He runs an after-hours gentlemen's club in the entertainment district of Osaka. It has four hidden rooms in the back. He offers me triple the wages of a teacher, to work security for him. Not only am I double the size of any Japanese man who comes through the VIP door, I am even more feared for my dark appearance.

All black folks are thugs or worse. Period.

I take the job and am witness to perversion like I've never seen
before.

All Aboard

On average, the Japanese workingman rides the train twelve hours
a week. Thus, it should come as no surprise that a few fetishes
have developed around train travel. One such perversion truly
swept the nation: the Chican. Originally, he was just a typical
letch, striking on crowded trains during rush hour. By wedging
next to women in jammed cars, he covertly strokes legs, buttocks,
or sometimes even breasts amid the confusion. The more daring
Chican has even been known to slide hands inside an un-expecting
passenger's skirt or blouse.

In the eyes of the Chican, the constantly pumping work machine
that is Japan seemed to supply a never ending playground. Even
better, the unapologetically patriarchal tones of the Japanese social
structure allowed the Chican to be fruitful and multiply. Within a
few years it was as if Japan was hit with a Chican epidemic.
Finally, after years of being forced to endure forty-five minute
train rides with ninja hands everywhere, Japanese women won a
small victory.

In 2002, Japan Rail introduced the "Ladies Only" train car. For the
first time in Japanese history women were given the option to ride
the train to work in a testosterone-free environment between the
hours of 7:00 and 9:00am. Usually marked by hot pink character
writing or a large flower, the "Ladies Only" car is always packed
to the brim during rush hour. Not one human being wielding a
penis is allowed to board the demarcated train car. The Chican was
left like a starving man, hands to the glass, staring through the
window of the best steak house in town.

Didn't anyone care about the Chican? Molesting women on the
train was his only excitement in an otherwise flaccid existence.

Not more than five feet away there was a whole train car full of prime, unsullied flannel skirts just waiting--just screaming-- to be lifted. No, some vindictive bastard scribbled the words "ladies only" in hot pink and purple all over the train car windows. They relentlessly provoked him from the adjacent car. How could the government allow this to happen? How could life be so cruel?

Relief had to come. Finally in December, 2003 it did. One man, one social philanthropist, one ingenious entrepreneur solved the dilemma. He first purchased a decommissioned train car from one of Japan's railway companies and had it placed inside an abandoned warehouse. The interior of the warehouse was then designed to resemble a train station. Next he hired around fifty women and dressed them up accordingly. Every evening the train car is packed with businesswomen, girls with pigtails, librarians, flight attendants, high school girls in uniform, French maids and the like. One cold winter night in the back streets of Osaka's Shinsaibashi entertainment district, Kaunami gave Japan its first Chican club.

That man is my new employer.

At an average ticket price of about two hundred dollars, our customers are allowed half an hour of unadulterated brushing, bumping, groping, rubbing, molesting, caressing, flicking, licking, pinching, blowing, petting and even biting. The fantasy is created with impeccable design. Every detail is attended to. Realistic train sound effects play in surround sound. Doors open and close while an ominous voice calls out station names. Even train attendants occasionally walk the aisle to collect tickets. You are allowed to grab them too, if that's your thing.

It is also a common game for the sponsor of an Enjo Kosai arrangement to board the train and search for his purchase. This is the girl who has auctioned off her virginity and the only one on the train who does not resist him, too much. As simulated rape is one of the most popular themes in Japanese pornography, there is usually a pretend fight on the train, a little struggle and then the girl is taken to one of the four back rooms in Kaunami's club. My job is to look over the scene making sure things don't get out of hand in public eyes. I wear a train conductor uniform. It is a very tight fit.

Faded Color

The summer heat has long passed and the autumn colors have fallen from massive maple and birch trees on the Kyoto hillside. Osaka has begun to grow cold, these changes go unnoticed. Every night I sit in my train security stall with fresh green tea in hand. Tickets are purchased regularly from the office in front of me where simply showing my face to new patrons accomplishes ninety-nine percent of my job.

They flock to the new club. Rich boys in school uniform take a break from studies. Band members before a show releasing some nerves. Friends sharing a rare night out. But most are drunk businessmen in full suits before a real train ride home to a wife. The ticket agent collects the fee and the revolving door spins. It seems to be in constant motion.

One night the cellular phone rings. It is large and feels bulky as I raise it from desk to ear.

"Moshi Moshi." The typical Japanese telephone greeting.
"Montgomery-San?" an unknown voice asks.
"Hai." The Japanese affirmative.
"Please come Room-Shi," it requests.

I leave my station and walk to the back of the club. Kaunami is there.

"Let me take your mocha, Montgomary–San," he insists as I hand him my glass of warm tea.

Security in the back is handled by Motoko Faiisan, a former Sumo wrestler champion who is both feared and revered by the clientele. In passing I notice he is not at his station.

Room Four is simple but spacious. It is painted bright white with white leather couches. There are two flat screens inside, one on the wall and one mounted above the bed. The same Japanese porn films play on a loop. There is an ashtray on the bed stand. The bed is made in a black silk sheet with two large pillows. I have only been to Room-Shi once before. A patron wished to see his prize penetrated by a black man. He tipped well.

Today the room is stained red.

"What happened in Room-shi?" I ask.
"What room? Kaunami responds. I glance back at him.
"Where is the patron?" My voice is shaking.
"What patron?" Kaunami answers again with a question.
"Where is the girl?" I survey the scene.
"What girl?"
"Have you called the police?"
"No." It is his first answer to a question.
"You are not going to call the police are you?"
"No."
"What am I doing back here then?"
"You are going to clean, Montgomery-San. This is why you are here." I notice the gloves he wears for the first time in our conversation.
"I will not."
"You will."
"But the po---"
"I will take care of the police," he cuts me off before I can finish.
"What if I go to the police?"
"You will not."
"I could."
He makes a hissing noise from deep within his throat.
"You are in Japan, Montgomery-San." Kaunami pauses for the demonstration. "Who will the police believe?" A smile forces itself through his black eyes as he puts my glass of tea down on the nightstand beside a pool of blood. Faiisan emerges behind him from the bathroom. "Me or you?"

In my mind I translate his words into their actual meaning: Human or Ape?

I am left without choice.

"Clean the room," Kaunami orders. "Be careful what you touch," he adds as he hands me a set of latex gloves and exits with my tea.

Like a proper Japanese servant I do as instructed. There is a large deposit into my bank account the next day.

Obosan

The novelty, the strangeness of it all pulled me in. Here I have grown comfortable in the dark. It matches. I am immersed in it full time, I grow callous and indifferent. I might blend in on the surface but only skin deep. When thrust fully into the shade of night, these dark practices that at one point interested me, that I wanted to witness and be a part of, that kept me employed, that kept me safe, that kept me in the shadows and away from the surf, that seemed to follow me my whole life, I am finally sickened by it all. I want out. I want a new path.

The answer comes on an emotionless day with my Korean girlfriend. There is about an inch of snow on the ground outside. We lay in bed after sex. She smokes a cigarette. I hate the smell. Her face rests against my chest. I will always remember how tiny she felt in my arms.

"Ayumi."
"Hai."
"I have just been paid my salary from Kaunami."
"So des."
"I am leaving tonight."
"Where will you go?" she asks coolly without opening her eyes.
"Everywhere. Nowhere," is my answer.
"I do not understand."

"I am tired of this Japan. The filth, the noise. I want to see the real Japan. I will seek Zen. I am going to find it the old way. I am going to take the path of an Ascetic."

"Deon–San, what do you talk about?" She still does not look up at me.

"I sold everything. I have two bank accounts now. One is in your name and can only be used to pay a good lawyer or bribe some corrupt city mayor. Kaunami knows people who will do this for you. Get citizenship for your family. You want it so badly. The other account is locked for a year. I am taking only what I can carry. Tomorrow I will disappear."

"Wakata, tzen tzen dijobu," she tells me. "Arigatou gozaimashita." Ayumi falls asleep. It is the last touch of a woman I experience for years. Over the next few months I travel on trains by jumping lines and over platforms. I hitchhike, although rarely get picked up. Mostly I walk. My feet become tough. I sleep on park benches and in subway tunnels. Cops harass me, guards shout profanities, people stare, fleas suck, dogs bite. I beg for food, pick wild produce and eat out of the trash. I visit hundreds of cities across Japan. The most impressive of all is Hiroshima with its decaying Atomic Bomb Memorial. I stare at it for days, the primary evidence of man's ability to destroy, then move on. I seek the natural beauty of Japan which struggles to survive in a country of concrete. In Nara I watch mochi being made by hand. I body surf the southern islands. I climb Mt. Fuji near Tokyo. I drink from the holy springs of Omizutori. I jump off waterfalls. I experience Sakura sitting under the cherry trees as they bloom. I watch people graduate school, watch people get married and watch people die. I hike through the snow-capped mountains of Nagano. I shoot an arrow down the distance of the Temple Sanjugsangendo where I beg the two thousand Bodhisattvas for help.

Eventually I find refuge in Koyasan. It is a mountaintop sanctuary only reachable in spring and summer. It is the place where the forbearers of Zen Buddhism originally came to Japan from the Chinese mainland. The monastery finds me. I help manage their gardens and farms. I eat only rice and vegetables. It is quiet for some time. I feel clean.

A Tidal Wave of Action

One morning I heard a different calling and left the place of Zen behind me.

It was a few days after the event when news of it reached the monastery. The Tsunami hit South East Asia just before Christmas 2004. Caused by the third most powerful earthquake in recorded history, which shook for nearly nine minutes, it was raw destruction. I felt the antithesis of Zen reverberating in me. The epicenter of the quake, just forty-five miles off the coast of Sumatra, Indonesia, created a wall of water which no one could have forecasted. The tidal wave engulfed and wiped out beaches from the southern tip of Sumatra, Indonesia, all the way up to Phuket, Thailand. It moved in other directions as well, reaching as far as Burma, India, Sri Lanka, Kenya, Somalia and many other coastal areas around the Indian Ocean. The entire earth's crust shifted just under a centimeter.

What most people do not understand about a tsunami is that the water line recedes quickly to power the shift in volume of the sea. To the average beach goers or villagers it looks like the tide has pulled all the way out and then some. That is why most people call it by its misnomer: a tidal wave. Reefs are exposed to the air and easy to walk on while fish and other sea creatures caught by the sudden change in water level are flopping about. So how do most people respond when viewing this rare event? They run towards the receded shoreline, dancing around with flopping fish. The only problem is when the water returns a few moments later it is exponentially higher than before the shift and people cannot breathe under water.

I got to Phuket the week after it all happened. The Thais had things under control; I learned the real mess was in Ache, Sumatra. A region of the country Indonesia, south of Phuket and far more exposed to the devastation. It took a week to get to Sumatra because transportation was so disrupted after the Tsunami. The wall of water made its way with incredible speed down boulevards, through buildings and flooded the entire area. Cars, bikes, hotels, villages, palm trees, dogs, people, anything near the shoreline was violently lifted and consumed by the sea.

In Ache, I finally got to put my college degree in agricultural sciences and my naval engineer training to work. After almost a year of volunteering in Ache, my group of relief workers and locals assisted in rebuilding six villages, a hospital, a mosque and a library all of which were washed away by the Tsunami. Most importantly, we rebuilt their agricultural base using a redirected irrigation and water filtration system. We had to move everything inland because all the topsoil was littered with salt, just as the ground water was flooded with seawater.

It felt good to do this work, but as with most opportunities it did not happen without consequence. Towns had to be motivated, gangs of thieves and scavengers had to ignore valuable materials lying around, magistrates had to be bribed and the money for reconstruction had to come from somewhere. We had claim to a piece of the multi-billion dollars raised worldwide for relief; it was getting access to it which proved quite difficult.

After weeks of dead ends, these hurdles were cleared over with the assistance of a man named Pak Hayarti. A military opportunist who transferred to the area just after the Tsunami, he had come to Ache to benefit from the suffering of others. A government sanctioned kingpin of sorts, Hayarti traded rights and permissions in dark corners during the reconstruction period. At times it felt he had fingers everywhere. In the end, he traded permission to rebuild, safety for my workers and even access to our funding because I was able to provide a bartering chip from my past: my Green Thumb.

Behind the guise of reconstruction and rebuilding fields of agriculture for those displaced, I was able to make Hayarti's newest business ventures grow. I was forced once again to earn my way by assisting the evil people of the world. Like in Los Angeles, like in the US Military, like in Japan; here in Sumatra it became my official trade. I do things for bad people so I can thrive. However, I realized for the first time in life, my success could also mean good things happening for innocent people who had no other way to survive. It is a delicate justification for my unique skill set, but it provides an application in the real world that I can live with. This dichotomy became my leading mantra as I departed from Sumatra.

As always in such ventures, the relationship with Hayarti had its complexities. Still, business went smoothly and our partnership blossomed. The nine month trail finished abruptly in a change of political tides and I was forced to leave my post hastily in the hands of the able volunteers who worked with me.

At that moment I desired only two things: good longboard waves and a hint of civilization. A flight from Ache to Jakarta is 45 minutes, a two hour layover at the airport, then Jakarta to Bali another hour flight.

Bali in Those Days

Bali has long been regarded as the surf Mecca of the world. The surfing hub of Indonesia, a chain of over 17,000 islands, it is one of the few places on earth that funnels swell, bends world class reefs and is blessed with trade winds that blow gently offshore all day during the cool dry season.

I check into the Balisani Padma Hotel in Legian Beach. It is a nice place built to accommodate some of the first non hippie/non surfer types coming to Bali in the 70's. After two years on my knees in the monastery, and nearly a year in the mud of Sumatra, a little luxury is appreciated. The place is designed in a traditional Balisese style. Limestone inlays on the walls and teak wood carvings depicting scenes from the Bhagavad Gita leading up staircases. The light aroma of incense from afternoon offerings to gods fills the entryway. My room has large vaulted ceilings and a massive plush bed protected by a mosquito net. The only modern addition to the hotel is the grand pool with swim-up bar where I have my welcome drink and then three more.

There is a case waiting for me in the room. Dad has shipped my surfboards from California. They are already at the hotel waiting, a huge board bag with two longboards. I have been riding Epic Shapes by Tim Phares since age sixteen. Tim has shaped a ridiculous number of surfboards in his lifetime and pours his heart into each one. They are not cheap but they are worth every penny. My boards are more like children! Giving them up all those years was excruciating. I spend the whole night grooming and then snuggling my babies, anxious for some morning waves.

The main drag in Bali is and always has been Kuta Beach. Just a stone's throw from the airport and a very classy beach break, the little fishing village of yesterday boomed into high-rise hotels, massive nightclubs, McDonalds, endless stalls and persistent hawkers. On what was once a black sand beach the locals imported white sand from Nusa Dua -- 27 kilometers away. Massive amounts of manual labor have kept it white since the 1970's.

As I walk down the streets first thing in the morning searching for a board repair shop, I am overtaken by endless drunk Aussies on their way home from the night's festivities. Shirtless, often trouserless and always belligerent, most are still holding one or two beers well past dawn. A pair walk by in matching hot pink booty shorts and fake tattoos of tits on their back. I manage to ignore most of the rabble but the ones buzzing by, three to a motorbike taxi and drinking from Viking helmets, force me to laugh. With the booming economy in Australia and high import tax, bogans flock to Kuta by thousands each day to spend their wages in a whirlwind of debauchery. Most of these Australian rednecks don't ever leave the four main streets of Kuta until their wallets and bank accounts are completely drained.

However, little things do remind me of Bali's uniqueness, even in Kuta. Daily offerings and Hindu ceremonies are more than background noise. Columns of women, beautifully dressed in traditional garments, gingerly pass the local beach boys first thing in the morning. The women balance on their heads many baskets of colorful fruits and vegetables as offerings to the gods. The shirtless beach boys are stacked with their rental boards and coolers for the day. It is a masked beauty here in Kuta, just on the edge of tipping towards mass development. One can see a delicate balance between the old simple ways and the new industrial tourism. Still the Hindus keep things in check. As much as developers would like to ravage the island, a few local laws keep things under control, such as the one which states that the tallest building in Bali must remain shorter than the tallest palm tree on the island.

All in all, the Kuta area is a great pit stop to work on surfboards, ride a beachbreak wave, grab a bite and then move on to better places.

During the first week in Bali I surf practically nonstop, hitting a lot of the famous beaches, using my motorbike to get quickly from one spot to another. I only slow down to eat or take a massage. If the wind changes direction on one side of the peninsula, I zip to the other.

Dreamland is my choice of beaches and the name is not accidental. A beautiful white sand cove just off the Bukit cliffs. When you look left, Dreamland has southwest-facing views all the way to Uluwatu at the very south tip of Bali's Bukit Peninsula. Looking in the other direction, it has a view of Kuta all the way to Tabanan in the West. Turquoise water laps over the white sand and meets green limestone cliffs on both sides. A few locals have set up warangs, which are local style restaurants with a room to rent above. Other than these wooden structures there are no signs of civilization.

Except for days when the swells are exceptionally big, the wave at Dreamland only works at low tide as the reef is very deep there. That also means hitting the Dreamland reef is rare, a nice alternative to other nearby waves where the reef is shallow or even exposed at low tide. There are actually two waves at Dreamland, a steep wedgy left wave that wraps in from Bingin Beach, and just down the sand, an A-frame which can sneak up out of deep water very quickly.

The A-frame is a fat building peak which can jack up quickly and make for a steep but very makeable drop. The left is good and quite racy, but always closes out at the end. This means a lot of swimming for my longboard if I surf without a leash. I prefer the right on the A-frame. It's a fun drop and then a quick 30 to 40 meter wall. Sometimes there is even a little tuck section, depending on how low the tide is. At the end you are dumped into a deep water channel and can paddle directly back without even getting your head wet. It is also the only wave around where a longboard has a clear advantage over a shortboard. The swell is running solid and despite crowds of nearly thirty surfers on the shoulder of the wave, I am the only one catching it from the peak. No one else seems hip to the advantage of a longboard here, meaning plenty of waves for me.

Surfing is the only time I find myself absent of mind. The past and the future seem to become distant entities and I can simply enjoy the now. It is tranquility and adrenaline together, an unlikely pairing. Surfing is my passion and my escape. It's the wave, it's the surfer, it's the surfboard, it all becomes one. Sitting on the board like the ancient Hawaiians, waves come rolling in. You turn, you lay, you look back and you stroke the surface of the ocean. A few paddles later you see it growing in size and power. You paddle faster because with every look over your shoulder you know you will need the speed to match that of the building wave. The wave begins to pick your board up from behind and every muscle in your body contracts. You stand to your feet and your body contorts in odd ways allowing both you and your board to drop down the face of the wave. For a moment all thought is lost. The world you know fades. Worries surrender to water. You are stoked.

I paddle out early on the second October morning of my trip. The sun is rising and I find perfect overhead peaks at Dreamland. I catch nearly a dozen bomb sets before realizing something strange: All morning I haven't seen another soul in the water. As the tide comes back the wave starts to shut down. I finish my surf very satisfied with about twenty successful notches in my board and the entire session completely to my lonesome. Both the sunset session and the next morning are eerily quiet as well. When the tide shifts high I jump on my bike and head into Legian Beach. There is only one guy out and we basically trade waves in each set. He is a blond shortboarder with a total SoCal vibe. He is really good and actually calls me into a few waves that I didn't think anyone could make.

"Nice wave, Big Dude," he half shouts and half laughs as I cruise by, five toes to the nose.

Jonah

We surf the rest of the morning and into the afternoon. Exhausted we decide to take lunch at Blue Ocean Café. When this place opened in 1969 it was the first bar/homestay on west facing Legian Beach, which was away from the headache of the Kuta crowd even then. Truly a hippie spot, the menu consists of food from all around the tropical regions of the world. Patrons take their food and drinks in giant blue lounge chairs with ceiling fans cooling things off when the ocean breeze is absent. The coffee is amazing, imported fresh from plantations in Java, brewed individually in a French press. All the produce is from organic farms nearby and the fish directly from the ocean out front.

Jonah and I become fast friends even though we have nothing in common besides surfing and California. But those are strong bonds.

Jonah grew up in the privileged life of a little Orange Country surf town called Laguna Beach. Laguna is famous for its live performance art show once a year and its multimillion dollar beach homes. Jonah is the quintessential California surfer dude. He is an amazing shortboarder. He is well acquainted with all the Newport Beach locals, especially after making surf history for charging the 'Wedge' at thirteen years old on the biggest swell of the 20th century. He could have gone pro at seventeen years old, but decided to go to school in Santa Barbara instead and join the surf team there. He surfed every day until a car accident with a drunk driver, which herniated his L4 and L5 discs in his back. This constant pain kept him out of the water until well after graduation.

When his father died suddenly from a stroke, his mother remarried -- a little too quickly some might say -- to a local real estate broker half her age. This guy then quickly made off with all the family money and skipped town. He was last seen trying to purchase a yacht somewhere in Europe. Jonah took a year off school to try and track him and his inheritance down but received little help from Interpol and gave up after several dead-end leads. Jonah's mom fell to drinking hard and moved in with her sister in Oregon. Back in California, Jonah finished university with a degree in sports medicine and a large financial debt for the first time in his life. He worked two jobs to save enough to have his spine operated on. After two years of sixty hour workweeks he had his spine surgery in Thailand so he could afford the cost and six months later was surfing pretty well again.

Bali, a world class surf destination, is only a two hour flight from Bangkok and once his back healed, it was the first stop on Jonah's adventure. He arrived the week before we met. I tell him my story in return, omitting certain darker details. It is a lot to learn about someone in one conversation, especially just after meeting, but we both feel genuine about this quick connection.

An hour before sunset I ask, "Have you noticed how empty the surf is out there?"

Jonan looks at me with slanted eyes.

"Where is everyone?" I ask.

"Are you for real, brah?" Jonah stammers more than usual.

"Yes, what's the deal?" I ask.

"Dude, you are in the surf bubble." He chuckles. "I was on Jimbaran Beach the other night for a little fish BBQ when, 'POW!' 'POW!' I thought it was firecrackers or something of the likes. Nope. Bombs, three of them. Some wacko, good times hating, turban wearing group calling themselves Black October decided to blow shit up."

"Seriously?"

"Yup. They hit like the three most popular tourist spots around. Duck that shit dude!" Jonah always uses the work duck instead of f**k, "They killed a ton of people too. Figure the safest place is in the water and that's where I plan to be."

"You got that right. So much for being safe on the island of peaceful Hindus in the most populous Islamic country on earth," I say.

"You not spooked? What if they start blowing shit up again?" Jonah asks.

"Not really, these things take months to plan, fund and execute. They already did the damage they wanted to do. Look at those empty streets," I say pointing to the beach road in front of the restaurant.

"No way, Big Ed, I am looking at those empty waves. Sunset Session, Brah!" Jonah grabs his board and I grab the bill. We surf well into dusk.

The next few days we see about the same number of people. All the tourists and surfers just seem gone. Jonah moves into my room and we are working triple surf session days, sometimes quadruple. I am convinced that if not for Balinese massages my entire muscle system would collapse. The week of Halloween I call the airline company.

"Can you repeat the question, please?"
"How long can I stay?"
"Do you realize that we have had hundreds of callers a day changing their ticket to the earliest flight out of Bali?"
"Even better. How long can I stay?"
"Well, how long do you want to stay?"

"Indefinitely."

Ketut

For a moment in time that is exactly how it felt, indefinite, without limit. Not only are the famous surf spots uncrowded but swells are bigger and more consistent than the typical season in the Indian Ocean. We get Uluwatu for a week with the same four Aussie rippers camping at the point. Our Junkin boat captain is glowing as the only surf shuttle of the day arrives and flags him down for transport to the outer reefs. Canggu is a ghost town. When the wind shifts during rainy season it is time for Nusa Dua, which we share with just a handful of fulltime ex-pats who couldn't be happier with the line-up.

The tourists have left, the hooded Jawas have gone home to Java, Asians are scared to visit, even the Norwegian hospitality university in Jimabaran takes a hiatus. It is empty and it is awesome. There are of course a handful of local Balinese surfers, who are undoubtedly the coolest local surfers on the planet, but still thousands of waves go unsurfed daily. It seems everyone surfs to exhaustion every day. No one smiles like a Bali brother stoked out of his mind on life.

Jonah and I paddle out practically alone at a break called Balangan one day. I am already out back behind the waves but Jonah gets stuck on the inside for a moment. On the third wave of a set, a tiny Balinese guy on a tiny board comes screaming down the line and nearly whacks Jonah. Jonah dives deep and the Balinese guy changes his near perfect course through the tube line just to be double safe. As he paddles back to the lineup he is singing, literally singing.

"Hey brah, I am totally sorry about ducking up your wave!" Jonah says. "I owe you a solid nugg and some bubblies."

"Hati Hati, me brodda." He sounds just like the Indo version of Jonah. "No worries."

"Thanks, man. Surf is up today, dude," Jonah starts to relax. "Didn't expect that set wave to be so big."

"Ja friend, surping bagus today, no?" he answers.

"Totally brah... super bagus, the surp is amazing." Jo laughs as there is no 'f' sound in Balinese so a lot of guys in the water call it 'surping.'

"I am Deon, this is Jonah," I interject a greeting which is very important in Balinese etiquette.

"Mi Ketut," he tells us. "Most Balinese names Wayan or Made because it mean first born and second born. Ketut is number four. It makes easy that way."

"Busy parents?" I joke.

"Yes." He smiles and points to the horizon. "Another good set coming, broddas."

"It is your wave Ketut!" Jonah insists while paddling backwards.

"Ok. Me go number two," he calls out in his Indolish accent.

"Good by me," I smile, "I'll take number one," I say while turning to catch the first in the set of waves. A quick rock back and two paddles latter I am cruising full speed ahead. Ketut is on the wave just behind, singing and laughing.

Turns out Ketut is local from the Bukit. He was a surf guide but without people to take surfing this month, he just enjoys the present tranquility. We quickly sign him up for the post. We travel together like the three musketeers yielding surfboards and chasing waves. Ketut is always with us except when there are Hindu ceremonies to attend, which is often.

"Yo dudes. We should check out G-land. The surf camp is about to close for a while cause no one is coming. Buddy says it is going off this week!" Jonah suggests enthusiastically.

"Cannot, have ceremony," Ketut tells him.

"Can't you get out of a few, dawg?" Jonah pleads.

"Cannot. Very important."

"What? K-Mart! I am talking G-land! It is empty right now. That sick ass left peeler Jerry Lopez discovered like 20 years ago. It's Ulu on roids, dawg! Tell me you've been there?" says Jonah.

"No," Ketut begins. "Waves here. Bali mi home."

One night we are invited to Ketut's home to join a ceremony. The colors and smells are incredible. If ever a people could invoke the gods' attention, it is Ketut's family. We meet Ketut's older sisters Wayan and Made and then the rest of the family. It is a full house.

"Tonight full moon ceremony. We must please the gods for making happy moon," Ketut's father tells us. Ketut's father is a Ketut also. Most Balinese families reach a Made and then cut things off. At most a Nyoman, the third born. Not this glowing family. "Full moon the time of most power. Things grow better now, people heal better." He goes on to explain. "Tonight we do Mapandes, ceremony for making Nyoman peace before marry wife."

Manpandes is the ceremony of tooth filing. Hindu Balinese believe that by filing away the sharp ends of the canine teeth, certain negative behavior such as anger, greed, and jealousy are removed from one's character. Several Balinese can undergo this ceremony at once and Nyoman is joined by a few cousins. The participants bring holy water, music, fireworks and many offerings. By tradition, Manpandes is one of the most important of the Balinese festivals and it ensures a good reincarnation. By the next full moon, Nyoman will be healed, spiritually and physically, meaning he is ready to marry his betrothed.

Jonah and I stay late into the night. Only a few guests remain. Some of the nephews play music on the Gamelan while we drink Bali style kopi with the family.

"Bali very special place. Surp is fun, work so have food, make new the sky first," Father Katut explains.

"You know gods make the universe, the planet, the waves, but in Bali we make it new. That is why we never leave Bali. Very important," our Ketut adds.

"Yes, must stay Bali for good Kama. Never leave or can be very bad," Nyoman says to us, drunk on pain. His smile glows nil aggression. We can't resist but to smile back.

So we stay in Bali.

Boys in the Rain

One rainy day at Keramas we are all sitting in a local Warang waiting for the weather to turn so it is surfable. Jonah broaches a new subject.

"De, all the girls are gone. I mean like all of them, bro!" he half jokes. "Think I am going a bit mental staring at your ugly mug every night."

"Jo, would you even know what to do with a real woman if you got your hands on one?"

"Oh for sure." He smiles. "I got the touch baby!"

I scoff.

"Ketut, you got a girl back on the Bukit?" Jonah asks.

"Yes, I marry one day soon. Already wife know Ketut."

"Very cool, my bro totally got his shit dialed in." Jonah offers him a big high five. They slap hands.

"OK, you guys. Top five things your girl must be?" Jonah throws out there. "Numero uno... ?"

Ketut is ready with the answer, "She must surp. Must be good surper. Very important."

"Number one in my book."
"Definitely."
"Bagus."
"Truth."

"Your girl surf, K-Mart?" Jonah asks.

"Yes. I meet her in water," Ketut tells us. "She is from village in Canggu."

"That's good, it's important she shares your greatest passion and you are happy doing it together," I tell him.

"Word."

"Why we haven't met her?" I ask.

"Cannot until after wedding ceremony."

"Very important?" Jonah asks laughing.

"Very important." Ketut smiles, showing his canines still intact.

I laugh.

"Deon. You are up on numero dos my man."

"Good sex. I'm not talking about a quick lay, girl's gotta be a superfreak, down to go the distance. We gotta have some serious chemistry. Talking get down sober goodness. Know one another and how to push those buttons. Don't get me wrong, she can have some boundaries. I can respect that, but when it's playtime, it's time to play. She's gotta give it up whenever, wherever," I continue. "Oh, and never ever ever ever get lazy bout it or let her shit slide."

"You put some thought into that one brother." Jonah lifts an eyebrow, surprised by my hoodspeak when it comes to females. We are quiet for a moment.

"My girl must smell good," Ketut interjects.

"Very important," I joke this time.

"Surf and Sex. Bagus!" Ketut laughs.

"Your turn Jonah," I say.

"Got it, girls have got to be self-confident and independent," he begins. "I am not talking cocky, but she should be able to joke and tease without taking serious offense. Both ways, you know? Some financial independence would be nice, too."

"Like you got cash flow independence at the moment?" I raise an eyebrow to Jonah.

"Well, at least a team effort. I am willing to scale things down to meet our means, sweetheart." He chuckles at me.

"Watch it, Jo. I could turn off that tap entirely."

"Jokes, right?"

"Also very important," Ketut jumps back in. "Able spend time apart. I go surp trips, she must be happy during time gone. Not sad."

"Truth," I say.

"Have at least one passion or interest which is independent of mine," Jonah adds to his point.

"What your second passion, Jonah?" Ketut asks.

"Girls," Jonah answers. "Duh!"

"Yeah, that will work out really well with the girl of your dreams." I laugh.

"My girl cooks Bali food, very delicious."

"That's what I am talking about." Jonah goes for another hi-five.

"She has got to have friends," I say. "If you are the only one the chick has around to talk to that can get a bit intense."

"Seen that happen to the homey, it's rough dude," Jonah says a little more grounded.

We all sit back pensive for a moment.

"Empat, number four, my girl must have same values me," Ketut establishes.

"Like what, Ketut?" Jonah asks.

"She must be happy with my family and want make new family."

"I dig," Jonah nods.

"Sure, and same feelings about how live life," Ketut goes on. "Only need simple life, surp, meet friends, make babies. Not more."

"Gotcha, if a chick is a party animal all night and I am up all early is for sure a conflict in lifestyle values," Jonah wedges his point into Ketut's.

"Cannot be princess and want, how say it? Castles. Very important."

"Hear you," I say. It's good to go out once in a while, especially if the waves are flat, but for the most part all the cool stuff happens during the day."

"Agreed braddah."

"Number five. Emotional stability," Jonah begins. "I can't deal with mood swings, hyper sensitivity, overt jealousy or any a that shit. When it is time to relax, listen and talk logically, both of us gotta be able to make it happen."

"I like the jokes with everyone. Laugh very important," Ketut says, a little out of context. "Must Laugh."

"Hear yas, K-Mart. Quips are a must." Jonah doesn't seem to mind the tangent from his unusually grounded statement. "Also, no power plays. Love is a team effort."

"Good call Jonah." I am surprised by his dead-on wisdom of relationships. "You nailed that point on the head."

"Thanks, De. Had a lot of thinking on this stuff. Really hope the next girl can hang with me and sticks around."

"I hope this also for you, Jonah," Ketut says.

"One last go," I jump in.

"That makes six, dude. Don't know if it can be allowed." Jonah is unsure about how he feels in breaking the boundaries he set for the conversation.

"It's ok, Jonah, I want hear Deon," Ketut defends me in breaking the rules. Then he smiles in teasing himself and says, "Maybe very important."

"You cannot expect your partner to change, or worse, that you will change your partner." I open the last point for discussion.

"Totally hate when chicks are all into it just to try to make you different than you are." Jonah is satisfied with my last point. "People are who they are. Straight-up."

"Agree. Little can change during one Kama cycle," Ketut concludes.

"All this sound like your woman, Ketut?" I ask.

"Yes, she bagus all six," he replies.

"Have a feeling it is gonna be a good wedding," I say.

"Yeah and in a few years little Wayan and Made are gonna rip it!" Jonah shouts as he jumps over the table to hug Ketut.

"Without question," I laugh.

"Does she have any sisters?" Jonah asks with a smile.

"No, sorry friend. Wish we real brothers," Ketut says a little seriously.

"We are, my brother from another mother!"

"More like Sister from another mister," I am about to slap Jonah upside his head. "God I hate it when you try to be all ghetto, foo!"

We chill at that restaurant for hours talking and laughing. The weather never allows us to surf. In fact, it stays flat and rainy through the peak of the wet season. Jonah starts to show signs of withdrawal from wave and girl. However I am content with the small days and truly enjoy every moment as it comes. It is the first time in life I understand the meaning of the word "friends."

Besaki

An area on the west coast of Bali known as Canggu seems to pick up the most swell this time of year. It has a racy, reefy beachbreak and a fun outside longboard wave. In other words, there is something for everyone. Over the next couple weeks we only see a few local cats and some Aussies working on their house. Then it goes flat for real.

One flat day, Ketut convinces us to visit the core site of Balinese Hinduism with him. Up toward the heart center of Bali sits Mount Agung, 10,000 feet above the ocean. It is an active volcano and home to one the most sacred sites in Balinese religion. Ketut drives at a pace which he promises will not disturb the sleeping gods. It takes a while. On the way he tells us that Agung last erupted about 53 years ago and the fingers of molten lava barely passed by the mother of all Balinese Temples, Besakih. Its salvation is still held as the most miraculous sign from the gods in modern history.

The original temple was built over a thousand years ago on a terraced platform, incorporating the natural slope of the volcano into its architecture. Since its creation, the temple has been dedicated to the dragon god of fire, Besakih, who, it is believed to this day, still inhabits the sacred mountain.

As it is the heart of all Hindu worship in Bali, every islander must make a pilgrimage at least once in life. This is part of the reason why Besakih is the only temple in Bali where Hindus of any caste can pray together.

Besakih is unlike any temple I saw in Japan. It is phenomenal to look at, ornate and unique. Every block that creates the place is hand carved and one of a kind. Every move of the eye draws attention to another artisan's work. The Stairs at the entrance climb through a monumental spirit gate and ascend up the multi-level complex. There are also countless lesser shrines, each one dedicated to a different god or goddess. In the temple complex, each regency of Bali maintains its own minor temple in the outlying orbit of Besakih. The stairway continues up level after level, leading to a vast courtyard at the pinnacle of the main temple: Pura Panataran Agung. It hosts the central shrine, with massive dedications to the Hindu trinity of Brahma, Shiva, and Vishnu wrapped in the checkered cloth of good and evil. Every shrine, every step, every block is covered with flower offerings. It boggles my mind to imagine what the temple looks like dressed up for a major ceremony.

Before we step through the spirit gates at the entrance, each of us wraps a sarong around our waist and a white shirt over our back. It is the minimal dress code to enter any temple in Bali.

"Yo, De, you look like a scary ass demonic Bali goddess in that skirt." Jonah laughs.

"Appropriate buddy. Really spot on."

"Gotta say, this place is pretty sick."

"Bagus, yes?"

"Definitely Bagus, Ketut."

The inner courtyards are reserved for worship and closed to foreign visitors. Ketut goes inside one to pray for the success of his marriage and the wellbeing of his first born. We wait outside for some time, lock-jawed in awe at the temple complex. Ketut returns, smelling a little sweeter. Then, just as the three of us turn to go higher up, Jonah whacks a mosquito sucking blood from his neck and Ketut forcefully grabs his hand.

"What gives brah?" Jonah asks, cockeyed.

"In Bali, cannot harm others. Small or big. Everyone family."

"Yo, K-T. It was sucking my blood. Is that not reason enough to put the smack down?"

"No. Not good reason. This what Mosquito do, how gods make them do. If you kill Mosquito for being Mosquito, you attack the gods. This bad Kama."

"I don't get it," Jonah states flat out, his wrist being held firmly.

"OK, explain again." Ketut carefully picks the pieces of dead insect from Jonah's hand.

"If you kill Mosquito there must be purpose." Ketut stops speaking to put the remains of the insect in his mouth. "I am hungry so you give Mosquito for eat." He swallows. "Now nothing wasted. You Kama clean."

"Gnarly."

Perks & Peaks

A few weeks later, Jonah appears to be going mad from the nil wave situation. Ketut and I scramble to find ways to pass the time and more importantly keep his mind off the flat ocean surface.

We scuba dive a WWII liberty shipwreck in Tulamben. Our dive master Putu is as wacky about diving as we are crazy about surfing. He is an Indian Ocean encyclopedia of knowledge. One dive he brings us to a station on the wreck where a colony of Scarlet Skunk Cleaner Shrimp live. When he opens his mouth near the reef, shrimp swim in and clean those pearly whites. On another dive he takes us through a trigger fish breeding area. Apparently they focus their attacks on the biggest threat, which of course was me.

I buy a small speedboat thinking we can use it to visit Manta Point and other dive spots, then when the swell comes back we can use it to surf outer island breaks. It seems like a great idea, until I let Jonah drive. Now there is a new shipwreck to explore.

We visit ancient ruins and loose our sunglasses to gangs of monkey thieves. We join a Yoga studio in Ubud where Jonah is immediately shot down by the first woman he has seen in weeks. We gamble on Cock fights and Oxen races where Ketut somehow manages to win quite a bit of money. He chalks it up to his ability to communicate with animals.

Probably the funniest single moment during the flat spell happens over coffee.

"Satu Kopi Luwak," I order from the counter at Kopi Pot, a super fancy spot on the highway between Sanur and Legian. The coffee shop is decked out in teak tables and cute baristas. Photos and sketches on the wall depict scenes from the golden age of coffee plantations. Maps pinpoint areas of Indonesia known for growing premier coffee beans. The aroma of the place is unforgettable.

The guys have gone to find a spot in the empty dining area and our table is in the back as close as possible to the barista Jonah is working hard to crack. She ignores him and continues working the delicate Chemex brewing process. As she finishes, a smile is passed and Jonah assumes it is for him.

"Ya brahs, see that, she is totally mine," he gloats prematurely.

"Good luck Jo." I laugh.

"Ya, semoga sukses," Ketut wishes him luck, knowing first-hand how hard good Balinese girls are to pick up.

"Oh laugh it up you giant Wookee." Jonah catches the sarcasm. "This is on."

She brings the freshly prepared pot to our table and stands at attention.

"Bagus kopi boss," Ketut says to me immediately as he detects the distinct aroma when the pot arrives at our table.

"They say it is the best," I tell the guys as the Barista moves in to pour us three espresso size cups.

"Yes, very bagus," Ketut says, enjoying his first sip. "Satu Lage!"

"What's so bomb about this?" Jonah takes a sip without taking his eyes from the girl behind me.

"Ketut, you wanna explain this one?"

"No. I just enjoy, Boss." Ketut gives that radiant smile.

"Well then, a few centuries ago, coffee plantations in Indo were all worked by indentured servants who were forbidden to drink any of that kickin' Dutch coffee. But, the slavers hadn't said anything against snacking on the processed beans laying around the ground. So, that's exactly how the slaves got their coffee drink on. Over time, they realized that a lighter bean lying around tasted quite a bit better than the darker ones which fell directly from the berries. They began searching these out more frequently, cleaned them and gave em a light roast before brewing."

I pause to finish my first cup of coffee, the boys do the same. Our barista pours us all a fresh round and I catch Jonah trying to make incidental contact with her hand as she passes him a fresh cup. I continue the story.

"Guess at some point a Dutch master caught them sipping away and tried some of their special roast. Having sampled both regular coffee and this one, he realized the flavor of the new brew was quite different than the regular roast they harvested. The slaves were forced to tell the secret. Turns out the white beans used to brew this special roast were pooped out by a large ground cat know as a Civet. Now, because of the unique flavor it is the most expensive coffee on the market.

Jonah stops mid sip and holds his cup in hand. "So what you are saying, man, is... that I am drinking coffee... directly from the butt of some giant cat."

"Basically."

"Duck you, Deon!" Jonah shouts. I dodge the projectile but the beautiful Balinese girl is drenched in a $20 shot of coffee. The cup smashes to the ground. Ketut and I roll on the floor just short of pissing ourselves. Minus that direct hit, Jonah completely strikes out with the cute server.

The swell drought pushes further into the wet season and Jonah is developing full blown signs of a mental breakdown. Even I am really starting to crave some real waves. Finally things change. The swell gets big time without much notice and Ketut talks of a place way up East Coast Bali. Supposedly it is a wave that only breaks when things are huge. He tells me I will really like it because it breaks like California waves in the movies. It takes a couple hours to drive it. Turning off the main road we weave through a coconut farm to approach the break. We arrive before dawn. The wave is insane and we surf it for hours alone. Might as well be surfing warm water Topanga or Malibu, just your boys.

We trade off waves, whistlin', hoopin' and hollerin' till our arms feel like rubber. This thing is so performance oriented that Jonah can smack the lip about fifteen times on a single wave and then falls because his legs are out of shape. Ketut shouts out, "Party wave," and all three of us drop in together, weaving in and of the pocket, giddy with joy. The smile reaches from ear to ear.

Then it happens. Three vans stacked high with surfboards all pull up at the same time directly in front of the break. I look at my watch; it is only 8:25 in the morning.

"There goes the morning bliss," Jonah whines.

Except, out comes the O'Neil women's surf team. Longboards, shortboards, fishsticks, in the water photographers, the whole range. They are hot and they can surf. One girl is from Newport and knows Jonah right away.

"Sounds like the Gods heard your cry Jo." I laugh.
"Good Kama brother," Ketut points out.
"Yooooo. I have never been so happy to get dropped in on my whole life!" His smile reaches longer than imaginable.

For a time, the three of us are inseparable. We explore, we surf and we fall in love with Bali. But all good things eventually come to an end. It is two very fast years before crowds start to come back. The thick traffic and fat tourists as well. Jonah is surfing top notch again and anxious to try the professional circuit. I have my own reasons to leave. Amongst others, bank accounts are empty, teeth are starting to decay and we finally decide that it is time to move on.

"Brah, we might a missed the pioneering days of surfing Bali by a few ticks of the clock, but we just got it as good as it gets," Jonah tells me before heading off to Ngurah Rai Airport.

"Truth." I smile. It was the best two years of my life.

Since Bali, Jonah and I went our own ways but always stayed in close contact. Jonah went on a semi-pro tour of Morrocco, South Africa, Nicaragua and Brazil. The first time around, he placed second overall out of fifty world class surfers. The next time it was third place. In his words, "You can only blame it on pussy swell, pussy judges and pussy punts." Jonah needed to place first in order to get a wildcard opportunity on the world tour. So, he quit the hustle of the pro-life and moved to a heavy beach break in Mexico called Pesquales.

I found the waves and crowds of El Salvador more to the liking of my 10 foot longboard. These are the volcanic beaches where surfer bums from L.A. came to film surf scenes for the Hollywood surf movie called Big Wednesday. A few never left. It's a country of warm water right hand point breaks with waves that gently caress your board as you slide over the large black boulders below. El

Salvador is a small country of just seven million. El Salvador recently ended its very bloody civil war, which put more firearms in public hands than in all of the United States. It has some of the roughest surf locals I have come across and a hardcore gangbanger scene. It reminds me of the hood I grew up in but right on the beach. It's just the kind of place I know how to live in, but that is a story for another time.

We always promised a reunion in Bali, which finally came to fruition in 2012.

PART II

According to the Buddhist tradition, there is only The Path to be walked. Personal Choice leads Karma closer to suffering or farther from it. Darkness is on one end, Enlightenment the other.

Reunion Trip

"Dude, he dropped in on you sooooo hard!" Jonah shouts as he comes ripping in the doorway. "Kook is from Austria, ducking Austria, the only waves they surf there are the ass ripples of 300 pound big chested blonde yodeling -- beer stein wielding -- mountain broads ... from behind. Duck it! Nations without surf should not be surfing! Done. Uluwatu none the less. Ulu-Ducking-Watu! Done. No really, unreal! How you feeling, Big Brudda Ed?"

"Pain, man, pain," I reply. "What happened?"

"So there you were, perfectly in trim, halfway to the nose and this Euro-Tard just dropped. Total disregard dude, the whole lineup was watching that wave. The rest is ducking history. Luckily, you were wearing a legrope today. I managed to get you halfway back on the board and tandem rode the next breaker back to the cave. Bunch of Ulu locals carried you up the stairs and got you to the hospital as soon as possible. Only took an hour to drive 12km ... not bad for Bali these days. Damn foo. What was that, like a 20 minute straight shot back in the day? Anywhoo brah, they have the whole thing on video, dude uploaded it to his iPhone and we watched it like a hundred times on the way here."

"And the board?"

"Ha. You would ask that, Big-E. Your stick is banged up but nothing the locals can't fix. I ditched mine to get you into shore, doubt I'll ever see it again."

"I love that board. I'll get you another board, Jo," I say as I touch the stitches in my chin wrapping around to my jaw. All seventeen of them.

"No worries, big guy, I got Ketut on it. He followed this little Euro shit, who totally tried to bail by the way, right back to this kook hole - $1000 bucks a week - European surf school in Padang. Shits me to even say that, 'surf school' in Padang Padang. Anywhoo, he got two black eyes and Ketut misplaced his passport till this mess is handled a hundred percent."

"Don't you think that's a bit much?"

"Have you looked in the mirror yet?" Jonah shot back. "Anyway he should not have run, would have saved himself some exorbitant eye makeup cost at the least."

"Hey, Jonah."

"Yeah, Bradda?"

"Thanks," I say, "I owe you a big one. Now get outta here and let me pass the hell out."

"Jokes from above. Sweet dreams beautiful." The door closes quietly as Jonah leaves. So do my eyes.

I wake up sometime later and there is just a little evening light coming through the window. I pull back the curtain and look out onto Jimbaran bay below. I am on the third or fourth floor. Thousands of tourists are eating fish BBQ just down the beach below me. The smoky aroma of the dried coconut husks used for fuel seem to permeate everything. I look around the room and notice curtains drawn on both sides. I can see by shadow that my room now has two more patients residing inside.

In the dim light I make my way over to the bathroom sink and flip the light switch.

I keep my eyes down, unwilling to face the mirror yet. My head hurts. A lot. Seems just the thought of thinking inflicts pain.

With a shutter of nerves I grit my teeth and start to piece together the incident.

It was the big outside set wave I had waited for all morning. Most of the hundred other guys surfing Uluwatu that morning could rip the inside, smack the lip and get tubed wave after wave. I needed a big one. The big ones at Ulu open up and wrap the reefy point with a huge wall of water. What looks like a three foot swell out back can easily turn eight or nine feet on the inside of the break. When I saw the wave my heart jumped into overdrive. No matter how many times you make a wave at Ulu, the next one is just as scary as your first. A dozen or so back paddles put me in a solid position for the biggest wave in the set. I turned and angled my drop. With my right hand on the front rail and left fingers guiding me backside across the face, I pulled into the wave of the day. I made it.

Then I remember the drop-in kook job and the guy coming over the lip. I was trying to go low on the wave to avoid the impact with this renegade fuck. I don't think he ever landed the drop, meaning he must have fallen vertically six feet or so, straight to my head. I trace the bandages on my scalp and what remains of my left ear. The fins they make these days are sharpened to a razor's edge. I sigh and look into the mirror. The third line running up my chin is not bandaged but stitched. From profile it kind of reminds me of a kid drawing a joker's smile across my face.

My right shoulder and hip burn like someone is perpetually pouring hydrogen peroxide into the wounds. That's where I must have hit the reef first. I pull back the hospital gown to find bloody cotton bandages wrapping my arm and waist as well.

"Doctors said they picked out at least four species of coral and a fish hook from your right side," says a husky voice from behind the curtain separating our sections of the hospital room.

I peer over my right shoulder in the direction of the voice. "They say anything else?"

"Yeah, you are lucky you missed your head on the reef, some of those corals and rock fish have neurotoxins in them."

"How about my recovery time?"

"Don't sweat that one kid, you'll be back in the water in a tenner, just gotta let those holes close before then cause that Indo Ocean is bloody cankerous."

"That's more than I could get out of them. Thanks, you speak Indo, too eh?" I ask.

"Been here long enough, but a Bulet is always a Bulet," he explains.

Bulet is a slightly derogatory Indonesian term for a foreigner, especially a white man.

"Must have taken a good fall, eh?" he asks. "The reef at Ulu ain't something to get dragged across mate."

"You are telling me."

"How'd her happen then?" he asks.

"Euro-Kooked. Swear, there are more and more of them every year. And not from the coastal countries like Spain or France. We are talking places like Poland and Austria, as land locked and potato fed as they come. Once upon a time surfers had to know how to surf and earn a place in the lineup. Now they hire local kids to push them onto waves and call it surfing. When did this all become acceptable? Did real surfers just give up trying?"

His laugh turns into a wheezing noise.

Realizing I am on a little bit of a rant, I pause to look back from the window into the direction of the voice. I can barely make out the curtain folding around the small hospital bed, bent by the gentle breeze of the A/C in the room. Whoever this guy is, he remains in bed during our conversation.

" 'Euro-Kooked' Ha, killer in me, that's what I overheard from the SoCal kid always comin here checkin in on ya. Your boy handle that business, at least?"

"You could say that. Jonah might be little but he has a way of getting things done. It's a sort of accidental responsibility," I explain. "What are you in here for anyway?" I ask in an effort to change the subject. I am still not entirely comfortable with the retaliation, even if it was warranted and proportional.

"Bit a madness mate, bit a madness."

"Aren't we all." I laugh.

"Not even a likeness," he stammers back. "Only those who have touched perfection know its dregs."

After his long coughing fit I don't hear from his husky voice for another two days. We hold a few more conversations but mostly I do the speaking and he does the listening. When I do hear from him, it is mostly in the form of ramblings or further coughing fits. Jonah comes by a few times over the week but there is plenty of swell in the water to keep him occupied. Mostly I try to occupy myself with books and newspapers about Bali and watch an occasional surf video. It's hard to be on lock down while there is good surf to be had just out the window. The anxiety grows and grows until it finally bottlenecks and chokes me. Plus, having Jonah continually coming by to tell me, "It's so ducking good out there, brah!" doesn't exactly help smooth the situation.

Paradise under a Bulldozer

The day before that European kook job at Uluwatu, I went to track down the family I once stayed with on Dreamland Beach. They were the first to show me the beauty of this land and the people. Then, happily lost in a time warp for generations, they were forced to relocate to a barren hillside this year, making way for another massive apartment development targeting retired Europeans and Aussies. They had lived on the cliff top hills looking out at the Bukit peninsula for as long as the family could trace its ancestry. For Balinese Hindus, this is a very long time. There is now a massive neon colored nightclub sitting on their land.

For twelve days now I have been back in Bali, seven spent in this bed. When the power is off, as rolling blackouts are something of normality here now, thoughts of our past life in Bali creep up and then they are smothered with the shame. This trip and sitting on this bed has given me ample time to reflect. I barely recognize my favorite little island on earth. The drastic changes over just the past five years are daunting and horrible. More than that, it has shocked me worse than ever into an understanding of the nature of people. Not just the greedy and evil people but humans as a species.

How could this be allowed? Where is the good in it? How could we consciously and purposely destroy something so fantastic?

Bali is forever altered. The high-end resorts of Jimbaran are just outside. The newspapers and Internet tell me details. I soak up information and search for answers. Uncontrolled business prospects under the Asian Free Trade Agreement have destroyed her beauty, gutted her hillsides into limestone quarries and put fifty new cars a day onto her intricate roadways through the rice patties. The magic of the religion, one that in past times was literally held responsible for the renewal and revitalization of the universe on an hourly, daily, monthly, seasonal and yearly basis, has been reduced to an arena show for hordes of package tourists.

I look around. I read on. I become ill.

Cheap urban sprawl dominates the once green island as seemingly endless investment money pours in from Jakarta, China, Russia, Australia and Europe. Financial sources both legitimate and otherwise. The vibrant red and yellow colors of Balinese temples dressed for offerings and ceremony gatherings has become more and more boxed in and bleached by the encroaching grey of concrete.

Developers are destroying the reefs and mangrove forests of Benoa as asphalt is being laid to create a floating car highway above water in an effort to connect Jimbaran, Nusa Dua and Benoa quicker. They are also constructing the Dewa Ruci underpass, a feeble attempt to move traffic quicker at the Sanur to Kuta roundabout, the most congested spot on the island. The construction project alone has created more traffic than the finished product could ever hope to alleviate. They are in the final stages of construction to expand the Ngurah Rai Airport, allowing thousands more to fly into Bali each day.

I want to scream, "Enough!"

Highways move at a crawl. Prices on everything have doubled or tripled. Real estate battles and bidding wars between investors are common, oftentimes raising the purchase price of desirable locations tenfold. Surf breaks must suffer double or triple their maximum capacity. Japanese 'surfers' hire people to push them onto waves. Brazilians flock in packs of ten or larger and bring their world famous etiquette and peripheral vision blinders with them. Unskilled migrant workers from Java squat in slums and garbage dumps where they try to earn two or three dollars an hour on multi-million dollar development projects. There are a dozen surf camps in Canggu.

There is no shame. It is just western progress of course.

Perhaps the worst example of these dramatic changes comes to the impact on the environment. Last wet season, when the wind blew hard from the southwest, hundreds of metric tons of floating plastic and trash, combined with the dead sea life killed by it, washed up on the shores of the west coast beaches. It took weeks for Balinese locals to make headway through the trash and the dead sea animals. Despite valiant efforts there was no way they could get it all before the next dry tourist season. So, when tourist and travel writers asked where the trash came from, investors and entrepreneurs told a plethora of different excuses and sources, not one of them pointing a finger at the real cause: unsustainable mass tourism.

Bali, once the island of the Gods, has become the island of Trash and Lies.

Discharge

Today I am to be set loose from the hospital. Most of my wounds are dry and semi closed. The stitches in my chin are the kind which will dissolve in a few days. I am still not sure when I can surf again. A new doctor comes into the room.

"How are you feeling today, Pa Deon?" he asks.

"You speak English."

"You are in Indonesia. You should not expect your doctor to speak English or that man likely would have wasted part of a medical education on language study," says the young doctor.

"I never thought of it that way. Guess I was kinda being self-centered. My Indonesian is just so rusty at the moment. How is your English so strong?" I ask, humbled.

"My Father is Australian and I have spent a fair amount of time there. Beautiful countryside," he responds.

"That's cool, so can you please tell me what's going on with all this damage and more importantly when can I get back in the water?"

"The stitches will fall out on their own in a few days, you should be good from then. Keep in mind the earlier you go back to the water the higher chance of scarring."

I could care less about scars.

"Thanks, Doc, anything else I should keep in mind?"

"Be safe. You have strong genes and heal well."

"So I can go, then"

"Yes."

"Terima Kasi!"

I turn to gather my things off the hospital bed.

"Oh, Deon," the doctor begins and pauses. "One of the other patients, he had this," he says as he shows me an envelope, crumpled but still sealed. On the back of the stationary is some scribbling. I know who left it.

"What happened to him?" I ask.

"His skin cancer went unchecked for years. It metastasized and spread through most of his face and neck. Yesterday he found the override on his morphine drip. It was most likely a pleasant way to go. How well did you know him?"

"Just from talking here in the room. He told me his name was Gabriel. I never actually saw him, we mostly talked about Bali. He seemed a little out of it."

"Do you know who he was?" the doctor asks probingly after a long pause.

"No. You don't either do you?"

"No, we don't. By the way he looked when we brought him here he had been in the bush quite a while. Well, he left the package for you. He told the nurse something like, 'only you will understand it.' Here in Bali we respect the wishes of the dead as we believe their spirits are still nearby." The doctor slides the envelope into my left hand and shakes my right.

"Good luck out there."
"Terima Kasi."
"Soma Soma."

With those words the doctor lets himself out. I follow shortly after. But not before I open the envelope. A notecard falls out, it reads:

There is an island. No one knows about it because the people who control it keep it that way and the people who stay there must pay for the secret. You cannot find it with a standard map. You cannot approach it in an orthodox boat. You cannot survive it with a straight mindset. There is no conventional life there. If you find it, embrace it. It will change your being. The wave there is as close to perfect as they come. Go find it, you owe it to yourself.

In the back crease of the letter is a map. Like all treasure maps, X marks the spot.

Long Live the Internet

Jonah and I stay at the Bukit Inn for a week before I tell him about the map. We surf all my favorite spots but nothing feels right. I am always pissed off and find issue with the swell angle, the size, the crowd, just about everything. As hard as I surf during the day I still have energy at night.

One of the business matters that must be taken care of is the sale of a property I own. Back in 2006, when Jonah and I expected to stay in Indo forever, I purchased a small house on the Bukit peninsula. Nothing special, but it was home base for over a year and it was cheap. It is a common system for bilingual Indonesians to pay high amounts of money to get jobs on international cruise ships where they earn western wages for common jobs. However, in order to be put forth for these jobs the families must pay quite large sums of money to the Jakarta mafia. It was from one of these families that I purchased a small two bedroom home with garden. The husband and wife used the money to buy a three year contract working on a European cruise liner. At that time the house cost me a month's worth of wages in Japan, including land assessment and lawyer fees. It is on the market for less than two weeks and sells for seventeen times what I paid.

My restless evenings provide time for research. From the map Gabriel gave to me, I have been able to locate an area of Indonesia about half way up the Sumbawa Strait, slightly closer to the Lombok side. The problem is that I cannot find any information on an island there, nor does it appear on any map on the Internet. I even search old Dutch trading records and find nothing. Nightly I update satellite maps and Google Earth but come up with nothing.

Night after night I look without luck until finally a blip. That is the best way to describe it: a blip. After zooming into a section of the Sumbawa Strait on Google Earth, the section of the satellite photo which I think matches the area of the map, the photo disappears. Just gone, as if someone had jumped on Photoshop and used the eraser tool to wipe it clean. A few minutes later it is replaced by ambient water closely matching that of the sea around it.

Someone is hacking Google Earth.

The next night I watch the same phenomenon occur and then the next night again. By the fourth I have done my homework and cannot handle the anxiety anymore.

"Jo, tonight you gotta stay up a little while, I got something to show you," I say over dinner after a day of mediocre surf at Balangan with 72 other surfers in the water.

"What's shakin?"

"If I show you now you won't believe me, you just gotta see it."

"Gonna keep me up past bedtime?" he asks jokingly.

"It's worth it," I assure him. "It might change your being," I think to myself.

Nighttime comes.

"Jonah, J-Bomb. Wake up dude…. You up?"

At 12:45 or so a very sleepy Jonah drags his way over to my bed.

"What do you got going this late, man," he asks sleepy eyed.

"Flick on the lights."

"It burns."

"Um, so you remember that guy in the hospital, the one in my room. Older, Auzzie. Rambled on in his sleep a lot. Wouldn't shut up about 'his paradise.' Well he left me a note and a map," I begin to explain and pass the papers over to Jonah.

Jonah flicks the lights back off. "Yo. Some crazy dude, who killed himself on opiates, gave you a scribbling, and you are waking me up at this hour like two weeks later to tell me about it. Dude, Big Ed: R.E.M. it is like so freaking necessary."

"Jonah, you should have heard him talking about this place. I thought he was nutz but the details of the wave, the water, the sounds, the island."

"You got hit really hard in the head bro, seriously. Kill the lights and climb back in the sack. Now."

"Wait, 10 more minutes," I plead.

As my laptop powers on, I explain all the research I have already done to Jonah.

"I looked at the code," I begin to explain. "At 1:14 each night Google Earth posts a satellite photo of the area. By 1:17 the island is erased and replaced haphazardly by water colored pixels."

"So the big ol' duck what brah? Kill the lights or I am gonna kill you, dude!"

"I took a screen shot last night just in time. The photograph is a clear aerial view of an island right there in the strait," I say with excitement as I show him the picture. As my watch alarm triggers, I click the refresh command on the Internet browser. Instantly a new map of Indonesia appears with fresh clouds and new weather patterns. I scroll over to the section we are discussing and zoom in. The island stares up at us.

"It's the same island from the screenshot," I say while handing him the printout. Then I click the refresh button on the browser. The island is gone. My watch reads 1:18. Holding up an antique map, I say. "This thing is nearly a century old. Printed off Dutch survey maps. It shows the Island. But nothing I can find on the Internet or any modern atlas shows this island. Is it freaking Atlantis? Someone is hacking one of the largest corporations in the world to keep this rock hidden."

"Then let these tards have it and go back to sleep, there are like 15,000 other islands in Indo," Jo rebuts.

"Actually 17,512, depending on who is counting them."

"Shut up, Deon."

"You are so annoyingly obtuse sometimes," I begin to lose my cool with Jonah. "Look at this satellite photo, there is a wave there, somebody is hiding it, think of the possibility."

"You are not gonna back off this till dawn are ya?"

"Nope."

"Recockulous brah."

"Jonah"

"What?"

"Let's find it," I say and then outline my plan. "No matter what, we will be passing by some excellent waves in Lombok."

"Dude. Sleep!" Jonah moans. He has little input towards the theoretical plan of action I propose and is super upset that Ketut won't be able to come, but in the end, he cannot resist the prospect of a real surf adventure. By 1:45 in the morning, Jonah is half convinced to leave Bali.

"Now for the love of Buddha and Poseidon and all those other godly dudes, please shut it down and get some shut eye."

Bye-Bye Bali Breaks

Ketut meets us at Balangan, a beautiful white sand and shell beach on the Bukit where most of the families dislocated from the Bingin and Dreamland takeover have moved shop. We would go to Canggu but the twelve mile drive alone could take two hours from the Bukit and then we would have to deal with the surf camp kooks. The wave at Balangan is a reefy quick moving left. It sections a lot which makes it really hard for a longboarder but Ketut and Jonah can just hop, float or tuck their way right through.

The peak is a narrow takeoff zone breaking fast over a shallow reef shelf. It can handle about 10 surfers on a consistent day, fifteen at best. There are forty by 7:00am.

"Hey, Jo. Know I have been bitching a lot about Bali lately…"

"Yeah, with good reason brah," he cuts me off short.

"Can you explain what happened to surfing?" I ask, sitting out back after a fun little set wave.

"Whatchya mean?" he asks.

"Surfing. The sheer number of surfers. The machismo. Completely forgotten etiquette. The Brazzos, the Kooks."

"Haha, been that way for a minute brah."

"Has it? Maybe I'm getting old but I swear I remember a time when you had to know how to surf to surf. It is headhigh and fast out here, for shit's sake. Half these guys out can barely duckdive their board. Every freakin wave turns out to be a cleanup."

"Oh brother, this is gonna be a long one, ain't it," Jonah sighs.

"Damn right, I am pissed. My last three waves have been cut short, not cause the wave closed out or I blew it, but because people are paddling like little fairies at fairy speed to get out of the way. Again, back in the day, if someone was riding a wave, everyone else paddled like mad to get out of the way for the surfer. Now the shoulder hoppers just sit and block the line, expecting the guy riding from the peak to dodge them like as if it is some kind of slalom course. I really don't even know what to say about it, Jo, but that's not even the worst of it. Peak etiquette has gone to shit, too. Everywhere I look Brazos cut people off and paddle right past the line-up. This dude a minute ago went straight to first position and then Kooked the drop. Think he went to the back of the line? Hell no! Guy is right back at the front by the time the next set shows up and then he pulls off a brilliant repeat of his first attempt. No one says a word. If some douche pulled that shit at second point back in the 90's, you bet their ass would get kicked right out of the line-up and onto the beach."

"Wow, crankypanky, Big Ed," Jonah pokes fun at my rant.

"Don't even get me started on the drop-ins."

"Oh, no way. After Ulu, you got that sealed tight, brah."

"You gotta agree, right?"

"True, it used to be about good times with a couple a friends."
Jonah splashes me with a fist full of water. "We'd even have those
days with a crowd back home. But the ultimate was that day on the
east coast with Ketut. That shit was prime. Now anybody who
thinks they can pull off a hard bottom turn thinks they have the
right to paddle places they simply aren't ready for. Then you have
the new generation. For them it's all about the fluff or the macho
shit. If it's not worth a photo or some suit back at headquarters
can't bottle it and sell it, seems nobody cares. Guess it's cause of
big marketing, surf corporations, hype of the tour, Hollywood,
shaping machines and all that. Everyone who can put a stick under
arm, thinks they are the next Taj." Jonah pauses to reflect on his
response. "Even I got sucked in for a while, brah."

"It's too much, Jo. Did all this happen in the last couple years?"

"Naw, it didn't. Been changin up for a while. You were just out of
the game. Remember the super commando shit you signed up for?
That literally stranded you in the jungle of Panama for three years,
and then you went off chasing all that Japanese honey. Started to
get demented around then. Those blissful years in Bali we had
were sheer lucky timing, mi amigo. Then you went back to hiding
in El Sal."

"Guess that could be true. I was landlocked in Panama those years.
My commanding officer only let me fly the chopper out of the
bush a few times, and trust me it was never to a white sand beach.
He was too busy watching over the coke trade coming out of
Colombia. Oh, and El Sal the last few years, even that gnarly dump
of a country got crowded with Brazos."

"Brah, did you know Coca–Cola used to be made with real cocaine
back in the day?" Jonah questions me.

"You are so on target hilarious sometimes."

"It's true."

"Hence the name Coke."

"Oh. Right."

"So it was all in a matter of those ten, fifteen years I missed."

"Yup, oh and longboards came back in style too!" He laughs.

"Ketut, when did it turn into a shit show here?" Ketut is paddling back up the line to us.

"Long time, Deon. Many many surfers now."

"Doesn't it bother you, Ketut?" I ask. "I mean you are the real local."

"No, I share, no worries. Have family now. More surfers mean more business," Ketut smiles at us with his recently filed grille.

"I see your logic. Bummer it seems to be the business model for the zillion dollar corporate surf industry as well," I point out.

"No worry man," Ketut says as he starts to paddle. "Still get good waves." And he goes in deep for a tightly bending wave, takes a steep drop and makes three sections before the thing closes out.

"Look at Ketut. Nothing phases the guy. It doesn't matter how many Euro-Kooks drop in or how many Brazos back paddle him, the unchallengeable master of the reef always rocks that pearly grin on his face," Jonah throws back my way.

"Looks like you are up for the next wave," I say to Jonah, noticing the set on the horizon. We turn to paddle farther out for a large outside wave. He puts himself in first position and takes a screamer down the line. He pulls into a little barrel and gets covered, barely making it through. On the way out there are three perfectly spaced Japanese guys sitting straight up to watch with googly eyes. There is no way to avoid an impact. Jonah paddles back to the peak missing three inches off the nose of his 6'2 thruster.

"You are right, De. We really need to get out of here."

"Told you."

"Duck it. Let's find this magical surf island."

"Let's leave tomorrow?" I ask.

"Sure thang, foo." Jonah sneaks in his little ghetto slur, knowing that I am pleased he agrees to go. "After the morning sesh, of course."

Gili Trawangan

Gili Trawangan is the largest of three islands off the West Coast of Lombok, now popularly known as "the Gilis." Traditionally three small fishing islands, the shallow reefs and crystal waters attracted scuba-divers initially in the early 21st century. A thirty minute jog can get you completely around Gili Meno, the smallest of the three. However, the small size and lack of infrastructure has kept government entities such as the police out of the plans. The island population and tourism have grown exponentially, especially with the 'do anything' crowd over the last ten years.

Walking the island at mid-day with a googly eyed Jonah, we laugh at very sunburnt and drunk Germans gloating about scuba diving incidents during the day. Russian tourists straight out of the Moscow winter, pale as snow, ride their pushbikes in little bikini bottoms, men and women both. In the reggae bars, Aussie bogans are double fisting magic mushroom milkshakes and hallucinating around the clock. Every drug on the black market is pushed by Muslims wearing traditional Hijab in the square directly in front of the Mosque. Ironic and a tad dangerous in spite of clear religious violation and a capital sentence.

There is a reason why we have come to this place, only a small detour from the path I laid out to reach our ultimate destination. This is the same reason the police stay away from the Gilis and the drugs continue to be sold. Tonight we are meeting my old boss from Sumatra. Ex-Indonesian naval commander Pak Hayarti.

Hayarti was sent to Sumatra to keep order after the disaster, which he did very well. At first, Hayarti was not inclined to give me the things I needed in Sumatra. Mainly, he took issue with my water purification program in the village as he could not understand why I would dedicate so much hard work and personal funds into a system that I did not directly benefit from. His distrust was quickly put to rest after recruiting me to work on a more profitable agriculture project. I was only granted freedom of my work with the villages in Ache under the agreement that I secretly tended Hayarti's fields of Marijuana plants.

Hayarti was no longer needed after the Ache region regained its infrastructure and a standing police force. Because he was feared for his hold on the region, certain government entities had Hayarti removed to the farthest sectors of Indonesia. However, without any direct evidence of corruption, Hayarti could not be held in jail past his trial hearing. He was nevertheless stripped of his military title before being set free. Since then he has found the fringes of Indonesian society quite to his liking.

On record, his company earns a great deal of money and powerful connections by providing impeccable security for high profile Indonesians visiting the islands who want to remain anonymous in both their presence and doings while on Gili Trawangan. However, Hayarti keeps a file on each of his clients for possible future needs. Off record, it is no surprise that Hayarti manages a great power share of the black market here in the Gilis. Nothing happens by chance in Indonesia. There is a reason why drugs are sold on the doorstep of the mosque in a fundamental Islamic area and nothing is done. There is a reason why Indonesian celebrities don't overdose in the night; they have early morning scuba-diving accidents. There is a reason why police fear the island and it is not by chance that 100% of the weed smoked on the Gili islands is directly imported from Northern Sumatra.

For the last of those reasons I am granted audience with Ali Watara, Hayarti's second officer.

I leave Jonah in the company of two Canadian girls who recognize him from a surfer magazine. The bar is about fifty meters down from the villa entrance. The snakelike pathway leads to a wooden door tucked into the only hill on the Gilis. Hayarti's compound is mostly built into a bunker. Only the villa itself sits above land and has a 360 degree view of Gili T. and her happenings. After knocking twice I am pleasantly greeted by two Pygmy size footmen. They are dressed in all-black fatigues and are very closely shaved. By the folds in the uniforms it is clear they have brought a small concealed arsenal.

Hayarti once told me that he prefers these miniature men for his personal body guards because they make a far more difficult target to shoot from a distance. Plus all the anabolic steroids he keeps them on, combined with their low center of gravity, makes for a very tough fight. These two could probably take down Arnold, even during his most fit days. I certainly never want that fight.

The Pygmy guards speak only Indonesian. I am led down the hallway and into a meeting room where they tell me to strip. I know the drill having held audience with Hayarti's office before. One of the miniature gorillas meticulously checks my clothes and belongings while the other maintains a steady glare on my naked body. When I jokingly tell in my limited Indonesian that there is little place to hide weapons in board shorts they are not amused. Next I am instructed, mostly in grunts and pointing, to lift, pull, reposition and show various body parts and cavities which theoretically could be used to hide contraband or weapons. After they are thoroughly content with the search, I am asked to dress and they leave the room.

Watara enters the room and takes a seat on the table's corner where I am dressing. He speaks English.

"The boys tell me you have quite an impressive banana for Bulet."

"I am happy to impress. How have you been, Watara? Still pleasantly working as number two?"

"Proud service has its own rewards, something you might not understand from your short time in the American forces."

"You serve a psychotic criminal mastermind."

"Like Allah, he keeps his words simple and maintains strict order in this chaotic archipelago of tribes and lesser monkeys."

"And I love how you justify it." I scoff.

"Why have you come back to see us, Deon? Was our arrangement not clear and concluded in Sumatra?"

I pause to say the line I have practiced in my head several times.

"I want a handgun and three clips, nothing more."

Watara is taken back, a rare thing for him. "Why would you need these tools?"

"A Beretta is my choice, you know that. They are military issue in Indonesia, I believe."

"Why would you need these tools?"

"That is my business but I promise it does not concern you, your company or your divine mission to bring order. I can pay for it in cash or you can take it from my holdings in the company."

I am not exactly sure of the value of it, but I assume a working handgun on the black market is worth a small fortune. It is also a huge deterrent on the outer islands of Indonesia, where bandits, mercenaries, and pirates can only afford knives and machetes. In fact, the waters of Indonesia recently became the most pirated region of the planet. I choose not to discuss our larger plans with Hayarti or his inferiors as I fear curiosity and suspicion could lead them to sabotage our plan.

Watara sits unmoving in his thoughts.

"You know my word is firm. I have no cause or desire to disturb your fiefdom," I assure Watara.

"I will of course have to discuss this with the boss. Please be patient," Watara says as he leaves the room and the two miniature gorillas return. An hour passes before Watara comes back.

"The gun will be delivered to your hotel the day after next at noon. As for payment, Mr. Hayarti now considers his debt to you balanced for your services rendered in the past. When you receive the gun you will leave Gili Trawangan and never contact us again."

I am a little surprised at the steepness of the terms but agree with little hesitation. Watara leaves without parting words, I am led back to the wooden door and into the evening sun outside.

I have no doubt the gun will be delivered.

A Roller Coaster Ride through the Cosmos

"You were gone for a minute. What was that all about?" Jonah asks.

"Just wrapping some things up for the trip. You look like a man in fine company."

"I am indeed, my large Hawaiian friend, I am indeed." Jonah laughs over what must be his third or fourth beer. "Meet… ah duck it, forget their names."

"I'm Deon," I say.

"Helen."
"Josie."

"Really, it's Josie yeah?"

"Yeah, isn't she awesome!" he begins. "I always wanted to scream my own name in bed!"

"So, the cute one is taken," I think to myself.

"We are going to Sunset Beach for mushroom shakes. Are you coming?" Helen asks.

Jonah looks at me. After the stress of the day I decide to give in to a bit of fun. Plus I have never tried magic mushrooms.

After having dinner and about 20 minutes scouting, we find the bar. The sign outside actually reads, "Fucking bloody fresh sexy magic mushrooms." Josie, taking command of the mission has four brown and pink shakes at our table by 9:40. At 9:46, with our hands over our noses, Jonah yells, "Bottoms up, all."

The mushroom shake tastes like a dirt and strawberry Jell-O mix. Before I move on to the rest of this story I'd like to say that time is very important to this experience so every chance I have to note the time, I do. But mostly, my concept of time is based on how things occur in sequence. What I mean by this is that time is a huge factor in the altered reality which we experienced this night. I bring this to attention not only for the purpose of the story, but also because time has always been an elaborate human construction. Time is why the ancient Hindu Shaman preferred the hallucinogenic drug Soma to invoke the gods. Without such a profane tool of cosmic organization, perhaps they never would have had such a profoundly unraveling experience in the ditches of India.

We are on the beach in front of the bar. At exactly 10:32 Jonah begins to feel the effects of his shake. The four of us are alone on the beach, which is perhaps a good thing because he is really starting to freak out. He is rapping off gibberish at a rapid pace as he is storming up and down the same stretch of beach in about seven different directions. He keeps on saying, "Everything is cool. Everthing is cool," and we assume it is all cool, until he peels over and starts dry-heaving like a cat which has ingested far too much fur. A few moments later and he goes back to pacing mode, then back to coughing cat mode. When I run over to help him he pivots and launches both his dinner and the mostly digested shake all over the sand.

"Thanks for the courteous gesture, Jo," I say barely avoiding the projectile vomit.

"Brah."

Now don't think Jonah is out of the game this early, on the contrary it appears his body ingested just enough of the drug to keep him ringing the whole time. It just chooses to kick the excess out.

By 10:41, all three of them have chucked out the excess fungus and strawberry Jell-O. I still am not feeling the effect, whereas Jonah is on a ranting trip about the sand and the sea, and this is when it kicks in for the girls. As they begin to trip, they both freeze in place to observe the jungle's edge breathing. Just after, Jonah notices the lights of the bar are pulsating. We definitely are not going back in there again. When I notice the breathing forest seems a little odd, I assume it is about go time for me too. We all lay down on the wet sand and stare up at the illuminated night sky. On the first and one of the best trips of the night, Josie figures out that she can move the universe around with the tip of her pointer finger.

So, for a while, Josie and Jonah trade stars like they are baseball cards. They go wandering from one point in the sky to the next, yelping and giggling as they trade the Big Dipper for the North Star and so on. Then Helen pokes the half-moon in the sky and it starts bleeding cheese. I can't believe my eyes. When I tell Jo and Jo, they question me, but after a moment they see the oozing cheese too.

That is really the coolest thing about doing this drug with friends. When one person gets going on a positive trip they can simply vocalize it and everyone else can join in on the hallucination to some degree. At the same time, if it is a negative trip only your friends can pull you out before things get really bad. Otherwise you would have to finish the scary voyage out on your own. This is another lesson I learn tonight.

After the cheese incident I look at Jonah and his face quickly turns into an alien from the X-Files. So I look away but Helen's two front teeth are HUGE. She becomes one of those inflatable punching bag clowns I had as a child, with that big freaky grin and no matter how hard you nail it right in the face it always pops up from the ground for more.

I am about to throw a right hook at her when Jonah yells, "De, you look like Skelator," and they start running off lines from the old cartoon show. The more we look at each other the more freaked out we all get. So when I really start to wig out I just get up to walk away. As I do, Jo and Jo turn back up to the sky and get on a roller coaster with tracks running through the cosmos. I am on a bad trip, and at this point I am destined to finish it by myself.

I walk more than a safe distance from the pack and look out at the bay in front of Gili Trawangan. What I see really starts to make me crazy. It's as if my mind's eye can snap a photograph and then slowly but subtly that photograph contorts and mutates itself. The ocean became a blanket. Sand became a million fleas. Palm Trees howl and hiss. I see the boat from a surrealistic videogame I played in my youth, and then it calls my name in an angry ghoulish tone.

Stars become spotlights from giant ghetto birds and I have no escape. Finally, I just sit down and put my head in my hands, resting each elbow on a knee, and watch it all in third person. With time I became comfortable with the new reality as the drug really kicks in full force.

This was the pinnacle of my experience, but far and away the least enjoyable. I am fine as long as I stare out into my picture, where I realize that not being in control of each transformation is kind of thrilling. I begin to relax and actually manage to lay down for the first time since I left the others on the far end of the beach, but I don't take my eyes off the developing photograph.

A fair amount of time passes like this before I see It approaching. It walked at a slow but melodic pace, approaching at a ninety-degree angle to me. Then It gave a cool and muffled "heellooo" as It stepped through the black cloud of night. I sat up, shooting It a quick glance. Taken back for a moment I realized that It was Jonah, but at the same time It was very new and I wasn't ready for new. There was no place for It in my photograph, so I ask It nicely to sit down behind me, out of my eyesight. I told It to sit but also that I was unsure of how I felt about It, and that I could change my mind at any time, "15 seconds, 15 minutes or even 15 hours," I say.

I begin to wonder how much time we have spent looking at my picture, I try to explain to It just what I am seeing. I power through an explanation of my hallucination, but my words must have come out just as contorted as what I was seeing. Not a moment too soon I hear Jonah say, "OOOkay Brooo, I'm gonna go see how the other guys are doin," and with those words It left just as quickly as It had come.

After his departure, I come to the conclusion that reality is not a matter of control, it's a matter of balance and boundaries. What fits into normal space we think belongs and what does not we simply discard as unreal. That is what the balanced mind does. It is the inability to differentiate between sensual reality and possible reality that scares us. From this duality I begin to think about the idea of Oneness. There is no other, no duality. There cannot be reality and unreality. If it is created for the mind or even seen in the mind's eye it is all still part of the same reality. Is this what it is like to be insane, to be out of balance, to just let go of sensual reality? Or is this a touch of emptiness?

I was diving deep into these Buddhist thoughts when my Bodhisattva returned. But it isn't his presence that takes me out of this profound state, it is the chick who walks by moments later. She wears only a long beach sarong. She said something as she walked by us, but I miss it. Anyway, from where I lay, my sight is set at a 45-degree angle fixed on her path down the beach, so there is no avoiding her figure. She is a part of my night and I am a part hers. As she moves away, her dress is flapping in the night breeze enunciating her pristine figure in a stylized saunter like something out of a 1920's deco print. I watch every step of her brisk but casual pace as her figure becomes smaller and smaller, then in an instant she simply disappears. I decide that I have had enough philosophy for one night.

I jump to my feet, and a very anxious Jonah joins me.

"De. This is your first time on Mushrooms, huh?"

"Yeah," I answer but cannot look him in the face.

"OK brah, three rules. Number one, no throwing things. Number two, no swimming in the ocean. Number three, no being loud." By the end of the night I will break all three rules. I try to look at his face as he says these words, half ignoring my baby-sitter's speech, but find that still way too new. In fact I never look at Jonah's face again the whole night, so I don't have any idea what he really looks like.

The others see us standing and come running down the beach. Helen is eager to show us her cigarette trick, where she spins her arm like a windmill and this leaves an orange glowing trail in the air. I have to admit it is cool, but then she does figure eights and that is just too much for me.

"We gotta go, Jo." I grab Jonah and briskly walk back to our resort on the other side of the small island.

The casual banter we have brings me to a good state of mind. Jonah is curious why I had taken off and I try to explain the whole, 'new' thing to him but he misses the point and keeps saying, "Dude. Big Ed. It's me, Jonah…you know your boy Jo," and I would say "Yeah, but you're the new Jonah now, bro." Even after making it back to our hotel we go back and forth like that till we just give up and look at a tree.

This is no ordinary tree. It is growing at the corner of a retaining wall which separated our resort from the beach and its tidal surge. It has roots going in and out of the wall. Together we stare at the layers of roots weaving in and around the tree, making out several images in it, including a woman's legs entangled in a giant spider. We find this fascinating and just stare for a while. When we recover our attention, Jonah looks down the beach and proclaims, "Dude, this beach is huge! It goes on forever!" I look down the beach and have to agree, "Jo, you're right, it does go on forever!" After a moment of awe at the beach's foreverness we turn and climb the steps back into the resort, where we instantaneously meet our next challenge.

Sitting by the volleyball net in a little café, is a group of backpackers also staying at the resort. Jonah decides that they all have four eyes, the normal set and then the ones in the forehead. He is determined to poke them out one by one. I try to compose myself to a state capable of talking to sober human beings; well at least they were human until I lifted my gaze for a moment to look at them. The heavyset guy at the end of the table has a bulldog head resting on his shoulders and yet speaks perfect English. The light-skinned girl next to him is wearing an octopus for a hat. I try to keep myself from screaming at them and regain my composure when Jonah attempts his most brilliant feat of the night and totally distracts me. He tries to hurl his water bottle at the group but at the same moment remembers his own first rule and refuses to let go of it. Instead of throwing just the bottle, his body is dragged under the momentum of the half-toss, and he stumbles over himself for a couple yards, barely catching his balance before running into the volleyball net. Our audience found this very amusing, as did I.

Jonah, entangled in the net, does not laugh. Low and behold Jonah is now on a bad trip. He is completely convinced that I have thrown him to his death into a giant spider web. When I approach from the short distance he thinks I have eight arms.

"Get off me, you nasty thing," he shouts. "Go suck someone else's blood!"

Luckily, like I said before, friends have the power to make or break your experiences on mushrooms. I look at Jonah and in a soft but stern voice say, "DUDE, you are not stuck in a spider web and I am not a spider." Following a giant leap out of the net and a quick glance at me he replies, "Oh snaps, you're right, brah," and just like that, the 6 foot 5 spider coming to eat him simply disappeared. I think it's kind of cool that your friends can eliminate an advancing monster with a single suggestive proclamation.

Spontaneous images are becoming more and more frequent now since I can't keep my mind on one thing for more than a moment. Josie somehow finds us and we all sit looking at the ocean with its gray, silky bed sheets for quite a while. Jonah starts to doze a bit while Josie and I go off on a tangent about an old McDonalds advertisement campaign for the Big Mac. The commercial featured a cool jazz-playing, lunar-faced mack-daddy wearing a sleek zoot suit. In the old advertisements, the Mac would cruise the galaxies in his oversized Cadillac convertible spaceship, with thick black-framed Ray-Ban sunglasses covering his crescent moon face as he hunted his Big Mac prize. When he found the Big Mac he sought, his face would glow in happiness and he would lift his shades giving you a slow star-glittering wink. The image was a perfect allusion to the half-moon illuminating the black Indo sky. When

Josie and I see the Mac drive by in his blue Cadillac we fall over ourselves with laughter.

At that moment some random guy walks out of his bungalow near us and says he can't sleep. We ask him if we are being too loud and he says, "Niet," but I know he is just being cool. Wearing only a Speedo and a pair of swim goggles, the guy runs out to the ocean's edge and jumps in. We hear the splash over the music, and Jonah wakes up a bit. We talk about the different jungle sights and sounds but I can see Jonah isn't going to make it much longer. Looking out over the beach we see a series of ripples and then, like the Swamp Thing, our friendly insomniac emerges from the black silk blanket in front of us. Because of a feeling somewhere between awe and sheer fright, none of us can say a word as he walks by, but shortly after ol' swampy is out of earshot Jonah says, "Now that was weird."

As much as I enjoyed my little adventure with Jonah and the patio table overlooking the beach, it is the water that moves me into the fourth phase of the night, by far the most enjoyable. He has long gone to sleep, alone, leaving only Josie and I in the episode. Without a word I get up and walk down the steps to the edge of the ocean. I remembered Jonah's second warning, so I just put one foot in it. I watch in awe as my foot disappears into the dark silk. It is just then Josie changes the music to a mellow electronic group called Postal Service. My whole outlook on the world changes again and I know what has to be done. I strip down to nothing. Giving off a primal scream, I ease my way down the slope of the sandy floor and watch my body disappear until the wet blanket is well above my shoulders, leaving only my head in the world.

The water lifts the sand and sweat from my skin, washing away all the impurities I have collected during the night. I lift my arms up through the water's surface and watch the dark-silky beads fall from my body. Finally I let myself fall, giving way to the subtle movements of the changing tide. My last experience on that beach is nothing like the philosophical phase I had earlier in the night, nor fear of the world changing before my eyes. My mind becomes a clean slate. I look out across the bay and take in everything I can.

The hills of the bay form an elliptical wall around the beach, lined with palm trees and craggy rocks. The water still seems to be made from a dim silk blanket stretching through the valley and holding within it a whole different world of mysteries. Only what is at the surface is accessible. A fleet of fishing boats move into the picture, each with a brilliant spotlight on board. At the far edge of the scene the world collapses at the horizon. I remain still for quite a while just experiencing this scene without bias. Perhaps it's why such a slight anomaly turned into the most moving vision all night. The lights coming off the fishing ships formed a series of ladder-like illustrations on the surface of the ocean blanket. Each ladder then melts into the moving tide and breaks off, slowly but methodically making its way toward the shore. When the luminous shapes reached the tidal swells in the center of the bay, they calmly rode over and under each ripple. Even the smallest wave formed a tsunami for these particles of light to surf. I can't help but smile at each miniature little surfer. During this time in the ocean the poison finally finishes its course through my body. Even when sober, I continue to watch the night-surfers.

When I return to the Bungalow, I see my travel watch lying on the nightstand next to the bed. I turn to Jonah and even though he is totally asleep I ask," Wonder what time is it now?" He gives off a grunt. I bend down to pick up the watch, thinking to myself, "It's gotta be at least 4 or 5 in the morning." It would be impossible to have experienced all we did in less than six or seven hours. I look down at my watch. It is 12:25. The entire experience has taken place in less than two hours.

That night on Gili T gave me not only the most abstractly existential ninety seven minutes ever, but also that profound feeling of a total lack of control for the first time since youth. The drug unlocks childhood memories filed so far away that they were as good as forgotten. Things like cartoon characters, commercial jingles, toys, and faces, which become vivid in the mind's eye for quick moments and random glimpses. I probably had a thousand different trips, but they all melted into four major phases. The first and most painful was sitting on the beach contemplating reality. It was as if my body was at 10% but my brain was running at 300%. Without such a daunting experience I don't think I could have emptied my brain to the extent I did while lying naked in the surf of the bay. Perhaps I will never have such an empty mind again.

Jonah and I wake up shortly after sunrise and to my surprise there are no side effects from the hallucinogenic drugs. We take breakfast on the deck outside Jonah's bungalow.

The gun arrives in a brown package. In my room, I unwrap the Beretta and slip a clip into her. With a slide of the hammer a bullet is chambered making a sound long unheard. She feels heavy in my hand yet familiar all the same.

An hour later the three of us are on a private speed boat for Lombok.

Lombok

Lombok and Bali are considered sister islands because of the geographic similarities, size and proximity. In reality they share very little. Separated by only a 45km wide strait, Lombok and Bali have some of the most picturesque beaches, reefs, hills, and waterfalls in Indonesia. Most of Bali is wetland and rainforest whereas Lombok is more dry and arid. Bali has three smaller volcanoes whereas Lombok has the largest volcano in Indonesia, Mount Rinjani.

Regionally there is a shift as well. Although very close to each other, Bali is considered part of Central Java while Lombok is in West Nusa Tenggara; Bali is much more urbanized since the Central Java region of Indonesia, especially Jakarta and Bali, have had a more stable economy and liberal social policies. The province of West Nusa Tenggara has had a more tumultuous history that includes vicious tribal fighting and natural disasters.

Another difference is religion. Lombok is Muslim, like most of Indonesia, while Bali has remained a Hindu sanctuary.

There has always has been a difference in the number of tourists coming in. Development in Lombok has been slower than Bali across the strait. We used to joke about Lombok being in Indo, just twenty years behind. The white sand beaches in Lombok have remained virgin compared to Bali's beaches with skyscraper hotels and multimillion dollar nightclubs. Lombok did not even build an international airport until 2011. Fewer people means less negative impact on the local economic program of the island, the beaches are not crowded with drunken tourists, over aggressive hawkers and petty criminals. So Lombok has a more serene and relaxing setting, similar to the Bali I choose to remember. However it is changing rapidly as well.

From notes in the letter I received from Gabriel in the hospital and my own research, it seems there is a chance of military presence on the island we seek. This means we'll have to approach it with as much stealth as possible. The craft cannot sit too high on the water or it would be spotted by lookouts. Engines and electronics are easily detected these days, so the craft must be manually powered and navigated. In other words, we will have to keep a low profile or else risk being identified, intercepted and sunk on the barrier reef I can see from the satellite photos

We hire a car from Mataram, the capital of Lombok, and start gathering provisions for the trip. At the hardware store I select the materials needed to build our trimaran paddle boat.

Waiting for swell to die down is usually not a bad thing. Kuta Lombok is different from its namesake, Kuta Bali, in almost every way. Kuta Lombok consists of two roads running parallel to the beach, one is paved and one is not. A string of beach huts double as both homes and seafood eateries on the beach road where guests can stay in local huts for little more than the price of a beer. Unlike Kuta in Bali there is no surf in Kuta Lombok. This means you need transport to the waves, which provides a whole new world of problems. For one, the roads are bad. On any given day you can sit at the bar and watch blond tourists wipe out on the unpaved roads, about two trip-enders a day. It's even more frequent with a little tropical rain.

Having to watch out for a 'rent a run' scam is another hazard of surfing near Kuta Lombok. It is a very nifty system the Lombok locals came up with, where unknowing tourists hire motorbikes to visit the beaches in South Lombok, only to have them stolen a few hours later. The renters then have to pay a hefty police fee for the bike's recovery while it sits safely in some back road shack the scammers run.

When you see the waves here, you start to understand why people make the trek. Jonah and I grab our boards and head to Ekas Bay.

Unfortunately for Everyday Joe surfer, some capitalist asswipe bought all the land in front of the Ekas surfbreak. Then he built an Eco resort – which is really just a fancy excuse to charge exorbitant amounts for sleeping close to a wave. However, they also closed the road access to the break to sweeten the deal for their guest. By doing this, land access to the surf is closed off, which limits the number of surfers who can show up by motorbike from Kuta Lombok, where people pay normal rates to sleep. Luckily the wave is still there and just a somewhat pricey boat ride away.

So, Jonah and I make our way to Awung, a local fisherman village 10km from the break and hire a boat for the day. The rough road situation does provide one benefit to the local economy. Fisherman, in traditional Indonesian Junkin boats, make about double to triple what they would earn in a day of fishing and environmentally speaking a couple fish get a second chance at life.

The wave itself is a chaotic, powerful left that jumps around from set to set. The peak is wedged against steep cliffs on the eastern headland of the bay. It consistently pulls in more swell and power than anywhere else in South Lombok, making for high speed walls and a very odd tuck section that can offer up the occasional three or four second tube ride. Not only does the wave itself shift around but currents are strong and hold-downs are long, making it even more challenging and important to consistently make the peak wave after wave. I can see Jonah getting more and more excited.

"Bro, you are the oldest grom I know," I tell him.

It doesn't matter how many world-class waves he has surfed, you can smell his excitement every time he comes in contact with a classy wave. Our guide flips the motor and before he can even throw the anchor Jonah is jumping overboard behind his surfboard. Moments later he is in the Ekas lineup and positioning to challenge it. A five wave set begins to corduroy on the horizon. Out at sea the swell is about overhead but when it funnels into the bay and slams against the rocks it grows at least twice that size. I witness some set waves are as high as four meters. I can see two surfers in the water ahead of Jonah and a third attempting the wave which shifts and pitches him as he tries to drop. The other two surfers take a pass at the next few waves and Jonah jockeys into position for the fourth wave.

A few fluid paddles later, Jonah is thrown to his feet and starts dropping down the face. In the time it takes me to blink twice, he snaps off the top, lands an aerial and glides to the bottom of the wave. At this point the wave looks about double his size. Jonah reaches his left arm back to drag it across the face of the wave while using his right to hold the front rail of his board. Water begins to gather around him as the wave is doubling up. The maneuver stalls him just in time for the lip to cover both surfer and equipment entirely. For a moment Jonah vanishes inside the wave, then quickly is spit out again. Two more rapid snap turns and the wave begins to flatten out into the channel. Jonah kicks off the back and I can see his smile reaching from ear to ear.

'So pitted!" I shout, full of excitement for him.

"All yours, Big Ed."

It takes quite a few paddles to get my board moving against the offshore breeze. As I start to feel the surfboard tail lift, my back arches in anticipation of wave size. I look back. The wave has not shifted and I know I am in position to make the drop. I relax my abdominal muscles and momentum slides me forward. I land the drop about halfway down the face, digging my right heel into the tail for additional lift. As I feel my board correcting itself, it begins to rise up the wave. I whip it around my left side with all my muscle energy. In a precisely timed moment I run – one never actually walks – up to the nose and crane my back into a soul arch, full trim. Anticipating the double up section ahead I turn around to run again, crossing my feet three times to reposition at the tail where my big toe leads my entire presence, body and board into a critical top turn. The nose of the board begins to carve into the right turn. As I reach the bottom of the wave I can see it beginning to double up so I slam my heel back into the tail, squat down and grab both board and wave in a similar but altered maneuver to Jonah's. It pays off and for a moment the wave swallows me, sound and light are lost. That deceptive moment always seems timeless. On the far end a keyhole grows and I am allowed passage out of the green room.

It is my first good wave since Uluwatu, nine weeks ago, and it feels incredible.

"Rock on, Big Boy!" Jonah shouts at me as we paddle back to the peak.

We surf another three hours at least. Not all the waves go so well but there are some real choices. Keep in mind Ekas is a temperamental beast at size. I get axed once or twice and so does Jonah but for every wipeout we take that day, there are two or three great waves to compensate. By the end of the session I think we have taken double the waves of the entire lineup. At about the moment my arms feel like they will fall off, I am sitting on the far outside of the channel and watch the set of the day come in. Jonah also sees it and is in a much more strategic position.

While everyone else in the lineup is scrambling as hard as possible to get away from the heaving monster, Jonah gets closer and closer. It jacks up to the size of a horizontally moving Mack Truck.

As he makes the last two paddles, Jonah yells out a battle cry which echoes off the cliffs in front. The drop is steep and even Jonah has to take it at a conservative angle. He drives hard off the bottom and looks back at the wave behind. I know Jonah wants to set up for the pitch section but he has too much speed to stall for the tube. Pumping the whole wave he makes one last turn and shoots off the top of the wave for a huge launch like Evel Knievel off the ramp.

"Nice wave, bro," I shout out.

"Yeah, not a bad one," he raps back with a huge smile.

"You ready to get back?" I ask. Even after that last wave I can see he wants to stay for more.

"To what?" he asks. "This is awesome." Just like that he makes his way directly to the front of the lineup. I watch him get three more waves before he makes his way over to the boat. He is sunburned.

"How many days is this swell supposed to last for?"

"It has a 3 day run on the charts, might be small enough for us to sail in 4 or 5 days," I tell him.

"Sick."

As we motor away, Jonah's eyes remain fixed on the wave until it is absolutely out of sight.

Brawl Boys

There is still at least one day of double overhead swell running before things start to back off. One of the best Indonesian longboard waves at size, and there aren't many, is called Grepuk Inside. As a further introduction to this part of the story perhaps it would be a good idea to distinguish what makes a proper longboard wave in general.

Broadly speaking, longboard waves run waist to headhigh but it is not the size which makes then longboardable, it's the way the wave breaks. The waves peak slowly and run down the line in clean sections at a gentle angle. Usually these waves break over hard packed sand or cobblestones. Often factors such as seaweed or protected bays slow the wave as well. The steepness is not too radical and there are no close-out sections you have to thrust your board to get through. A simple glide does the trick from take-off to kick-out. The clearest determination of a longboard wave is when having a big flat longboard also carries a clear advantage over a small shortboard. Often the waves are simply too fat to paddle a shortboard into. A shortboard wave would be the opposite of this.

At Grepuk, yet another picturesque bay flanked by sheer cliffs, swells come marching in from the Indian Ocean and sweep across seaweed beds. This slows the open ocean swells and smoothes them before approaching a headland. The wave builds slowly to a peak and wraps down the headland sometimes for a hundred meters, right into a deep water channel.

The local Sassaks here really found a gold mine with this wave. Charging an exorbitant eight dollars a head per trip, they shuttle kooks from all over the planet by the boatloads who cannot make the paddle to the wave. It takes a big board or a lot of explosive paddling to get on the wave at the peak but certain tides can offer some aggressive push once fully formed.

It takes convincing but Jonah agrees to one day of, "Mushburger longboard waves."

Grepuk is one of the most popular surf points in South Lombok as most of the new surfer generation equate a longboard wave to an easy wave because it moves slower and when they mess up the wave, the hold down is not so hard. A longboard has sufficient volume to tap into the slower breaking wave's inner energy before it is fully formed. A surfer riding a shortboard has to paddle very hard to catch the slow building wave and has to sit way far inside the peak so the wave has more power when you try to get it.

Add up the few local Joes who surf the wave every morning plus fifteen Eastern European backpackers and another dozen Japanese paying high prices to local guides to push them into waves, trying to get one to yourself from the inside becomes a real shit show. Knowing this, Jonah takes my second longboard and we make the three kilometer paddle well before dawn.

In the grey light of a new day we are sitting out back waiting for the set waves to come in. I am farther out than Jonah and a couple long paddles glide me into the first wave with ease. I drop my right knee to hook the bottom turn on a head high wall of water just as Jonah goes paddling behind me. Shooting off the bottom with some speed, I run up to the nose and throw my left foot over in a Cheater Five stance. I reach out my right hand to caress the wave. My fingertips track the across the silky surface, the only disturbance to the morning glass, a clean line across the face of the wave. When the wave starts to run quicker I am forced to remove my hand and run back to the tail where a few pumps and a driving top turn help me regain speed on the wave. Looking back at the peak where Jonah sits there must be a football field of distance already between us. Not bad for the first wave of the morning. A twist of the hips propels the board into a launching kick-out and I begin paddling back to the peak

"Good morning lines yeah, brah?" Jonah laughs.

"This one is coming right for you," I say to him." Looking back at the building water behind us.

"Score."

We trade off in this fashion for a few set waves. By the time the AM crowd arrives by boat, we have had about a dozen waves combined. To my surprise not one other surfer joins us at the peak. Instead they all sit about thirty meters inside mostly chatting and picking up the shoulder sections where the wave is a little steeper. They do catch a few good little ones, as well, that totally bypass the peak. On the big set waves though, the inside group watches us glide by wave after wave. A couple guys paddle down to the peak and right past us, but they mostly blow the take-off or don't have enough board to get into the building wall.

Jonah has a few kooky moments himself, as always, when he rides one of my big boards. On one wave he tries to run to the nose and ends up running right off the front. His longboard just about cleans up the group of shoulder hoppers. By the time the sun is just starting to get hot, we are fried. The paddle back to shore seems double the length it was in the first moments of the morning.

One of the French expats in town opened up a great restaurant in Kuta Lombok called The Spot. Using local food and French flair, the menu is simple and delicious. He is shocked that we are ordering fish at 10:30 in the morning but after a short argument on food etiquette, we are served what we want. The Mahi Mahi is caught fresh and braised in a white wine cream sauce, fried garlic cloves and capers. Stacked high over carrots, potatoes and other greens it's a post-surf protein delight. We sleep by the pool at the hotel the rest of the day.

At first Jonah was super against longboarding as it was very uncool in the OC when he was growing up. 'Shred till Dead' mentality. However, after I got him on some of my sticks he swears it has improved his surfing. We talk about it over a beer that night at a local bar in town.

"It's like the amount of force needed to pull off a bottom turn on a log just carries over to your power drive on a shortboard. My snaps always get stronger after a few days of logging hard."

"So why do you bitch every time I call a longboard day?" I ask.

"Not every time, Big Ed, just when there are real waves to be had," he says facetiously.

We are not there long when a couple guys I recognize from the water come in. The mood of the bar switches immediately. A group of three guys start walking directly to the area of the bar where we are chatting. We hear them coming. They are pointing and gesturing halfway to our mark. Jonah appears to be indifferent. My senses are on alert. Lombok is full of angry Aussie silverbacks, chased out of Bali by the crowds and mad inflation rates. They are not happy watching the masses spill to Lombok next.

"Well if it isn't the two longboard Marys from the morning session," one of them says.

"Enjoying our waves did j'ya?" says another.

"First of all, I am NOT a longboarder!" Jonah clarifies. "I only longboard on longboard waves. You should try it sometime, given it is YOUR wave and all."

"You are right matey, I could bring out one of them cheater boards but not really my style to kill the break for everyone else," the first angry guy shoots back to Jonah.

"Yeah, our surf break," the Napoleonic one chimes in.

"Hate to break it to you dumbasses but surfing started on really big boards riding waves just like that one out front. Ever been to a little island chain called Hawaii?" Jonah is not going to finesse this one.

"Ever been to a place called 'common fucking sense?' How bout a little etiquette you pompous cunt," the old guy shoots off.

"You guys took all the bombs, left all the scraps," the Napoleonic one chimes in again.

"Then paddled right back to the peak," says the first.

"See that guy," Jonah points to the bartender down the way, "He called me off two waves this morning. You think I lost my cool at him, hell no," Jonah says.

"He lives here, do you take me for a moron?" says the second.

"Should I answer that?"

'I wouldn't," he replies infuriated.

"Either way, dude got those waves first cause he either brought the right equipment for the wave or he is simply a better surfer. Doesn't make me angry or frustrated like you kookballs, just forces me to try and surf better," Jonah explains.

"Look all you guys. Why don't you join us for a beer or two, on me," I say. "We had a lot of waves today but we are moving on to another beach soon, maybe even the day after next," I try to reason with the group.

"No Ducking Way, Big Ed! It's one thing if a surfer keeps paddling deeper than you, blowing the wave and then paddling back to the peak. That's bullcrap. But if a dude is catching - and riding - more waves it's either because he-slash-she brought the right equipment for the day or is simply a better surfer. Either way I would keep my mouth tight," lectures Jonah.

The mob does not seem happy with his sound logic. After a moment of silence and swelling emotion Jonah decides to throw a little more fuel on the fire. "In fact the whole paddling deeper with a scowl on your face then totally blowing the take-off section … Ha … Saw a couple of you boys do that today for sure."

The Napolean looking dude shoves Jonah in the back. He doesn't move much.

"It's my wave. Mine! Got that?" Napoleon is heated.

"Look angry dude. I understand your position and the necessity to hold down your break from the hordes of Kooks mobbing everywhere. But, I stick by my point that if you know a break as your home wave, one or two traveling surfers, who stick to basic etiquette, can't mess up your whole session," Jonah rebutts as he spins back around on his bar stool to finish his beer.

"You paddled past us, you fucks," One curses.

"You were not even at the peak, you old fart loosers."

"You had longboards."

"You are the one who brought a knife to the swordfight,"

"Longboards on my wave," says Napoleon.

"It's a ducking longboard wave!"

"Get up and face me."

"Get over it."

No one backs down and Jonah is not turning around. The old Aussie looks over his shoulder and makes eye contact with a fair skinned older guy walking into the bar. I recognize him from the morning session as well. The Aussie chuckles and points.

"That's Jaques Montaigne, he's French, which means he don't like Yanks and he especially don't like you or your giant friend there taking his waves."

"That is Jonah, he is fresh from the tour. He was the first one in the water today and kooked one wave the whole time cause we were having fun. He got more waves because he brought the right equipment and could take off fifty meters deeper than you guys who could only mush into the inside section. Like I said before, have a beer on me and lets get over it." It's my last attempt to defuse the situation rationally.

"And like the big man says we had the right equipment for the day. I am sure if we were at Desert Point this morning, you would have surfed circles around me. That wave has way too much pitch for a longboard to take off on the peak."

"I don't give a god damn if he can surf circles around Slater. This is my town and theys is my waves," says the Aussie.

The French guy joins the pack of angry old men. He is now fully in Jonah's personal space. I can see there is not much time for reasoning left. "Let's go, Jo." I start to make my way to the other end of the bar. Jonah doesn't move. I hale to him to follow but he is already engaged with the French guy.

"Webber, I really do not like this guy and his blonde hair. He thinks he is better surfer than me, does he. Maybe not so much without such the pretty face, no?"

"Hey French guy, how about a little breathing room, no one here is looking to play tonsil hockey with your Froggy asshole mouth."

"I will fuck the shit out of you, Kelly Slater," Montaigne stammers out.

"Oh is that your plan?" Jonah starts laughing. "Remind me not to bend over on the way out of this dump." Finally Jonah gets up to leave.

Clearly realizing his error in English diction and Jonah taunting him about it, Montaigne shoves Jonah hard. His is pushed back onto the sunken floor of the bar. I start making my way to him quickly.

"I spit on America." And then he does exactly that. The saliva hangs from Jonah's chin for a moment before he wipes it off with his hand.

"Yo, Big Ed, you stay out this round. I got this guy myself." Jonah motions to me by holding up his saliva dripping fingers and palm in a halting gesture to me.

"As you wish," I respond.

"OK, Froggy, let's get it…" Before he can finish the sentence Jonah is met with a right hook. He is knocked back two steps by the blow. After recovering from the shock he steps back to the match. His retaliation jab is parried and then Jonah is hit square in the nose. Surprisingly the French guy can fight. Jonah's nose looks broken. The rest happens quickly. Jonah comes back hard and tries to tackle him but only manages to grab a leg and drag Montaigne down. They both end up on the floor. There are elbows, feet knuckles, knees, fingers, forearms and toes flailing everywhere.

After about a minute, Montaigne starts to get off the ground where Jonah remains still in fetal position. He is taking repeated kicks to the side.

"Ok, he has had enough." I move in to break up the fight but the three Aussies move to block my path. I can hear Jonah grunt with every blow.

"Fuck off, Biggy. There are three of us and only one gigantor."

"Yeah, the loud mouth Yank is gonna get his till it's got. I'll tell you when it's enough."

Assuming an old school boxing stance, I have my left arm up in a defensive position. I have a longer reach than anyone in the bar and plan to use it to my advantage. My other hand is resting on my hip, ready to unholster the metallic threat that will quickly end the conflict.

"You have to the count of five to get out of my sight," I say.

"One."
"Two."
"TWrrrrrrrrrrrrrrrrrrrrrrrrrrrrrrrrrrrrrrrrrrrrrrrrrrrrrrrrrrrrrrrrrrrrrrr."

Everyone covers their ears in surprise. The bar owner has brought the local magistrate just in time. His whistle blows and a second fat Indonesian security officer comes charging toward the two brawlers. The Indo security man kicks the French guy off Jonah.

Just in the last tick of time too. My weapon stays concealed. Yet, at nearly that same moment, someone on the bar ledge above smashes a chair over the large Indonesian and he stumbles to the floor of the pit as well. The bartender hops over the bar and smashes a bottle over the new attacker's head. The man is knocked out cold and the bartender is now in the pit as well. Everyone watching is shocked for a moment and I use the advantage of the break in action to jump down to take sides with my two haphazard Indonesian allies.

We surround Jonah's unconscious body. All the angry Aussies and Frenchies form up across the pit to face us. They number at least seven but probably only outweigh us by about sixty kilos. I pull Jonah off the floor.

"We need a little scrap on this one, bro," I say to him.

"I can see that."

I don't know exactly where the first punch came from but I know it was them. We are backed against the bar so they cannot surround us. The younger magistrate is holding his riot baton in one hand. He is jabbing with his right fist to set up cracking blows with the baton in his left hand. The war rages for what seems like a long time. In reality it's probably about three minutes.

Finally a warning gunshot is fired into the air by the older magistrate standing in the door and everyone feels the bullet moving swiftly though the air above our heads. The fighting ceases. He is standing near the door with an exit sign above. His hair and uniform still in perfect order.

The air smells of blood and sweat and other broken body issues.

Several of the bodies strewn around the floor of the pit start attempting to get themselves upright. Two or three don't move expect for a soft breath. I make my way to the center of the mess and reach down to help Jonah from the chair he is resting on. His face is gashed open in a few places, probably from the diamond ring the French guy was wearing during the fight.

"Looks like we are hanging out in Lombok a few more days." It is going to take some time for Jonah to heal up.

Jonah throws his arm around me and I scoop him up like a bride being carried over the threshold. He moans.

"Nevermind, think I can walk."
"You are pretty messed up dude."
"You should see yourself."
"You should see the other guys."
"Just walked over one of the Frenchies. He won't be up for a few hours."
"Love it."

"I cannot believe I just got my ass kicked over that stupid ducking wave."

Healing Up. Again

When we stumble back to our villa complex, the receptionist cannot muster a word at our appearance. The security guard knows not to allow anyone into our villa area. We give him extra rupia to hire a second guard for safe measure. The medical clinic down the road closed hours ago but the doctor is always on call. The receptionist tries to reach him, except with eight or nine people calling at once, he doesn't make it our way until daybreak.

Morihiko Awaza is a retired physician from Japan. Two women follow him through the door. They carry the doctor's tools and assist as nurses. They look Indonesian mixed Japanese and they are stunning. Jonah perks up for the first time in hours.

"Salamat Malam, doctor," I greet him.

"Evening. These are my daughters, Kari and Mieko," he tells us in perfect English with a slight Japanese accent. "So you are the two Gaijin stirring up the town? I thought you surfers were supposed to be a peaceful lot."

"Talk to the local kooks about that one doc," Jonah spits out through the pain.

"We are just guests," I tell him.

"Well, we should get started. I still have a few more faces to patch tonight," Morihiko tells us.

"How did the Indos make out?" Jonah asks.

"Not as bad as you," he begins. "A concussion and a few stitches for the big one. That was quite the... How do you say it in American, 'Showdown.'"

The doctor moves toward Jonah first and starts cleaning the gashes. "You, on the other hand, are going to need much more attention. Hold on, this will sting."

Jonah recoils from the pain.

"You must hold still," Morihiko tells him.

"Sure, can I hold Mieko's hand?" Jonah smiles at one of the daughters.

"You can hold big hand if it make you feel better," she snaps back at Jonah. Kari giggles.

"Sorry," I say, "too swollen for that, dude."

Jonah whimpers as the alcohol swab reaches his eyebrow. The doctor and the two nurses work on Jonah for at least a half hour. He persistently flirts with the girls the entire time, completely ignoring the fact that their father has a needle passing through the flesh on his face. I give up apologizing for his crassness. Kari stays on Jonah's side of the room to finish working on the smaller abrasions, while the doctor and Meiko begin threading my face back together. Exhaustion is the only reason he finally shuts up as he falls into a deep sleep.

"Thank god he is out," I mutter to myself.

"Your friend is quite persistent." The doctor laughs light heartedly.

"Yeah, it's like traveling with a child." I laugh. "Nonetheless, I love him like a brother."

"So tell me, what are you really here for?" Morihiko asks me as he sanitizes exposed flesh. "I have seen you two in the water. Surfers of your ability do not stay in southern Lombok often."

"Like I said, we are just passing through Lombok."

"Really? Passing to where? Don't tell me you are chasing after a surfer's paradise."

"What do you mean?" I say feigning naiveté.

"The Island. People are always seeking the Island."

"What island are you talking about?"
"The one you will die trying to get to."

"Maybe we aren't afraid of dying in the quest for paradise. What do you know about this island of peril?" I say mockingly to belittle his concerns.

"Local fisherman out of Awang say that boats have been purchased and never seen on the water again. Jet skis have been launched and lost. They say the walls of the island are impenetrable." He pauses to focus on a large gash on my cheek. "This one will need a couple stitches." He signals to Mieko and then resumes talking to me.

"You know, I have personally treated a few of the people who survived attempts to reach the island."

"Any of them make it?"

"People who talk about it too much around here have a way of disappearing. A lot who try to hire boats in Awang are sent away and never seen again. Nor have I heard of anyone venture alone and come back. Those who are lucky end up in my clinic a few days later for dehydtration and heat exhaustion and then go back to Bali."

"Ever meet anyone who actually made it?"

"Not exactly. I have only spoken to one person who whispered tales of setting foot on the island and surviving."

"Really?" I stop myself short to hide my excitement. "I have yet to meet anyone who claims to have actually been to the island. Can I meet him?"

"I figured that would be your next question. He actually came to southern Lombok just this year. Older gentlemen. Very sick. He was by far the craziest survivor of the bunch. A delusional and most likely rambling schizophrenic. He also suffered from advanced skin cancer. We clearly do not have the facilities here to treat this, so I sent him to Bali where the doctors would have a chance at helping him."

"But was he on the island?"

"I do admit that based on his skin cancer and level of dehydration he appeared to have been somewhere in the wild for a long time."

"I would love to hear what he said about this place."

"I have nothing to tell you except the ramblings. He could have been anywhere in Indonesia. We got him on the first boat off

Lombok possible. I hope you and your friend will reconsider searching for this perilous place."

The doctor finishes stitching me in silence and the three medics bid us farewell. Jonah sleeps. As exhausted as I am, my mind won't shut off. I know the island is there. I have satellite photos. It exists, but is it anything more than an disintegrating volcanic crater that kills? For the first time since Bali, I can't shake the idea that this paradise only exists in the mind of a mad man.

The Path out of Lombok

We lay low on the outskirts of Kuta Lombok until the stitches come out of Jonah's face. By day twelve of hiding out, a little insanity starts to creep up. We hire a driver and by sunset we find a Sasak fishing village on the East Coast of Lombok that looks quiet enough. I pay the driver for the day and promise a little extra after asking him not to gossip back in town.

We unload all the gear from the truck bed and set it down near the shore. Jonah is quick to make friends with gifts of deflated soccer balls and hats from one of his old sponsors. I can always count on him for these kinds of gestures. It helps get our business underway and lowers the suspicious thoughts of onlookers. I take the opportunity to ask questions about our destination.

"Permisi Pa?" I ask one of the elder fishermen. He is working on a net. I show the map and the satellite photo. He looks at me and then turns back to his work, eyes down. Our entire conversation is conducted in this manner. When I return to the staging area, Jonah is playing soccer with the kids. It appears to be the seven of them against Jonah. With one boy flung over his shoulder and another holding on by his sleeve and long hair, Jonah asks me, "What did the old dude say?"

"Loosely translated, Jo, He told me 'Allah would not wish that place of death on anyone.'"

"But it's there, right?"

"It is. About 40km up the strait between Lombok and Sumbawa. Same as in the photo. We can't get any closer by land than we are now."

"So what gives?"

"He won't go anywhere near the place. That means we have to paddle the difference."

"What do you mean?"

"Hope you got a good rest."

The boat construction is anything but normal. Using rope, bamboo and other natural materials, we convert wood and surfboards into a seaworthy structure. The light wood hull is flanked by bamboo shoots three inches thick for light buoyancy, creating a lift frame to float us. My longboards slide easily between each rectangular structure and lock into place. This creates our stationary platform to generate power, a two person paddle station. Between the frames hangs a mesh net to store our gear during the voyage. Jonah's shortboards are tied off to an outlying bamboo shoot, creating a stabilizing boom on each side of the central hull. They are attached by cross ropes. The design loosely mimics a Trimaran construction in the physics of stability.

We pack provisions, a backpack each, plus bare necessities for surviving at sea. Of course our surf kits are there too with repair resin, fins and other accessories needed for a long surf trip. Sun protection is a must as the Indonesian sun is detrimentally hot by 10am. Everything perishable is loaded into dry locking bags and placed on the raised net between our longboards.

All in all, it takes six hours to assemble the rig over the shallow reef. Jonah climbs onto the rig first, stabilizing it with his bare feet over the reef.

"Jo. Your feet must be made of sandpaper. How are they not shredded on this coral?"

"Remember who was rippin' while you were restin in the Bali hospital, brah."

"Recovering."

"Same as."

At first light we board the boat of the fisherman who has agreed to tow our rig out to sea. Based on the currents in the channel I estimate we will need to be dropped twelve kilometers northwest of the Island so we can use the quickly moving water to our advantage. The diesel engine kicks alive and slowly takes us out of the bay into the sea and up the Sumbawa strait. Quite a few of the Sasak Fisherman come to watch us launch in silence. We receive blessings mixed with warnings as the shores of Lombok fade away.

Breakfast is light rice with mackerel and peppers. I tell Jonah to fill his belly with as much water as he can fit. At some point in the voyage, our Indonesian captain informs us that we are at the point of drop off. I remind him that he has agreed to venture out twenty five kilometers southwest of our current position the day after next. He acknowledges by nodding while his eyes look in the opposite direction. It is clear that there is not a secure rescue plan in place.

Luckily, the rig has fared excellently on the trip. Jonah jumps into the dark water below and I follow. We climb aboard as the captain quickly severs our ties. We are buoyant enough so that each stroke creates quite a lot of glide. With the two of us paddling at full strength we manage about two or three knots. Eventually even the Rinjani, the highest peak in Indonesia, starts to fades away.

Jonah seems carefree and ready to follow but I am a little worried as the leader of the expedition. So many things can go wrong out at sea, especially on a makeshift rig. The major straits of Indonesia are notorious for whirlpools and sinkholes, a phenomenon where boats just disappear below the surface, never to be seen again. We are also approaching the Eastern side of Indonesia, where the water gets deeper and tiger sharks are far more notorious for attacking people. These are just some of the major issues I can think of. The less glorious ones, such as heat stroke, dehydration, physical exhaustion, rogue waves, getting lost, or just a simple rope breaking, loom over us far more ominously.

The waterproof GPS mounted to Jonah's longboard station guides us on the most linear path possible. It has thirty hours of battery life. Open ocean swells come rolling through, lifting and then dropping the rig in a gentle rocking motion. Sometimes we are greeted with a four or five foot rise in the sea, which is still insignificant compared to the week before but far more than forecasted for today. It appears the Indian Ocean is not on a break after all.

Old Saint Nick

We focus our paddling to maintain as straight a line as possible, but with each passing swell, we rise and fall, shake and shimmy.

During the paddle my mind wanders in and out of thoughts and my mind's eye bounces between events which shaped my past and led me to this critical junction. The places I have seen and the people I have met, helped and aided, or hurt and destroyed. All in order to 'live' freely along a path of my choosing. Jonah, who knows nothing of this life, quickly takes me from this pensive state of mind.

"Hey D, think I am starting to get a little sea sick or something."

"For real Jo?"

"Could be, def claustrophobicky, probably a dash of vertigo and might be kicking up a bit of psychosis."

"Jo, you grew up in the water. These are just little bumps on the pond for you."

"I know but there are so many and they just keep coming. Never done a paddle like this before, brah."

"Distance you mean? Ah, too many private charters and corporations taking you right to the break."

"You know it!" he replies proudly.

"Wanna go back, princess?" I scoff.

"No, Daddy."

"Then will you please paddle, sweetheart?"

"How bout we go back and get a motor?"

"Already told you. Can't get there with a motor. Plus it would tear the boards apart."

"I know, but it would be so much easier with a motor."

"Are you really getting sick, Jo, or is this just a whine fest?"

"Naw, brah, you know my shit is in order. Paddle for me?"

"Nope, rig only works if we BOTH paddle."

"Sing me a song?"

"Shut up and paddle, Jo."

"Ooh, tell me a story, Big Daddy."

"Paddle."

"I'll paddle if I get a story."

I give in. "Ever hear the legend of Nick Gabaldon?"

"Nope, is it a good story?"

"Start paddling!"

"Geeze, get telling!" Jonah takes his first real strokes in a while.

"Nick is kind of a hero to all us black surfers. During WWII thousands of black Californians joined the military to die for home and country and all that Uncle Sam nonsense. In the Navy, Nick got wind of this new crazy thing called surfing and was itching to give it a go. When he got back from the war his folks had moved to Santa Monica, which was awesome because there are waves just 20 blocks out.

"On the flip, his local break was regulated to an area of the beach known as the 'Inkwell' which comprised a 200 square foot area of sand, roped off, where 'negros' were allowed to bathe and surf. The Inkwell was super crowded with black folk from not only Santa Monica and Venice, but every brother 'n sister in the greater Los Angeles area wanting to spend a warm summer day at the beach was jammed into those little ropes.

"One of the lifeguards assigned to the area was a white guy from a navy family. After befriending Nick, he let him borrow his surfboard while on duty. Once he got going, Nick was hooked and saved up for his own stick, a 13-foot redwood log.

"As he spent more and more time learning to ride in Santa Monica, Nick started to really get the new sport dialed in. About the same time, whispers of new surf spots up and down the coast began to reach his ears. Just a 15 mile drive north of Santa Monica, this new cult of wave worshipers discovered a beach called Malibu. They had found a perfect wave and Nick wanted to surf it.

"Getting to the wave proved to be the challenge. Hitching at the time was totally normal, except no one, even other surfers, would pick up this ripped black dude and his 13-foot piece of wood."

"Haha, sound familiar, De?" Jonah draws the parallel.

"Gets better. When Nick did borrow his dad's car to cruise up the coast, Malibu PD always pulled him over a couple miles short of the break and then were sometimes nice enough just to send him back to the Inkwell.

"So, for Nick, there was only one surefire way to get to those Malibu peelers: paddle. Well before dawn, Nick would make his way from his home on 19th Street in Santa Monica and begin paddling. Malibu old timers Matt Kivlin and Mickey Muniz always talk about the first time Nick paddled his surfboard the 12 miles up the coast to Malibu and just appeared like a dot on the horizon at daybreak. He rode the waves like a true local. Then he paddled back home."

"Dude must have been ripped!"

"He was, definitely would not whine about the half mile paddle at Kuta Reef like some foo."

"What a stud," he interrupts. "So one of the pioneers of logging the Bu was a brotha!" Jonah says ecstatically. "Why does no one ever talk about this guy? I mean what happened to him?"

"It was the first big south swell in June, 1951. It was point to pier. I mean the lines were peeling from the top of third point, through second, connecting at first and racing by mid pier. People say it was a solid eight to ten foot day. Most surfers were out of shape from the long winter or just straight up too scared to be out. Only a few surf specialists sat out back for the sets. Among the crew to challenge Malibu at its fiercest was Nick.

"It was a big one, the kind every L.A. surfer dreams of. I've actually talked to a couple people who saw it go down. From third point right past first, Nick came flying down the line and shot the pier like it wasn't even there. Then he just disappeared, sucked up into the shore pound at the very end of the wave."

"What? Dude managed all that, only to get grinded down by the pound?" Jonah asks despairingly.

"Well, nobody knows if Nick actually died because of an impact with pier, a freak heart attack or if his soul simply floated off in that ultimate moment of joy and accomplishment. No matter what, he will always be a surf god."

"Respect."

We paddle.

Mordor

It is about four hours into the trip when Jonah starts to tire. I slow my pace to match his. Eventually the heat catches us and we break for sun protection. We each have long sleeve cover and hats but I also brought light brown sheets which a Lombok local tailor turned into cloaks. Now we can cover head to toe and have a layer of insulation in the heat which helps to fight the effects of dehydration. Sitting cross-legged on the longboards we take a break to hydrate and eat. It's only 10:30 in the morning and it has already become too hot to continue paddling efficiently.

"We are going to stay here a while and let the sun pass over. It won't be efficient to go on paddling while it is this hot Jonah," I tell him after taking a long pull on my water bottle.

"Big Ed, you look like a giant surfing hobbit." Jonah laughs.

"Ha, is that Luke Skywalker of the Indian Ocean?" I joke back.

"This shit is hilarious man, how did you come up with it?"

"Marine engineers bro. It's a basic survival raft using my longboards. However we need to carry more than our bodies. That is where your boards come in. They provide the stabilization to cruise with swell rises. If you look at how the Indos build their open ocean Junken boats, the booms made from your boards provide outer balance to the hull which also helps provide equal propulsion in the water. As we paddle, the rig glides forward. When the rig hits open swell the craft can bend one section to ride up an incline while the rest bends down to come down another. As long as the swells stay under four feet or so we are all good. The most important thing is the craft is small enough and low enough to the water when we lay on it. That way we will avoid detection by radar. Whoever is watching this island will not see us. Crazy dude in the hospital explained how important this is. Even if they do see us, I bet we will look like a big piece of floating trash. Well, that is the overall idea." I explain.

"Crazy Dawg! I followed none of that. Hope it works. Ain't no chance I'm paddling back to Lombok now. Gonna grab a siesta. You should rest up too, brah." Jonah rolls over so he is completely shielded from the sun.

"I will try," I say with sincerity and throw the anchor I have made from surfboard leg ropes and a piece of scrap iron found in Lombok.

Out at sea things start to change. Let me say here that I have never been sea sick in my whole life except right now. I look around and there seems to be no end to the vastness of water. The motion is a complete beat down and it is ceaseless. No matter how hard I try to ignore it, the battle of stabilization rages on. Up and down we go, up and down. The heat beats on us. My cloak blocks the sun's rays but does little to shield me from the oppressive heat. One moment I am flying and the next drowning. Up and down, down and uP, Up and DoWn, dOoWn and uP.

"E, Big-E. Get up!"
"Huh?" is all I manage to say.

"Let's get moving dude, you might feel better." He has already pulled in the anchor.

Finally the sun starts to cool a little by 3:30 which means we have about three more hours before dark. Sure enough with each stroke I feel vitality and sanity return. I flick on the GPS and look at our position every fifteen minutes or so. We adjust course with the power of my stroke against Jonah's. It feels good to be moving. After an hour or so we take a short break to uncloak and dry a bit. It is a quick break and we are soon gliding on. According to the GPS we have managed quite a few kilometers by nightfall. Most of these were in the correct direction as the bird flies. We are still 8 or 10 kilometers southeast of the island. I turn the GPS off to conserve battery. Jonah throws the makeshift anchor.

By the time it is dark we are exhausted.

"Let's paddle through the night," Jonah says.

"Neither of us has that kind of strength right now; we need to eat and rest," I tell him.

"It's only a few more kilometers to paddle isn't it?"

"Only if my calculations are correct."

"You are always right Eddie."

"Then trust me, let's rest at least a few hours."

"OK, but what about the sharks?"

"What sharks?"

"The ones who have been following us some time now. When they circle around, doesn't that mean they are getting hungry?"

"Shut it Jo, there are no sharks out here."
"Than what is that coming right for us right there?"

"What where?"

Jonah splashes me with water.

"Quit the jokes. You had me for a sec."

"I did eh? Just wanna keep moving."

"We got to pace it, bro. We will get there tomorrow."

"When?"

"Tomorrow. Let's sleep a bit and see. Wake me up round three in the morning if I can snooze that long."

"Hey, Ed."

"Yeah?"
"It's three, can we go now?"

"Go to sleep."
"Can we go now?"
"Go to sleep!"
"Can we go? Can we go? Can we go? Pretty Please, Daddy!?"

"I swear I will toss your ass off this rig!"

"No you won't."
"No I won't."

"Gnight."
"Kisses."

A couple hours later I awake to Jonah splashing me in the face with seawater.

Sunrise

We paddle through the rest of the night. Jonah spots the land mass on the night horizon first. It is just a dark grey lump. My spirit is lifted with the sight of the island. So is my seasickness. Soon the shadow grows to be a fissure between Neptune's ocean and Uranus' sky. It is not until first light that we know for sure that the GPS has steered us correctly. In the grey and purple light of dawn there the island sits, directly northeast of us. We throw the anchor in front of the gap in the cliffs and watch. Even from this distance the island is stunning, with white limestone cliffs rising out of turquoise water. Jonah and I sit to stare for a long moment. It is raw beauty. The small opening in the cliff seems tiny compared to the caldera isle. It is also partly blocked by a single pillar of stone. It stands strong and unshaken, whereas the forces of erosion have long since kicked down the cliff face on either side of it, providing an entrance to the bay. The pillar that guards the entrance to the bay is backlit by the rising orb of fire.

The approach looks a little heavier than I first thought. Despite the fact that there is minimal swell running, we can see the surge breaking against the bluffs and a current running hard due south over shallow reefs. Even anchored a mile out to sea we have to work at keeping the rig stationary against the current. When our tether comes loose we begin to paddle hard. I can tell Jonah understands the seriousness of the approach as well as I do.

"You ready for this?"
"Ready as can be."

We paddle harder.

On our first pass the rig comes up about fifty meters short of the gap between the pillar and the opening to the right of it. No matter how hard we fight the moving tide we are losing. We are caught in the current and swept down the cliff face. I feel the rig scraping against the shallow reef. It is a good thing we removed the fins from the surfboards or they could have been buckled and destroyed. With the two of us floating on top this could have ruined the journey quickly. We are swept back out to sea south of the island about 3km from where we started.

"That could have gone better."
"That could have been worse."

Once we are far enough down current I tell Jonah to throw the anchor again. I think about breaking the rig apart but then we would lose half our boards and all our gear. I look at the river of free flowing ocean water. I realize what needs to be done.

"To get into the bay we are gonna have to paddle up current as far as we can from the northern gap and really gun it to get through that rip."

"I know."

"Water?"

"That's the end of it." I toss him the bottle.

"Better make this round count then." He throws me the bottle back with just a sip left in it. There is none for the return journey.

"Let's do this thing."

Slowly but methodically we get the rig much farther up the coast than the starting point of the first attempt. I take a deep breath and look at Jonah.

"Ready?"
"Ready."

We paddle.

"We are not gonna make the first gap."
"Paddle harder."

"Its not gonna happen!"

"Paddle harder!"

"We are gonna slam the ducking pillar."
"No we won't, DON'T stop paddling."

"DON'T STOP!"

Jonah breaks from his paddle. He has nothing left. The rig is heavy. I stroke as deep and strong as my elongated body can handle and at the same time allow the inside rip current near the pillar to pull us. We gain speed. The rig starts to turn on its axis and the nose of my board now faces the right gap. We are moving quickly and I do my best to keep the rig angled in the direction of the gap. Like Jonah warned, we have lost the chance at the first gap. We are coming up against the pillar, fast. It is a titan of sheer rock covered with urchin-like creatures, which are now close enough so that we can make out purple and teal barbs everywhere. I throw the anchor over my left shoulder.

Just as our line pulls taut in the current the boat is jerked hard and swings again on its axis.

"Paddle NOW!" I shout to Jonah.

Using the momentum from the sling shot effect of the anchor throw, followed by our full paddle strength, we are propelled forward. I cut the rope. We have made the second gap. As we break the current the water calms. For a few strokes but we are so wound up with adrenaline we just keep wind-milling at full pace. I notice the surge waves come through the gap the same as we did and then reform on the inner reef into a wave. The first wave lifts the rig a few feet into the air.

"If we paddle hard enough, I bet we can ride this next one to shore."

"Let's do it."

We do exactly that. The wave carries us forward another couple hundred meters or so, bringing us to the shallows. Then the rig washes right up onto shore. We jump from the rig and lay down in the white sand. It feels like powder. I stare at the open sky for a long time.

"Brudda Eddie. Dude. Sit up. Yo, you gotta see this place."

Using the miniscule strength left in me, I sit up and open my eyes wide. Tears fall to the sand as my senses absorb the hidden beauty of the place finally discovered.

The Beach

"We ducking made it."

The rig has landed on the inside of a crescent bay. The beach is at the innermost strand stretching most of the oval bay with only a slight opening in its protective cliffs. Since its volcanic inception, presumably millions of years ago, giant arctic swells have been smashing the southern cliffs and eventually made their way in. Over time, a fantastic bay is created, and like a man with a camera: this is the moment captured in time.

The sand all around is white powder. I run my hands through it, a collage of limestone decay, broken shells and coral. Standing up to throw a handful back into the ocean I swivel to take in the panoramic view. The beach wraps both sides of us and tapers off into the distance. The sun is at about ten o'clock and radiating over the turquoise water. It is stunning. Farther in the distance, the sandy beach morphs quickly into the rising cliffs. They push against the horizon and out to sea. The wall provides an oval shell around the bay, protecting it from the raw ocean outside. A perfect defense except for one glorious flaw: the pillar and the two gaps in the cliff we passed. They face south to the open Indian Ocean, allowing only a select few to pass through.

And then there is the wave! The swell comes in the gaps facing south – southwest and past the rock pillar which guards the entrance. The waves are nearly identical to the one we caught and rode to the beach. Although some of the energy seems lost on the outer reefs, waves pass the currents and make their way into the bay. Then they hit a deep water area past the entrance, where they back off into swell again and continue pushing on toward the inner reef. There the swells build and reform into waves. The wave picks up momentum on the inner reef and peaks in the same spot. Every wave! Set after set, the open ocean swells march into the bay and mechanically form waves on the reefy runway.

This phenomenal design of Mother Nature makes a perfect horseshoe A-frame. The right is almost identical to the left as it wraps the reef. From the peak the wave throws over into a double barrel. The steep but makeable takeoff section seems to slow down and speed up in several places as they form a very vertical wall across the reef. The wall seems to last for over a hundred meters of workable lip in each direction. Finally the end section bends to a sharp degree that you must tuck for the lip or kick off the back. There is a channel on each side between the reef and the shore, allowing an easy paddle back to the peak.

The wave is perfection. There is not a surfer to be seen.

Exhausted, I fall asleep under the morning sun.

PART III

According to Hindu tradition, the duality of Dharma clearly separates all things into the categories of good and evil. Both major epics of Hindu scripture depict Dharmayuddha, the war that must be waged to establish and keep Dharma pure.

Contact

That feeling of being alone, it was false. I wake to the sound of a falling coconut shell in the distance and then muffled footsteps. I force my head from the daze it has slipped into. At full attention I roll over and one hand slips into my gear bag.

"Don't move," a male voice shouts at us from a distance.

Jonah stands up quickly.

"I said don't move. Lay back down or I will shoot you down ya," the voice shouts again. I detect an Afrikaans accent.

"If you could hit us from that far away, you would have shot us while we were asleep," I reply.

"Maybe that was my only mistake. I will not make it again. Now get down," he orders as he steps out from the tree line. A black, very black man holding a makeshift weapon shows himself. It is some kind of hybrid between a standard hunting bow and a crossbow constructed from natural jungle resources. He is tall, has a skinny build with lean muscles clinging to bones. He is nervous. He continues to make his way steadily toward our position.

"Be cool," I say. "Even if you did shoot true, could you reload and re-aim before my partner here is on top of you?"

"Don't get me mixed up in this, brah," Jonah says.

"I never miss." The dark African boasts. He stands at a distance with a quiver of arrows. One is notched and the string drawn. The tip is pointed directly at my chest. I pull the Beretta from the dry bag and aim it directly at his heart. I click the safety off. He stops moving forward.

"Look man, you are not going to shoot at me. Why not? For one thing I can see your trigger finger is trembling. You are holding a bow and arrow, not exactly the ideal of accuracy at fifty meters, whereas I am holding, well, something slightly more effective."

"Where did you get that, Ed?" Jonah's voice cracks loudly.

No one speaks for what seems like a long time.

"Ed, you have a gun."

"Bet you are glad about that now, Jo."

"Ed, he is coming closer."

"Stop. I will give you to the count of five to put your bow down on the ground and walk slowly towards us," I shout loud.

A moment passes. "Do you follow?" I ask.

The African nods his head once. The arrow remains aimed.

"Ed. You have a gun. Here? How? Why?"

"Doesn't matter now, really happy to have it. Listen, Jonah. When he puts his weapon down you go get some boat line so we can tie his arms back and feet together."

"You have a gun, Ed!"

"Focus."

"Duck it."

"You got this, Jonah?"

"No," my friend stammers.

"Not really a choice in the matter, dude," I say. "Breathe, cause here we go."

"One," I shout.
"Two," a little louder.
"Three."
"Four."
Ping.

The aboriginal-looking guy fires his weapon at me. The arrow buzzes about two feet over my head as I drop quickly to the ground. He noticeably missed. In the time it takes me to gather myself and re-aim the pistol he has already turned and is dashing for the woods with sprinter's speed. His path is thought-out and quick. A moving target is nearly impossible to hit at this distance with a handgun, especially a target that moves diagonally. At the edge of the tree-line, safely behind a large teak, he looks back at us. I have a clear shot.

I hold my fire.

"Why does no one ever let me finish counting?" I say out loud, letting off a little edge of the moment.

I turn to Jonah, he is frozen with shock.

"Get your shoes, Jonah."
"You have a gun."
"You sound like a broken record."
"A gun. Here."
"We need shoes, we are going after him."
"You have a gun."
"Jonah."
"How the hell, where the, why the - 'H-E-double hockey stick' did you bring a gun?"

"We'll talk about it later, get your shoes on."

"I'm not going anywhere, you're gonna get me shot, dude."

"We can't stay here. The longer he has in the forest the more time he has to prepare for us."

"Bullcrap, you dragged my ass all the way here, we are sitting on the shore of the most awesomely perfect wave I have ever seen and you are gonna tell me I can't go surf it? Duck that! Better idea; let's go chase some wild jungle afro man with a crossbow into the bush."

"Yeah. Basically," I say placidly while lacing up my right shoe.

"A jungle that he knows and we don't. No-Way-Brah!"

"So you want to wait here. No water, no food, at least one person intent on shooting us. Why not just go surfing, brah?"

"Finally, you have a good idea."

"Jonah, get your head on."

"Deon, look at it."

"I saw the wave. I also felt the wrong end of an arrow moving a hundred miles per hour."

"Going in there is a mistake, Ed." Jonah stares at the tree line. He is calmer now.

With both of my shoes laced I stand up and grab a black T-shirt out of my gear bag. It's still wet from the trip. The shirt sticks a bit as I put it on. What little food and supplies I have left I toss in my shoulder bag and I start up the beach. The handgun is holstered in my jean shorts, the second and third clips in my right pocket.

"Do what you wanna do," I say to Jonah.

At a light jog it takes about three minutes to reach the top of the beach incline before the trees begin. The air is immediately cooler in the shade of the trees. Light has a difficult time penetrating the canopy, even at the border of the forest.

"Wait," Jonah shouts from a pant as he catches up. "Wait, I'm with you, Big-E, no matter what."

"Fine, don't slow me down again."

"Fine, just promise one thing."

"What is it, Jo?"

"Don't get me shot."

I laugh. Jonah does not. His eyes convey the seriousness of the situation. I turn back into the tree line at the edge of the beach and take a few steps into the forest.

There are five of them. It is a motley crew. There are two men wearing only shorts patched multiple times to keep the fabric intact. One of the men is very tall, with a German look, a shaved head and impressive muscle definition. He wears a kilt-like bottom made from random pieces of fabric held together by jungle vines. Two of the women are in converted board shorts haphazardly paired with frayed bikini tops. The third, a tall brunette, wears only a skirt made of natural fabrics and a necklace of seashells. The sun beams radiate through the tree tops and glisten across her bare golden skin. They all have makeshift weapons pointed at us.

A sixth character approaches from my right flank.

"That was a warning shot earlier on the beach to avoid bloodshed. You know I will not miss again, ya." he says in a heavy Afrikaans accent.

"OK, where do we go from here boss?" I ask. My gun is still holstered on my right hip.

"Recognize my authority in the situation you are in ya. Get down on forest floor. Knees first. Your right hand on the ground like a three legged dog. Your left arm raised above the ground pointing straight forward. Lift your right leg pointed straight back. Head down. Clear ya?

"Crystal."

"If you run, I will shoot. If you reach for your gun I will kill you," he says calmly.

There is a command in his voice which carries the fact that this man knows how to kill. He is also no longer nervous.

"I will give you the same count which you gave me ya," he says with the accented English. "Begin."

I follow the directions given to me. In the time it takes to count to five my body has assumed the awkward position instructed. Once there, the African walks at a brisk pace, removes the Beretta from its holster and immediately pistol whips me with it. The last thing I hear before the blow knocks me unconscious is:

"See, I told you we should have gone surfing."

Bondage

Most people don't know how unpleasant it is to be bound. A little itch on the nose goes unscratched and makes its way to your ears, then down to the back of your neck. Eventually it splits off and makes its way down your spine, shoulders and every extremity. That is just the beginning of the discomfort. Despite your greatest efforts to ignore the spreading itch and contain it with logic and superhuman control, you pull at the wrists and ankles with all your might. No amount of reasoning keeps this at bay. Skin reaches a point of tenderness which then turns to blisters and blood. Despite these warnings one cannot stop pulling on the raw skin or ignore the spreading itch and the vicious cycle grows. As terrible as the physical discomforts are, nothing is worse than the psychological distress of being bound.

I have been bound three times in my life and it is always just so. At least this time I have the company of Jonah to share the misery.

Consciousness slowly returns. We are in a hut. I can smell the mud mixed with palm fronds. It is dark and my eyes have a hard time adjusting to the lack of light. The air is hot and humid as the summer rain makes its way through seams in the natural roofing. The ground soil is flat and brushed, but we have not been provided any kind of padding for sleep. My wrists and ankles are on fire. Somehow I feel well rested. Must have to do with being knocked out. The spot where the pistol struck me is throbbing and inflamed. I can do nothing for it. I sense Jonah stirring next to me.

"How is that big head of yours feeling, 'Sir Sleeps A Lot'?" he asks.

"Any idea how long we have been in here for?"

"Not really. They blindfolded me and tied me up before carrying us and throwing us in this hut. It must have been about midday. I slept a bit, but you have been out the whole time. It is totally dark outside so it must have been a while."

"Wondering if they are outside chanting 'ugachakakaka' with a giant boiling pot of water to throw us into at midnight," I say.

"Yup, always armed with jokes, eh?" Jonah is not amused this time. "Eddie, we better get out of here. I'm serious, brah. I cannot die knowing that wave exists and I never got to surf it."

The doorflap on the other end of the hut opens. A little starlight sneaks in and a man holding a torch enters. The light makes me squint. He is light skinned with a close shaved head and tall. Perhaps in his mid-40s. He first places the torch in a holder near the entrance. He is wearing shorts like the other guys from the jungle but he was not with the group that captured us.

"Mornin' boys. You been out a long time. The trip to the island on that rig of yours could not have been easy aye." He speaks in an muted Aussie accent. Probably from Sydney.

"Getting pistol whipped helps one sleep, as well," I say.

"Yeah, from what I hear you got on real well with Marcello. Be glad it was just one whomp to the noggin," he informs me. "I'm Howard, resident doc to the island. Here to make you more comfortable. Want me to take a look at that head wound?"

"We are tied up. That's not too much fun now, is it? Jonah points out.

"Yeah, and you are gonna be that way for a little while. Not always the way we handle biz around here, but you did rock up with guns flash and all."

"How long are we gonna be hog tied in this hut?" Jonah asks.

"Well, I reckon when you are rested and feeling up to it, sometime round noon, the council with come have a chat with yas," Howard begins. "Depending on your response they will decide what to do next. I reckon it's best to be honest, and anything you can offer to the Tribe will help your cause, but gotta tell ya, everyone is pretty worked up."

One word sticks out. "Tribe?" Jonah and I ask simultaneously.

"Yeah, that's what we call ourselves here on the island. Don't know exactly how or when it came about, but at some point we graduated from happy survivors to full blown tribe."

"How many of you are there?"

"On our side, thirteen members of the Tribe, since Gabriel..." he pauses, "... left a few months ago."

Jonah asks, "Why are you telling us all this?"

"Well, they are either gonna dig a grave for yas or let yas stay. Either way filling yas in a bit won't hurt," Howard explains.

Howard makes his way over to the spot where I lay. He has a coconut shell filled with a milky looking liquid, herbs and disinfectant. Even the bandages are fashioned from local shrubs. His treatment is quick and methodical. Howard has been trained professionally and is well practiced in his art.

The liquid drips in my eye and stings a bit. I recoil. Then I remember I can't wipe it off anyway. The way they have me bound I cannot even touch my eye to my shoulder.

"It's a little hard to rest while my hands and feet are all roped together in a demented position," I complain.

"Again, not much to do about that mate."

"Would it be too much to ask for some water?" Jonah puts forth.

"Aye, not at all. Nely, mayim bavakasha," Howard shouts in the direction of the door.

A few moments later a girl comes in. She hands him a couple coconut shells filled with drinking water. She is petite, dark and pretty. Her olive skin undulates in the torchlight like a dance over defined muscle. She was with the group in the forest. She tries not to look at us and then quits the hut with haste.

"Who was that?" Jonah asks the doc after pounding his bowl of water.

"That is Nely. She doesn't say much."

"That's OK, we don't need to talk," Jonah jokes and then asks half seriously, "Could she change my shorts?"

"Sure, but wouldn't recommend any funny stuff if you want ya pecker to remain intact."

"Never mind. I am too dehydrated for funny stuff anyway," he graphically adds.

"I still don't know your names."

"I'm Deon and this is Jonah," I use my nose to point.

"Well, Deon, don't believe that wound on your head is gonna require stitching, but ya better keep it clean and dry."

He puts down his medical tools and lifts the coconut shell to my lips. I am so thirsty I forget how to swallow. A little dribbles down my chin and is wasted on the floor.

"Yeah, sure the Tribe wants you as healthy as possible before they throw the big Hawaiian ass-up into the boiling pot," Jonah chuckles.

"Never know what the council will decide," Howard says half jokingly. "Well, yas all wrapped up, more ways than one. Anything else I can do to make it more comfortable in here?"

"Hookers and a bottle of Cristal."

"Be careful of what you say around here, not everyone takes a liking to condescending or male chauvinistic words. It's a tad bit of a PC world this place has become."

"My bad," Jonah says.

"No worries, tends to be hard on all us Aussie boys, too."

I laugh.

"How many women on the island?" I ask.

"Ha. That's kind of a good question, ya see. Guess there is technically seven females of the species among us."

"OK?"

"One more question, Doc. Who is Gabriel?"

"Gabe was with the first group to find the island, but he was alone for years before Tex and Goldie landed. Having paradise and not being able to share it, well, it changes a person. He was a bit schizo and manic when I got here. I did all I could for him and he was stable for a bit, even in control of his outbursts. Then, over the last two years things started to change for the worse. Fights, stabbings, fires, mostly hurting himself. The council voted he was too unstable for the Tribe and he was, well, banished some time ago."

"Older guy. Husky outback accent?" I ask.

"Could be. Why?"

"Has the Tribe picked through our gear off the beach yet?"

"I assume so."

"Check my dry bag when you get a moment. Wonder if you will recognize Gabriel's map."

"I will ask Nely." He pops his head out the door and says some words in what I guess are Hebrew. She replies. After a moment he walks back into the hut.

"It turns out that yas were one of the few to actually be invited to come to the island. Unfortunately, it was by the only man we have ever had to excommunicate. The council will weigh it all tomorrow, hey. Until then, good night." With that the doctor makes his toward way toward the door.

"So, no Hawaiian BBQ?" Jonah looks at me and jokes.

"Not tonight," Howard takes his leave.

Jonah and I don't talk much the rest of the night. When they come for us it's well into the day. Howard comes in first with water. He helps us drink. Soon after him enters another new face followed by Marcello who carries my gun in open view.

"Afternoon there. My name is Tex. We are here to escort you outside to meet the council group. Hoping this goes smoothly," he tells us with eyes down but mainly speaking to Marcello.

Our legs are unbound but not arms. I try to stand and all the blood rushes back to my feet causing me to fall to the ground again. Howard helps me up. Once outside, the sunlight forces us to squint for a while. We move slowly. Tex and Marcello keep a short distance. Nely is just outside the door holding yet another makeshift weapon. She follows a few more paces behind. We are led down a short path to what I assume is the village center. It is a clear area shaded by the lush jungle. I can see a large hut and several small ones, all with open doors. The thirteen members of the Tribe are gathered on a covered platform in the center of the square.

The group is split in two factions. Howard tells us that the council members are on one side of the deck, probationary tribesmen on the other. We are asked to sit on chairs made of bamboo and teak facing the deck. Tex then binds our feet to the chairs. Nely and Tex join the others sitting on the deck. Marcello stands nearby. Tex sits in a central position among the group and begins speaking.

"As you all know we are gathered here today to discuss the newest arrivals to the island," Tex begins speaking in a quiet tone so we cannot hear the rest of the address.

While Tex is speaking out of earshot, Howard sits back and begins explaining that the Tribe council makes all official decisions for the Tribe. One must be on the island for five years to be a voting member of the council. "It is composed of seven members: myself, Goldie, Tex there, Monica, Marcello you have met. Tasha and Svet are the newest voting members. If you make it that far, you get one of these," he says as he lifts the tattered shirt from behind and shows a burn scar in the shape of a musical C note. It is on his right shoulder blade. "The rest of the Tribe is allowed to watch, observe and propose questions if they wish," Howard finishes.

Howard seems to be an advocate for us, however the rest of the council gives ambiguous looks and vibes as Tex speaks to them. It is a while before Tex stands and turns to us. He begins speaking loudly enough for all to hear.

"We spotted your boat on its first attempt to shoot the gap in the cliff. Most of the Tribe was out surfing and Goldie saw the rig first." His eyes turn to a yellow haired man sitting with the group and then back to us. "It has been over two years since anyone made it into the bay on their own. Standard protocol is to get all of the Tribe out of the water, take cover and make sure the new arrivals have friendly intent. Marcello is the marshal of the Tribe and thus the first to make contact with you. He did not expect a gun."

Jonah coughs.

Tex continues, "We have found the map and understand you were invited to the island in a sense. That issue is void however as Gabriel is no longer fit to be a part of our community, so his invite has no impact on your being here."

"Gabriel is dead. He poisoned himself with morphine in a Balinese hospital a couple months ago," I tell them, "Just after inviting us to the island."

There is chatter and commotion among the group. Goldie stands and softly redirects everyone to the topic at hand. While he does, someone on the other side of the platform shouts, "Enough idle chat, get rid of them!"

"We must give the marooned a chance to explain," Goldie says calmly, "That is our way."

Jonah looks at me. I begin telling our story with a little of our background. I talk about rebuilding villages and agriculture in Sumatra and our early days in Bali. I continue by explaining how I came to meet Gabriel and how we came to the island. I skip over certain details like my Military training, drug production, connections in Gili Trawangan and the shadow of trouble that seems to follow Jonah and I throughout Indonesia.

"We have to consider the risk of your character to the Tribe. Not to mention the simple mathematics of having more bodies on the island means more mouths to feed which stretches our resources further and draws more attention from the Gentleman, especially when we have not heard from his faction in so long," Tex tells the group.

"There's not enough to go around as it is. Get it over with," a girl chimes in from the Tribe.

"We're having a rough production year," another interjects.

"There must be some way we can have a chance to stay," Jonah pleads.

"We cannot stretch the resources any further," Goldie says in his clear Kiwi accent.

"If they stay, we all starve," someone points out.

"We don't need your group or your provisions. I can provide for the two us just fine," I say to the group. "We don't need your assistance."

"And what, set up a separate faction on the island? No way, cowboy!" Tex denounces.

"Everything is done together here. There is no alone," one of the women on the council explains.

"What can you offer?" a blonde girl asks.

"Nothing!" someone shouts.

"It is dangerous and a drain on us if they stay!"

"The big one is a serious danger," someone says in a German accent. "It would take the whole Tribe to hold him down."

"Pas bien," the topless French girl curses us.

People just start shouting out randomly. A few comments support us. Mostly they condemn us. Chaos of the situation grows. Some are standing now and making full body gestures. A few walk off the platform and have separate shouting fits.

"One surf," Jonah says.
"One surf," Jonah says louder.
"Just one surf," Jonah looks like he is going to cry. No one notices.

Jonah shouts more. No one cares. They just go on bickering. Tex stands and calls for order. Everyone starts to gather again on the platform.

"One surf then, just one and we will be on our way home, just one," Jonah pleads.

"No can do, we cannot threaten the safety of the group so you can surf. We also cannot let you leave, either, risking that you jeopardize our location. It's not the first time we have had this dilemma," Tex explains.

Everyone is guarded and eerily quiet after this is said.

"The reception would have been a lot friendlier had you not been armed," Goldie adds in.

"Je ne l'aime pas!"

"Send them to the cliffs," an overly panicked voice shouts. "I vote Death."

Jonah sighs.

"I never fired," I yell out. "I could have but I did not. Marcello did."

"This is childish, we are getting nowhere," Tex says. "Sit down y'all."

Most of the group has retaken their seats.

"It's my turn to speak," Jonah says.

"Let him have a go," Howard insists.

The group is quiet for the first time in a while. Jonah takes a deep breath.

"All right, I got a joke for you guys. Used to tell it when I was a kid back home but definitely seems fitting to the situation you have us in:

"These three missionary dudes are captured by some wild, man-eating, Borneo tribe. They are dragged back to the campfire and then hoisted, buck naked, over the roasting pit. All this while the crazy native bone munchers dance and sing around the flames. Out comes the chief honcho. He must be three hundred pounds. Next to the chief is a little guy with a human bone stuck right through his nose. The little kook steps forward to approach the first captive and in broken down English asks, 'Death or UMUMPHAGUMPA?' The missionary guy is all like, 'I don't know what UMUMPHAGUMPA is but anything is better than death, I choose UMUMPHAGUMPA.' So, mini bone dude turns to the crowd and screams 'UMUMPHAGUMPA!' All the natives start chanting 'UMUMPHAGUMPA, UMUMPHAGUMPA, UMUMPHAGUMPA!'

"The chief gets up from his bad old throne and picks up a huge machete. He cuts the captive down and bends him over a nearby stump. He pulls aside his loincloth and proceeds to butt ram the missionary until he is way unconscious. The chief goes back to his throne while the poor guy is carried away by a group of natives and set free.

"The little man with the bone through his nose then approaches the second traveler. He gives em the same question, 'Death or UMUMPHAGUMPA?' The captive thinks for a moment and says back, 'As terrible as UMUMPHAGUMPA is, I choose UMUMPHAGUMPA.' Again, the little messenger chode turns to the crowd and screams 'UMUMPHAGUMPA!' The mob starts chanting 'UMUMPHAGUMPA, UMUMPHAGUMPA, UMUMPHAGUMPA!' The chief rises from his throne and the same gnarly ritual is on repeat. After, the second passed-out captive is set free.

"Finally, the third poor captive guy is approached by the little native with the bone through his nose. He proposes the same question as he did before. The man thinks for a sec and is all like, 'UMUMPHAGUMPA is too terrible for me. I choose death.' The little messenger chode with the bone then turns to the crowd and screams,

" 'DEATH BY UMUMPHAGUMPA!' "

Someone in the Tribe laughs, the rest do not.

"What was the freaking point of that, Jonah?" I ask.

"Sometimes you gotta take it in the ass for a little liberty, brah!" he says just loud enough so only I can hear him and then surveys the scene again, "And we better get out of this twisted Leonardo DiCrapio flick you got us in."

Jonah then turns to the Tribe and makes his best attempt to stand. He falls over into the sand. He lifts his head two inches from the ground and shouts, "We are willing to sacrifice to stay, just give us a ducking chance." He shouts louder than I have ever heard him shout on any wave.

There is silence for a while. A woman in the council stands, everyone turns their attention to her. "You mentioned your involvement in water irrigation and agriculture in the Ache region of Sumatra. I would like to see what you think of our farm."

"Yeah. Check it out. Deon here is a master in Agro anything. He is like the 'plant whisperer' or some shit." Jonah is still lying face down in the sand.

"Let me show the dark one," she says to Tex. "No harm can come from it."

"Goldie?" Tex asks permission.

"Yield is thin this year," she reminds the two men leading our trial. "Very thin."

"Yes, let them," Goldie replies.

I can feel the turn of tide. There is need in the group. A problem that I can most likely solve. But to what end?

As Monica makes her way over to our seats, Marcello perks up behind us. He has been silent the entire trial.

The woman starts unbinding our feet.

"I am Monica, Howard's wife. I was once a pharmacist but I was stranded here with Howard. We were not married then, strangers on a boat in fact. Maybe we can tell you that story later. I am in charge of pharmaceutical plants and herbs as well as second in charge of the planting. Goldie and the Swedish girl Svet manage the farm. I just make sure our pharmaceutical needs are met. Really no one on the island is an expert on agriculture."

Our legs are unbound. Monica and Goldie lead us to an area about two kilometers away. Marcello and Nely follow at a short distance. On the edge of the forest we pass a large pond with fish. I am told that the fish raised in the pond are used as a protein source when ocean fishing in the bay is not possible. We continue to a clearing on the edge of the forest. The field seems about three to four kilometers long and a kilometer wide. It has been well planted but poorly organized. The farmers are growing some tropical fruits and vegetables. Most of the field is dedicated to soy and rice. A small patch is left for Monica's plants. At several points I bend down and use my elbow and heel to sift through the soil. My hands remain bound.

"Hey Monica, let me taste a little dirt from that spot there." I point to the ground with my elbow. She looks at me with a perplexed look but I reassure her. After probing around in the dirt, she takes a pinch and places the soil on my tongue. I mull it around my mouth a bit, tasting both the acidity and the metallic nutrients. Then I spit it out. It's low tech but it gets the job done. We do the same taste test in a couple spots around the field. After a good look at the perimeter of the farm, sampling of the soil and observing the produce available, I let the guards know I am satisfied. We are led back to the square and return to our seats. The group has been disbanded, only council members remain.

"Did you get a sufficient look at the farm?" Howards asks me quietly.

"I did," I answer.

"Well then, tell us what you can offer. And then the council will make a final decision," Tex says.

Jonah looks at me with sincerity. I can hear his thoughts of guidance.

"Your farming system is highly inefficient given your resources," I begin. "The tomatoes could be growing in the shade of the mango trees. Rice sucks the water away from the citrus growing nearby. There is no central irrigation. I could give you a hundred more examples just from that quick glance."

"And you can do better?" Goldie asks.

"Yes, definitely. With some better irrigation and careful replanting I bet we could triple the yield."

"But wouldn't you have to dig up the crops we've got now?" Goldie asks.

"That is true but if we did it in shifts it would only impact your food supply for a few months. Especially if *'I'* do it carefully."

Goldie and Tex look at Howard.

"There is a second possibility in the meantime. The top soil is extremely weak in nutrients. You need a new system of fertilization for some of the more needy species. I propose an Aquaponic growth system."

"What kind of farming is that?"

"Well, it's not farming, it's Aquaponics."

"Aqua… what?" Tex asks.

"Isn't that how people grow Marijuana indoors?" Howard asks Monica.

"Kind of. You are thinking of Hydroponics, which is actually quite inefficient considering the amount of electricity it drains. Aquaponics is like a hydroponic garden done organically and outdoors. It uses a fish pond to complete an ecosystem that utilizes fish waste as organic food for the plants and in return the plants clean the water to provide a nontoxic environment for the fish." I pause to let the information sink in.

"Like a hydroponic garden, the Aquaponic garden uses no or little soil. The plants are organized into levels on a pyramid and allowed to grow their roots into a bed of rocks. This pyramid is then set on stands so that a drain can be installed at the bottom. Also, it is elevated so no soil depth is needed and it is easy to control growth. With the Aquaponic system, you don't have to worry about weeds or soil-based pests. Since there are no problems with these insects, which would typically eat away your crop, plants grow and grow. Also, there is no need for adding fertilizer. The fish provide all the fertilizer you need, allowing all of the nutrients to make it to the plants and provide for better tasting fruits and vegetables.

"Oh, and it grows a healthy fish crop at the same time," I add.

"That sounds like quite a lot to pull off with on an isolated island, mate," Howard says.

I think for a moment.

"Here's how we can make it work: We will utilize the pond outside the village you already fish in. We will have to gather shattered bedrock from the cliffs, enough to create a foundation higher than the waterline. Then using hollow bamboo tied together with vines we will create a scaffolding system for the plants. By recycling the water from the pond over the plants and back into the pond, the water will be cleaned by the plants and provide oxygenated water back to the pond. This complete system is usually powered by electricity or a solar panel and hooked up to a battery operated pump, but we will have to generate energy using human muscle to recycle and pump the water.

"In the end I can build a system which produces better fruits and vegetables easier than the typical garden. Additionally, you can eat more and more fish, a stellar source of protein, as their population will flourish in the enhanced environment. The pond will support a higher volume of fish. This is because the roots of the plants above clean it at a higher rate than the algae in it now.

"So there you have it, council members. With everyone's assistance I am sure we could have it up and running in weeks. This could be a real weapon in your arsenal for maintaining health in paradise," I conclude snidely.

"There is another thing. Can you bring the dry bag?" says Jonah, using his nose to point at the waterproof backpack. Howard makes his way over to it and hands it to Nely.

"Please pull out the ding repair kit. Open the fiberglass sheet box and dig to the bottom. There is a small pouch in there," Jonah instructs. Nely rifles through it and finds what Jonah describes. Nely opens a small tin and smiles. Marcello speaks for the first time all day, "Mota."

"Don't waste that, yo. There are exactly five seeds in that dimebag. Good seeds. I know Deon can pull off a sick crop with just those five," Jonah urges.

"Bonus offering," I smile.

"We have a lot to discuss as a council. Nely and Marcello will take you back to the Jungle Hut."

After about an hour we hear footsteps coming towards the hut. The door flap opens. Goldie, Tex, Marcello and Nely all come inside. They have a mattress made of home grown cotton and twine. They also brought our hobbit coats.

"That was fast," Jonah comments.

"Yes, it was practically a unanimous decision," Tex begins more in an address to the other people in the room. "Marcello is now your shadow. You don't leave this hut unless he is escorting you. If he is unavailable, you stay inside. When he in not with you, your feet are to be tied up. When this new farm system is up and running you may be invited to join the Tribe. Maybe."

"How bout a quick surf, Goldie?" Jonah asks the more amenable leader. "We did come all this way just for that wave."

"Earn your place in the Tribe, earn our respect and trust. Then you can take all the waves you want," Goldie says coolly.

"Not a moment before," Tex adds.

"We will," Jonah smiles.

"Or else death by UMUMPHAGUMPA," says Tex and laughs.

HiHo HiHo... Off to Work we Go

Jonah is up before sunrise.

"Can't sleep dude?" I ask.

"No paddling, no Zzzzzzs."

"Wow, I think I am still sleeping off the crossing here." I laugh. "Maybe I paddled a little more than the rest of the crew."

"Very funny, De. Always got the jokes."

"You are the one wielding junior high comedy."

"You are the reason we are tied up."

"You are the one who wants to play ball with the jungle sadists."

"You are the one who brought a ducking gun."

"Touché."

"Get some rest, bud. Have a feeling we are gonna be working our asses off for the Tribe come sunrise tomorrow."

"No can do, Mi Compadre. Just picturing the millions of unridden waves before we got here. Before your crazy ass hospital buddy and all this Tribe washed up. Now we are here, too, and all I can hear are those perfect formed waves lapping over the reef. It drives me crazy, bruddah."

"You'll get it, bro, and riding it will feel so good as you will have earned it," I say mockingly of Tex and his charade. "I still doubt we'll ever be set free."

The morning sun is bright when Nely and Marcello enter.

"Goodda," he says in his South African accent. "Time for work, ya?"

My gun is visibly holstered on his hip.

"Let's get this party started," I say.

Howard meets us on the path. Before we get to the village, I notice two German-looking guys at the fire pit.

"Tschuess," one says as we pass. "I am coming with you to the work."

"Sure. I'm Deon. This is Jonah. What's going on with the fire pit?" I ask.

"Ah yes we bring the fire. We take turns stoking the fire and having fun. That way we always have fire. I am working nights this month. My name is Lars. Everyone calls us 'Z German' as only one of us is here at a time."

"Ha, you ever miss each other?" I ask.

"No, I have had enough of him already this lifetime," says one of them.

"Which one are you?" Jonah asks.

"I am Lars. Vero is my cousin."

"How did you two get to the island?"

"This is a funny story, yes," Lars begins. "Before we find this place it was lots of mountains."

Howard chimes in from behind, "Back in Germany they were kind of famous for summiting volcanoes and mountains in record time."

"Howey, you just love stealing other people's thunder, donchya, brah?" Jonah asks.

"Guess a little," Howard smiles.

"Mountain men from Germany. Makes sense," Jonah says turning back to the storyteller.

"Ja. Dis is true."

"The first to try for a summit on Mt. Everest were Germans, yeah?" I ask.

"Ja. Dis is true. Only ten days in a year you can try for this," he tells us.

"Really?" asks Jonah. "Not many peaks around here, eh?"

"Must have been Rinjani on Lombok? " I ask.

"Aye," Howard says.

"Howie. Let Z German tell it, yeah brah?" Jonah laughs at our only ally on the island.

"Ja. We were trying to set a record for summit on one of the clearest days of the year. We missed the record by two minutes. At the top we noticed the island in the distance," one goes on to tell.

"Ja, when we are asking the guide making his way to the top an hour later, he avoided the question profoundly," the other finished.

"Sounds right on point," Jonah says.

"Back at the bottom we find the lack of knowledge of most people and the avoidance of the locals who did know about it makes us so much curious we just had to come," Lars says.

"They brought their survival kit and have been responsible for keeping the fire burning day in and night out ever since," Howard finishes. "It is quite a luxury on island to have a fire these past couple years."

"No more mountains now."

"No. Now you are learning how to surf on the most perfect wave in the world," Jonah points out with a glaring look at me.

"Ja," they grin.

We walk through the village and get a few glancing looks as people are up to their daily chores. Our surfboards are thrown around here and there as well. To Jonah and I, they are the reminder of the agreement we made with the Tribe. They also look recently surfed. Jonah attempts to kick me as we walk by.

"This better work, Deon."

"I know," I say. "Really don't plan to get thrown off a cliff."

We make our way to the edge of the village, and then beyond. Howard continues to lead.

"Svet will meet us later. Monica is already there," he tells us as we breach the tree line.

Work is hard but we make progress. Time drags on. I lose track of the days. Nely often leaves her post to assist, but Marcello is always on alert in the shadows, day in and day out. When he puts us to bed at night, Jonah and I have hours to catch up, but mostly we are exhausted and sleep. He still blames me for our current predicament as opposed to holding it against the Tribe. Mainly, the lack of surfing weighs him down.

When the sun is not too hot we start the day off hauling rocks from the north cliff of the island. Most hard labor is done under the heat of the sun. After pleading with Marcello to do some work under the full moon, he eventually agrees to watch us at night. Lars and Vero take turns to help drag stones while the other is on fire duty.

"Yo, Ed, how much longer is this digging around crap gonna take?" Jonah whines while hauling stones one night.

"A while Jonah, a while."

"Really?"

"Yeah, better we get it right the first time," I say.

Slowly we start to show signs of being over used and under fed. Each night we are given a modest provision from the village. I start sharing my provisions with Jonah as we are both becoming weak, but he has less fat cells to live off. Luckily, after a couple weeks the fish are thriving and some of the tomato plants are starting to fruit despite being moved to the pond. Fish and tomatoes day in and out. It sustains us. I am not sure what the others eat as we still have not been invited to join them. One day we are served rice with our fish so, based on the time of year it is safe to assume they at least have a stock pile of it as it is not nearly harvest season. One day at the end of the dry season the mango and papaya start to fall off the trees. We gorge ourselves in the shade just out of sight so no one notices. The diarrhea that follows is especially unpleasant that night as we are still bound by ropes.

With the upcoming rains we must hurry to finish planting. Goldie brings me all kinds of species out of the jungle.

"Where would you place the aubergine?" he asks.

"If I had known we had eggplant on island I would have put it with the other nightshade plants under the cover of the mango area a month ago."

"Can you still dig it up?" he asks.

"Not in time for the rains. We will see how it does with the wild potatoes. Next year we can move it," I inform the chef.

He is not happy. Each time he finds new plants it goes this way. It also further establishes my necessity to the Tribe. So, I play up the part a little. The pond is working ahead of schedule. Its main purpose, creating fertilizer and breeding fish, is functional by the first rains. Many of the more needy plant species moved from the garden thrive like never before in their new pest free environment full of nutrients.

Soon there is more than enough food coming off both the farm and the Aquaponic system than expected. Monica focuses on her herb garden.

Take a Walk

We are fast asleep from the hard work of day. Tex, Marcello, one of Z Germans and a face I recognize from the day of our capture enter the isolated Jungle Hut. We are blindfolded. It is more than enough manpower to lift us in our current state.

We are carried through the village but not in the direction of the farm. It is a path I am not familiar with, especially blindfolded. I can sense most of the Tribe is present during the walk. The steps become softer and deeper. It is sand or light dirt. We pause for a moment. No one speaks. Even through the blindfold I can make out firelight, and can sense many people around. There are strange noises. An odd smell comes from the fire. There is a weird vibe in the air. Our escorts carry us farther. We are too exhausted to protest. I wonder if Jonah is still asleep as he is carried.

We are dropped to the ground with a thud.

"What's going on?" I ask, the restraints holding me.

No one answers.

"Jonah, you here?"

He does not answer.

My rope binds are released but the blindfold remains.

"Stand," I am instructed by the new voice.

I stand up.

"Turn."

I turn.

I take a deep breath, clenching my fist ready to strike as he approaches from behind. But then the moment for resistance has passed.

"Don't move," he finally instructs from behind as he takes off the blindfold. "You move, you're dead."

I stand at the absolute edge of the cliff.

"You are on Sunrise Point, ya," Marcello tells me from a safe distance away.

It must be 60 meters. Straight down. The swell surges below.

"There is only one way to end this. You must choose," Tex's voice rings.

I turn my head to them. The three stand weapons drawn.

"Really, it has come to this?" I say, looking at the water below. I imagine the silver tipped arrowheads piercing my dark abraised skin.

"It has," Marcello answers me. "We will give you until the count of five to jump."

"It will be better for all of us this way. Trust me," Tex says in a monotone voice.

There is no time to think. The moment of resistance is well past.

They all yell in unison.

"One."
"Two."
"Three."
"Four."
"Five."

At the five count I jump off the cliff.

I fall.

I have a lot to think about on the way down but for some reason these moments are always shorter than one has time for.

I hit the water.

Cut Loose

I am not dead. I am far in the depth of a break in the reef. It is a long swim up but I breach the surface and breathe. There are torches lit upon the cliffs equally spaced and leading back to the beach.

"Swim," Tex yells from the cliff.

Jonah is here in the water somewhere too. "Jo?!"

"Here. big guy."

He swims up beside me.

"Did you know that was gonna happen?"

"Totally. They told me yesterday," he says. "Really, just wanted to give your big Hawaiian ass a scare."

"You shit," I say. "Thanks for telling your best friend."

"And miss this precious look on your face. Duck that. Priceless."

We follow the line of the torches on the cliff, held by members of the Tribe. It is a long swim but the adrenaline and the incredible feel of being in the water again seem to carry us the entire distance of the cliff right up to the beach. We make the shallows, and I tackle Jonah and laughingly put him in a headlock. We roll around all the way to the sand, happy to be free for the first time in ages. The Tribe emerges from the jungle, torches ablaze.

Howard comes out of the tree-line first. "Yesterday you fell asleep a stranded survivor. A captive. When the sun rises today you shall wake a tribesman of the island."

By moonlight, everyone makes their way down to the beach. They hold torches and surfboards. Initiation is apparently a nighttime ritual. They make a circle of boards on the sand and set the torches into mounts around the perimeter. "Please have a seat. You earned it," Tex says pointing to our surfboards.

We sit.

"As you know, I am Tex, founder of the Tribe," he goes on. "Welcome."

"I am Goldie," Goldie has brewed an alcohol from coconut milk. "Drink up."

"Doc Howard at your service, mate."

"Monica, most call me Momma Mon. By the way, don't think you are gonna go on eating all my mangos."

"Trust in the Tribe," says Marcello. "Drink up ya!

Svetlana, the Swedish girl from the farm says, "Halo."

The moonshine hits hard. Not the one above my head but the one in my hand. Either there are some hallucinogenic qualities or we start flashing back to the mushrooms on Gili Trawangan. One or the other. People start to morph into creatures, plants and other fantastic hybrids.

"Minah Zavut Tasha." The ballerina takes a curtsy and gracefully walks back to her place. "Welcome to paradise."

"Sababa," the tiny Israeli girl says. "It means 'all is good.'"

"Name's Max. Really looking forward to that first surf aye."

"Tess. Pleasure."

"Je m'appelle Alice." She wears only her bikini bottom and a necklace of white sea shells. "I am French."

"Hope you had a nice swim," Amelia, the tall redhead giggles as she walks by Jonah and takes a seat near the water.

"Lars."
"Vero."
"We make fire!"

Marcello sits as far from me as the circle will allow.

Everyone chats and jokes for a while. Now with fifteen members of the Tribe, we finish the booze quickly. It sticks around my system for quite a while. Less so for Jonah. Tess, who sits next to me, starts to tell us her story.

"Before here, we bounced around following swells."

"How did you manage that?" Jonah asks.

"I do a bit of freelance photography."

"She is really good!" Max jumps in. "Now she gathers stones and other materials to paint scenes of our life here and the surf happenings."

"Max here is my little brother -- the most cocky semi-pro alive. After a photo shoot in Sumbawa everything went a bit Pete Tong. The plane had to make an emergency route back, due to a faulty seal. Because the plane was off direction, the island was just below us. Of course the little shit had the window seat so he noticed the wave first."

"We only had a moment. Luckily Tess got the picture. I reckon somewhere on a camera in Aussie town is the only photo still existing of it."

"So the wave, have you seen it big yet?" Jonah asks.

Max says, "Oh, it gets big. We had to wait a month just to approach the gaps in the cliff."

"How did you get through?"

Max says, "First we hired a boat in Sumbawa to take us as close as the Indos will go. Then we launched jet skis I borrowed from a corporate sponsor. Bunch a' wankers. Told em we were going to shoot some outer reefs on a big winter swell and they would have exclusive rights to the pics. Straight stole that shit from those deep pocketed cunts."

"Jesus… would you watch your mouth," Tess warns.

"I like your style, Max," Jonah chuckles.

"No matter, matey. The Gent's got the skis now. Not that we are going anywhere in the near future."

"Yeah, they would have to rip you off the planet kicking and screaming before you would quit this place, Max," Tess laughs.

"Who is the Gent?" I ask.

"The Gentleman," Max pauses. "Don't worry about it tonight, matey, sure you will be introduced to the munted fuck or his army of shit-eaters at some point on your stint."

"Intolerable," Tess mutters as she rolls her eyes at her brother.

People dance. People sing. At some point during this night I fall asleep. Jonah parties through with anticipation of waves in the morning. By 3am or so it is starting to rain. By sunrise it is pouring and windy. Jonah stumbles out with his board under arm.

"Where are you going?" one of Z Germans asks.

"SURFING, Duh!"

"It is shit out there now," I say with sleepy eyes.

"The worst day of surfing is better than a day without!"

"I agree," says Nely, who gets her board under arm.

The whole pack of farmers, Monica included, make their way to the waves in the same paddle out. We laugh and scream over the rain and lightning.

"We did it, Big Ed."

"We did," I think to myself.

"And here comes your first reward," Monica says.

As shitty as the windchop is, Jonah is on it like the lightning above us. He manages a shallow drop, a nice bottom turn and a few quick maneuvers before airing out the back.

"Def better than a poke in the eye," he says on his way back to the pack.

"Or getting shot at!" I say, making my way to the next wave: a solid chest-high wind-chopped ride. It isn't the wave we saw when we arrived, but it is damn fun.

Freedom feels amazing.

The Daily Grind

We sleep through most of the next day. Guess it is kind of the first day off in ages, but with all the rain the plants are plenty happy.

"Dude, it's like noon already," Jonah stirs me. "We are moving, bro, grab your gear."
"How are you alive, man? That coconut juice absolutely wrecked me." The hangover pulses through both bones and muscles.
"What da matter, big guy, can't hold yo liquor," he responds in an accent mimicking my own.

"Maybe not." My head throbs. "Did that shit make you trip out too?"

"Naw, you're just weak sauce." He laughs. "Lets get shakin', foo."

"Or what, you gonna get all ghetto on my ass, white boy?"

We move into the main lodge where everyone in the Tribe sleeps under one roof. The outlying huts are used for privacy or a quick escape. Turns out we were taking up one of the favorite locations for lovers. Monica and Howard pass us in the opposite direction on the path.

Not a moment goes by inside the main lodge before Max practically jumps Jonah.

"Mate, Tex says you are on fishing duty. Suit up and grab your board," he says, and barely a moment later Max and Jonah are in surfing gear with board and makeshift fishing lines and nets under arm.

"Dude, I am so super stoked to be off farm duty!"

"Yeah, and now you're in the water like full time." Max smiles.

Turns out Jonah is quite good at fishing as well.

As nice as fishing sounds or cooking or building new living structures appeals to me, I love my babies. I cannot think of another place on the island I would want to spend my time working. I tend to the farm every day from the mid-morning sun until sunset session. The hobbit cloak keeps those nasty UV rays off. Surf conditions are generally best in the morning, and because of the cliffs surrounding the island it is rarely too windy. And after a day's work on the farm, there is no better way to cool off than spending a late afternoon in the waves. Without fail, Jonah has been the first in the water every day since we joined The Tribe.

One day I find him absent and then it turns out he has skipped fishing duties even though it is a clear day. Jonah is out on Three Palm Point. He sits under the coconut trees gazing out to sea. An empty shell is drained of electrolyte rich water and the husk lies beside him. The sun is luminously setting over one shoulder, the gap in the cliff looms over the other.

"Haven't seen you all day dude, what's shakin?" I ask.

"It is so quiet, bradda De," Jonah says. "I love how quiet it is."

"Me too, Jo, me too."

Neither of us speak again until we make our way down for bedtime.

Another day I am turning up to the community kitchen with a bundle of produce from the garden for Goldie. Jonah and Max have just arrived as well.

"Looks like a good day of fishing," Goldie asks Jonah.

"Ask and ye shall receive, brah," he jokes as he drops three ripe fish onto the counter.

"Hey Goldie, whatever bounty we pull in, you sure can make some delicious creations," Max points out.

"True that!" Jonah puts out there.

'You should have seen him in the galley with unlimited supplies and a limitless budget," Tex says affectionately.

"Oh no, here it comes," Goldie sighs.

"Goldie was a chef to the movie stars you know. Studios contracted him for shoots all over the world," Tex begins as he puts his arm around his partner. "Even cooked for the heavy hitters while they were filming. That is how we met."

"He will embellish, watch," Goldie says in a whisper to us.

"I was boat captain on this huge luxury yacht in Southeast Asia. A company from Singapore owned that beauty. Anyway, Paramount studios was doing reshoots on this muck-up of a film Mel Gibson was starring in. If you ever make it to Hollywood, never hire a high-maintenance superstar for the main role. Especially not a star with a giant freaking family in tow. So Gibson, his menagerie of rugrats, their tutors and servants all take a charter on my boat. Of course it was paid for by the studio while he took a break from filming reshoots," Tex goes on.

"I was personal chef to Gibson for the shoot, all negotiated by his manager and paid for by the studio, so I got on the boat too," Goldie adds.

"That must have been awesome," Max says.

"Ha, not in any way. Allergy to this, I don't like that, no gluten, no tomatoes, no potatoes. Wah Wah Wah. It was a messy bloody headache," Goldie answers.

"Oh, the drama with kings and queens! My only break was spending the wee hours with this rugged boat captain," Tex grins as he concludes Goldie's story for him.

"Yeah, it was love at first sight," Goldie says with daggers.

"More like you were too tired to fight me off. Wasn't really difficult to convince this sexy and underappreciated chef to stay onboard full time," Tex says.

"Especially cause the Singaporean owners paid more than the studios," Goldie finishes. "Plus, turns out the studio finally got sick of paying for all Gibson's perks so I would have been cut soon anyway."

"Goldie and Tex cruising the high seas?" Jonah asks. "How in the hell did two gay dudes from New Zealand get stuck with cowboy nick names?"

Tex runs his hand through Goldie's blonde hair. "Well, the first is obvious." He grins. "As for me, I started my career as co-captain moving oil tankers in the Gulf of Mexico. During time off or breaks we would take turns riding longboards out the back because the big old boats would kick up a wake you could surf. It was a lot of fun in the carefree days of my youth but the ambition in me wanted more. More money and more responsibility."

"And more power," I think to myself.

"So I started running cargo ships through the Suez Canal right up until the Somali pirates stepped up their game. One time we got boarded and a couple broke into the locked down bridge. I took out two of them with a single shotgun shell. The bodies fell from the flight bridge about 50 feet. Despite the brilliant Kiwi accent I have, the boys on board nicknamed me Tex…"

"Like the old Hollywood westerns," Goldie finishes his story stealing just a little bit of his partner's thunder.

"Ha, aren't they cute," interjects Monica as she walks in with a bushel of herbs.

Jonah and Max look at each other with raised eyebrows. Jonah calls out, "Last one to get a tube does cleanup duty tonight." As they race out of the kitchen to the water they nearly take out Monica with surfboard fins.

"Sometimes I forget they are grown men," Monica says. We all laugh.

Days come and go, each one simple and yet significant as they pass. Weeks begin to blend. The biggest breaks we have in the beautiful monotony are the passing rain storms and amazing surf sessions.

The Aquaponic system is up and running at full production sometime in March, toward the end of rainy season. Tex asks me to teach everyone how important the balanced system is. We insist that everyone learns how to care for it. Tex declares that each tribesman must spend two or three hours of their week in manpower turning the wooden gears to create the energy needed to clean it. Really only about two hours a day is necessary to clean the tanks. The overshoot is needed to regulate people operating on "island time." I expect everyone to come to training over the next few days and they do. Lars 'n Vero in different shifts of course. One person does not show up at all. Tasha never comes.

I broach this issue with Tex and a couple other tribesmen but generally people advise me to avoid a confrontation or even an explanation. The most I ever hear is, "She works when she has to." Marcello, the supposed island sheriff, avoids the question altogether and simply walks away from me in silence. I decide just to let it go.

Svetlana gets really interested in the Aquaponic system and we end up spending a lot of time together. It feels like she never leaves the farm. She likes talking about plants with me but not much else. I learn that she is the only person to ever be invited to the island but when I inquire further she changes the subject back to tropical plants. The only people I hear her chatting about other topics with are Goldie and Marcello. It is not a rude stance or even a cold one. She just feels like she keeps things easy. Marcello stops by the farm occasionally, both for his man-power-hour and TLC time with Svet. Sometimes she even gets him to do a little extra work moving this or that for her. I observe the way they touch, the way they look at one another and mostly the way they laugh together. It is hard to hide affection even for two ultra reserved people. It is obvious to me that they have a romantic relationship going well before I see them head off in the direction of the old Jungle Hut together.

With all of my agriculture projects up and running, living on the island falls further into monotony. However things do happen. As slow as they come, life is not static. These events might be things overlooked or appear underwhelming to people in another kind of grind. But to us, the Tribe, it is the simplicity of survival mixed with the welcome blessing of paradise that drives our day. Even the most minor of events can skew to major occurrence here.

"Hey Howard, I have a new plant to show you."

"Can't say I recognize it," he says.

Yeah, most don't know what it looks like in its natural form. Found it growing wild in the bush a couple month's back."

"Can Monica use it?"

"Not exactly her type," I answer. "Think you might get more pleasure out of it."

'Really?"

"Yeah, let's go pay Lars and Vero a visit, perhaps they have something brewing?" I play dumb.

"I can smell it, but I don't believe my nose." He says as we walk up to the fire smoldering in the outskirts of the village.

"Hey Howard, mi amigo!" Lars and Vero hand him a cup of liquid from the pot heating above the fire pit.

All four of us have a cup in hand and one of Z Germans says, "Braust" as our cups come together. They make an earthen noise. "Cheers" I echo. Z Germans and I take a sip but Howard cannot take his eyes from the dark liquid for some time. He stands breathing in the aroma.

"Mate, I haven't had a cup of coffee in about fifteen years. Shoot, I forgot just how damn good it tastes," he says ecstatically as he sits and takes a small pull on his piping hot cup a' Joe. The four of us take a seat around the fire.

"Don't go getting all teary eyed on me now," I say to Howard.

"Yes, Coffee Good Yes!" says Z Germans half joking but very much serious.

"More probable I will turn 'Cornholio' on you guys from all this caffeine which I have not been in contact with for some time," Howard says and laughs.

"Yaaaaaaaaa. COFFEEE!" shout Z Germans in a hilariously stoked accent.

We all start laughing. Hopped up on caffeine Z Germans start arguing about who is going to head off for chow first. I offer to watch the fire till they come back. They are gone, fast. Howard and I sit for a while. He takes a second top up and then a third. It is the third cup, with all the grinds settled on the bottom, which he really savors. We sit long past sunset hour. We miss dinner. Howard is remarkably calm and composed now, minus a big right toe that won't stop shaking.

"Howard, have you noticed your toe, buddy?" I point.

"Haha," Howard begins. "See," he pauses to compose himself for the next line. "I am the Great Cornholio, I need TP for my bunghole."

We both start laughing.

"Hey, Howey."

"Aye, Deon."

"Wanna know the best part about today?" I ask.

"Aye."

"Nothing really exceptional happened."

"Maybe not for you mate, maybe not for you."

Monkey Business

More time passes and it has not rained in weeks now.

I am chatting with Goldie one evening while he cooks fish and veggies from the day's harvest.

"Actually chap, seems like a longer than usual rainy season. Turns out it was a good year to move crops around."

"Guess we won't starve after all."

"No, in fact there is about double the food we are accustomed to having already."

"Yeah, double down on the same," I think to myself, and then ask, "We eat a lot of fish and veggies. Ever get sick of cooking the same thing?"

"Do you get sick of eating?"

"Yeah, not really man. But you were such an artist in the kitchen, just like Tex says."

"Naw, food is food, with or without all the flair from an unlimited Hollywood budget."

"Speaking of food sources, how do things around here fare in the dry season?"

"Bugs are more common, plants can die from heat and too much sun exposure."

"Yes, same story everywhere in the tropics. I will keep an eye out."

"Soon it will be time to harvest the rice patty," he informs me. "The Swedish girl really works her little tush off then. Last year we would not have had a proper harvest short her help."

"How long does the rice last for?"

"A couple months, we store some, too, just in case we have a rough harvest."

"Have you ever been to the rice patties in Bali?" I ask.

"No, can't say I have," answers Goldie.

"It's really fantastic. Those traditional villages have it down to a science without using a single bit of modern technology," I say. "It's totally archaic with huge oxen, flat line plows, hillside terracing created by hand, geese, scarecrows like the old days of farming. It's so cool."

"What are the geese for?" Goldie asks.

"The geese control the insects that can destroy a harvest. Oh, and when the oxen aren't working the Balinese put them to races for sport. That is a sight, man."

"Wish we had some geese. Good for the pests and Christmas dinner."

"No geese here?" I ask.

"Nope, no geese."

"Wish I had proper hindsight of what to bring."

"Deon, we all wish we thought of one thing or another before washing ashore."

"What would you have taken with you?"

"Whatever kitchen knives and sharpeners I could have fit on that little half submerged tender before Tex launched us. Oh, and really big mixing bowls."

"Figures. Slicing through fish guts with dull knives and stone utensils can't be that easy, even for the master chef, huh?"

"This is my curse," Goldie sighs. "Oh, and for Christmas dinner, Deon..."

"Yes."

"It will be fish with veggies and rice."

I laugh. "Can't wait!"

"Soon enough my friend. Soon enough."

"Food is food," I think to myself on the way back to the farm.

Sometime later in the week Marcello meets me at the farm. It is toward the end of my shift. He has a pair of those hunting crossbows I have been so well acquainted with.

"Talked to Goldie the other night, hey," he begins. "Says you are ready to mix up the grub a little."

"Yeah, a dripping juicy red t-bone steak would be nice once and a while."

He tosses me a bow. "Do follow."

We head northeast from the farm. On the walk we have a little bit of time to talk.

"No hard feelings about before ya," Marcello starts. "The Beretta you had flash right off the boat really threw my ass back to basics."

"No, you were just looking out for the group," I reply. "But I owe you one for the thud to the dome."

"And looking out for my own skin man," he adds. "Don't you plan on collecting that debt any time soon ya."

"How bout we call it all a truce then?" I ask.

"Good by you?" he replies.

"Good by me."

A few steps later I ask him about his history.

"How did a large black Saffer end up on this little rock?"

"After getting released from the Ranger Corps I stayed away from all the South African nonsense," he begins explaining. "Turns out I got a passion for athleticism. Got really into Ironman tournaments and long distance swimming."

"That's how you ended up here, huh?"

"Sure is. I was gapping several Indonesian islands for training. Found the island by mistake. Just swam ashore," Marcello tells me.

"You get the same greeting I got?" I ask snidely.

"Not exactly. Tex was looking a bit weaker than he does today. He came down unarmed to say 'hello'. Things grew from there ya."

The dense jungle around us starts to become sparser.

"You and Tex get along well then, 'ya'?" I tease him by adding the Saffer ending to the sentence.

"It's true. We hit it off quickly. He convinced me to stay. Things needed building and I know how to use my hands. Goldie actually got a bit jealous of us for a stint but even after being stuck on an island with four guys and a married woman twice my age, I remain straight as that arrow you are holding."

"Bet you were happy when some chicks washed ashore then?"

"You could say that. I enjoy my work. I enjoy this island. No racism, no bullshit like back home. It feels free. I love working with my hands, construction, and like any good African, I never tire of the hunt, no matter what the game. The island sheriff thing just kind of happened as more and more people washed up the last few years. Also really hated being the one to throw old Gabe off the island ya."

"Max does a little carpentry with you as well, right?" I ask. "How do you drag him out of the water?"

"With pride, Deon. Everyone in Aus knows how to use their hands," he begins. "After Max and Tess came over, we organized the Tribe to build the central hall out of wood and actual insulation for a proper sleep. A community should lay down together and rise together. That is the way of the Tribe."

"Before, you all stayed in those old huts of mud and palm fronds, then?"

"Ya, we still use them but usually for more private affairs."

"Like you and Tasha?" I pry further. "I have seen the way you two interact or better worded: don't interact."

"We had a thing once. It is over now," he says in a flat tone.

"The Swedish girl a bit simpler then?" I don't know why but I am really enjoying pushing his buttons.

"You could say that ya."

"I heard she is the only one ever invited to come for real. How is that?"

"Svet spent most of her teen years on her grandfather's farm in southern Sweden. He rescued her from an abusive father. As you have sorted, she knows a fair amount about plants and such. After finishing Uni she took a vacation to Bali. It was her first ever opportunity to escape the brutal Swedish winter. Some beach boy in Kuta Bali, originally from Sumbawa, told them rumors of the island but would not dare take her. She followed a similar route as you did but alone and by very different means. In the end she was about to give up when she met Tex at a store in Lombok. Tex and I were out on a secret mission getting emergency provisions for the island during the worst harvest season yet. It's the only time anyone ever left the island and came back.

"Svet was used to growing stuff in harsh conditions and I thought she could help out. But also we needed more women to balance the population before madness set in. I convinced Tex to invite her. Told him I would not return unless he invited her ya. Three of us on the makeshift rig with all the rice and canned goods. We almost died on the ride back. Luckily she has paid that debt and more. Plus, she gets along brilliantly with Goldie which kind of got him off my---" he stops short. "Shhhhh." Marcello crouches to one knee. He is in hunt mode.

We are about a kilometer into the jungle which is supposed to be off limits to the Tribe.

We listen. A pack of something starts making noise in the distance.

"Here they come." He motions to the area of bush from which the source of the noise moves toward us.

First a large male shows himself, then several more and then the females carrying offspring too young to walk on their own.

"Monkeys?" I ask in surprise.

"Bloody hell! There are heaps at the moment ya."

"Monkeys? We are hunting monkeys?"

"There is no other wild game on island, Deon."

I count near a hundred in the group of primates.

"That's a lot of monkey, man."

"Sure is. Their numbers have swelled big time ya. Hasn't really been reason to go hunting with all that food coming in off the farm."

The monkeys start to come closer toward us. We continue speaking in hushed tones. The pack is nearly in range of our weapons.

"See the big one in the back with the gashed up ear?" Marcello asks me. "You see him?"

There are so many. I squint my eyes. "Big saggy balls?" I say jokingly.

"Slight gimp. Rear of the pack," he checks me.

"Yeah, I see him." I start to raise my weapon.

"That's the alpha male," Marcello says. "Don't shoot him. Any of the other biggins are fair game."

"Why not shoot him?" I ask.

"We don't shoot him because If the alpha dies then all the others start fighting for position and it can turn into a bloody mess. Half the pack can die from mortal wounds or complications of a scourge. Less monkey means less food for us in a crunch," Marcello explains.

"Got it," I say. "It is my first time on safari after all."

I aim at another monkey. I fire. I completely miss. The monkeys freeze for a minute. A couple break from the pack to look around.

"Try again, Deon. The trick is not just to hit one. It is to get to the carcass before the other feral buggers drag it off for their own meal ya."

I aim at one of the big scouts. He is close. I fire. I miss again. Marcello raises his crossbow and hits him square in the head. The monkey makes a pathetic noise then hits the ground with a thud.

"Told you, I never miss. Now go fetch dinner, honey. Fast!"

I make a dash toward the fallen monkey. I pause when I come upon it and see part of its head missing.

"Hurry, Deon!"

You would think the wild animals would be scared of the human carrying a dead family member under one arm and a crossbow under the other. Nope. Not these monkeys. They start hissing and throw things at me.

"Mate, let's dash!" Marcello shouts.

Most of the monkey pack is in hot pursuit. A small stone hits me in the back. I pause for a moment and turn only to be pummeled with more stones and sticks flush with thorns on them.

"Keep moving east," Marcello shouts.

I am out of breath.

"Haven't used my legs this much in years," I shout ahead.

"Keep moving east. Don't stop or you are monkey chow ya!"

"Why east?"

"Trust me."

"Says the fucker who enticed a pack of wild monkeys to chase my ass," I shout.

"East!" he shouts back from at least two football fields in the clear.

The jungle grows lush again. My sprint turns to a jog and then a quick walk. I expect the monkeys to jump me at any moment. When I finally catch up to Marcello he is reclining on a large tree.

"Well done, brother," he says to me. I throw the monkey carcass at him. He picks it up off the ground by grabbing the arrow tip.

"Don't mess with your dinner." He laughs at me.

I am way out of breath.

"They... stopped... chasing... me. Thought I .... was gonna... have to ... jump off a cliff or... some... shit."

"You should have seen your face ya!" Marcello is now laughing furiously.

"My arms still work." I drop the crossbow and making my playful intentions clear I go to tackle him. "Gimme my monkey, foo!"

Like a ninja he uses my superior weight against me as I charge at him and I end up wrapping the tree instead. I am quickly put in a choke hold. Marcello knows hand to hand combat as well as weapons.

"I got it fair and square. Gimme my monkey, cheetah boy."
"I shot it ya." Marcello points out.

With a light pummel of my elbow to the kidney, Marcello recoils and I manage to wrap my arms around his legs. I get him down and we roll around on the jungle floor like siblings trying to pin each other. Only thing is, we have both had advanced combat training.

Marcello finally gets me good and I yield. We start walking back to the village.

"Getting chased through the bush by a pack of wild monkeys is not exactly my idea of forging a new friendship."

"Ha. Guess now we are really even ya."

"We will see, my fellow tribesman."

"Game on?" Marcello asks.

"Game on," I answer. A moment later I ask, "So why did the pack stop chasing me anyway?"

"That's the trick ya," Marcello begins explaining. "There are two rival packs on the island. The one you shot at today is from the smaller pack. Their territory is the northwest bush. The group to the southeast guards the fresh water source and the flush banana sections."

"So, one gang will not venture into the area of the other for fear of conflict. Not unless one proposes all out war."

"Exactly."

While I Was Asleep

What up all you stellar dudes & dudettes!

Deon has been down for hours now. I mean passed the duck out yo! Snot nosed and snoring like an ogre. My boy can sleep. I mean who doesn't appreciate the beauty of the nap... just seems a little 3 hour midday snooze might be seem a little pre-madonna, you big goon.

So, anywhoo, we are all here and shit like that. Big–E's little quest for surfer's paradise paid off fo shi'izle. Couple bumps along the ride, like almost being dead five different ways, but nothing a homie can't tap out on. He packed some heat for real, that kinda sucked. Would have rather not been tied up in the mess which unfolded shortly after our imminent arrival, but seems to be all cool now. Thank you Baby Jesus!

Oh and being tied down for a couple months, literally, that shit is wack for sure.

On to bigger and better. This rock is crazy wild. Like we rolled up in some cheesy ass 70's flick and stumbled upon a forgotten dinosaur island. Time warp. Bunch of cave people banging on sticks, monkeys, talking birds, stone tools, ugachaka around the fire. Crazy wild. Post apocalyptic at moments too. Still trying to wrap my head around this thing.

Oh and taking a dump twice daily in that gnarly jungle hole out back ain't exactly in my picture of heaven on earth but guess we are still human and all.

Wait! Gotta jam about the chicks round here for a minute. Girls are fly. There is this one, Alice, she is all, 'I am French. I don't wear stupid bikini top.' Awesome right? No. She is totally lesbo'd out. Bummer. But there are more pickins fo sho. Monica, she is a total MILF by every standard measurement known to mankind. But, she is also a little married to Howie, who is THE MAN, so cross her off the list. Unfortunately, big African homeboy with the handgun has his eyes all-up on that Russian hottie. So does Alice I'm figuring. Gonna steer clear of that mess. Well the first part at least. The second part could be fun. Hopefully navigate into those waters on a catamaran at some point. Now don't think I am out of the game like that early. Tess, not really my style but super chill and YO!, she can surf. Svet, the Sweetish farm girl. HOT! Genuinely hope to be milking some of that soon. Oh wait, one more. There is this deliciously fine strawberry blonde, Amelia. She is always in the water. Like 24/7. Haven't exactly got her wired yet but have a feeling that could be game on. Once in a while she sends over a look with those emerald gems of hers and I totally pop a semi – no lies. Anywhoo, we got time. Better watch my back cause there isn't really a change of scenery coming for a while.

OK, the wave. Oh my great god of surfing, thank you for blessing me with your wave! Jah Praise. The divine thing peals like a dream. A-Frame. Set up like a machine. Tube section right at takeoff. Jah Praise. Sick covers. I mean sooooo pitted. Then you get spit out and it is all like 'Wapahh!' off the lip. Then a couple more times too if you want. 'Wapahh!' 'Wapahh!' Thing walls up for days. Rippable all the way down the line and then an inside barrel section. Its all, "Excuse we waiter, Green Room with a table for two." Totally Epic. Kick out, paddle channel, back for more. Un-ducking-believable!

Only thorn is that I gotta put up with this total kook and a half. Day in and day out dude is on the wave. Total goober. Always talking like, 'Hey watch this one mate.' 'Bet you can't pull this one off Cali.' 'Did you see me on that nugget or was I moving too fast for your munted old man vision.' Kid did a minute on the tour back in the real world. Got his photo snapped a few times and now thinks he can hang with the men. Dream on sucker.

Alright, well that about sums up my position on all that. Signed, sealed and delivered. Oh wait. This here is Deon's diary thingy so figure he will be the only one reading it. Oh well, guess I best go out with a bang then.

Luv ya my Nig!

Kisses,
Jonah

Sunrise Session

It's a vivid purple and red sunrise over the North Cliff with offshore trade winds putting just a tiny hint of texture on the surface. The A-frame is peaking head high and running down the line in splendid form. As usual, Max and Jonah are first in the water.

I make my way to the lineup just in time to watch the two shortboards splitting a good set wave. Jonah takes the right and Max goes backside on the left. They carve and snap the thing like a lumberjack on a piece of wood first thing in the morning. Both are incredible surfers.

"Jonah has finally met his match," I think to myself.

Tess and Monica take the next wave and I sit up on the big board in the center of the bay to watch both. Monica is a solid surfer but I am always impressed by Tess's grace on the wave. On one part of the wave she runs her hand across the face to enter a short stall section. The spray glows yellow in the morning sun.

"Morning, Deon," Tex greets me first.
"Morning Tex."
"Guten tag," Says one of Z Germans.
"Sleep in a bit ya?"
"Bon Jour."
"Da."

"Sets are about five minutes apart plenty of waves in each one."

The Tribe is generally super chill in the water and actually follows good surfing etiquette. Most of the time. Another wave in the set starts to form on the reef.

"Go, Girl," Goldie calls Tasha into it.
"Spaciba," she shouts back while paddling into position.

"She rides an elephant gun from the 80's that Gabe left on the island but she is so small it flows like a longboard," Howard tells me.

"Groovy," I laugh.

"That looked like a fun one aye, Tess," Howard says while she is making her way back up the left side channel.

"Meh, it was all right," Tess says to us a little out of breath from paddling.

"Looked good from my angle. Catch a little shower did you?" Tex says.

"Yeah, maybe a little bit," Tess says as she blushes.

"For someone who spends so much time on the sand 'photographizing,' you sure got a lot of style in you," I say.

"Guess it's genetics. Oi, don't look now here come the jokers," Tess cocks off.

Max and Jonah are paddling straight up the middle. The two make their way back pointing and yelling between duck diving inside waves.

"Mine went longer!"
"I was backside and still got more turns in, you wanker."
"Ha, I would give you a six score! At best!"
"Get munted, Yank scum."
"Bogan trash."

"Hooligans!" Howard laughs. "Just what the doctor ordered first thing in the morning."

"Here comes another set, shut it you two," Tess instructs. "NOW!"

They shut up.

"Have I ever mentioned that I love the way you handle them," I say to Tess.

"Little brothers." She sighs.

"Brotha from anotha mother," Jonah says smugly looking my way for approval.

"God I hate when you try to be ghetto."

"Words!" Max says trying to be both black and American at the same time.

"I said pipe down, you Barney scum," Tess yells at Max then turns to me. "Sometimes those genetics scare me as well."

I laugh.

"Set coming. Hey Jo, lets split this one," Howard says from out back. "I'll go right."

"Left," Jonah calls. They both start paddling into position for the first set wave.

"The left is mine," Amelia calls from just above the water surface. Jonah kicks out the back just as Amelia drops in from priority position. Her Monofin bodysuit helps weave her in and out of the wave face. It reminds me of dolphins surfing back in Cali.

"She is awesome," Tess smiles.

"Oui," Alice answers. "Je l'aime."

"Its like body surfing on roids," I joke.

Jonah comes paddling back to the lineup. He is not happy.

"Mate, you just got called off by a Mermaid," Tess says.

Max laughs obnoxiously loud.

"Duck you."

The Dorm

My house back in the hood smelled like surfboard resin and moldy soil. The college dorms were bad enough with two stoner roommates and late night munchies everywhere. The barracks in Texas reeked of rotten socks and day old chow. I won't even talk about the perpetually feral scents of the rainforest in Panama. My apartment in Japan hovered in a balance of Pinesol, beer and air freshener mixed with Ayumi's cigarettes. Sumatra was dirt. The house in Bali: a fantastic blend of cloves, incense and sunscreen. But nothing can describe the smell of our island quarters.

Fifteen island squatters under one roof. Beds made of natural fiber over Kayu decks. Hammocks made of jungle vines. Sandbag pillows. Mildew that hides in every corner and every crack, no matter how hard one tries to clean. Air that doesn't move for months at a time. The fragrance of a people sleeping shoulder to shoulder. Fish, digested and otherwise. Herbs. Saltwater. Never drying feet. Coconuts. Homemade candles from recycled surfboard wax. Ocean air. Smoke off the fire. Palm leaves that line the roof. Jungle. Drying clothes. Men and women.

Tex, Goldie, Monica, Howard, Marcello, Tasha, Nely, Alice, Svet, Amelia, Lars, Vero, Tess, Max, Jonah, Deon. We sleep together, we sleep like a tribe.

It is a smell to cherish forever.

Bearings

I have now been on island long enough to get a lay of the land.

The entire island is a sunken caldera, partly retaken by the elements. It is easiest to describe from Sunrise Point, on the south east cliff, where I stand now.

Looking over the ledge in front of me, it is about a forty meter jump to the inner bay. Back behind me, a seventy-five meter fall to the open ocean.

I make a circle with my hands by connecting the pointer fingers and pressing firm. My thumbs are just short of touching, with maybe an inch of space between. This mimics the circumference of a clock, broken between 5:30 and 6:30. It also serves as the outline of our island. I rotate the entire face of the clock clockwise, about an hour. The Gap now opens at 7:00, southwest. I look at that gap between my thumbs and then down at the opening in the cliffs where Jonah and I came through all that time ago. The opening would be a lot larger and easier to pass if the guardian pilar did not stand watch.

Back to where I am standing, I make the circle with my hand again. Looking at my right thumb joint, not the first joint, but the one closer to my big ol' hand, that is Sunrise Point. It faces out about 5:00, southeast, and has an unobstructed view of the rising sun over the ocean. The North Cliff is more rugged and tougher to walk. It faces a western direction with a hint more north than south. It has an unobstructed view of the setting sun.

There is a half sand and half dirt path leading from the powder sand beach up to each of the two cliffs. They continue to wind down to the Sunset or Sunrise Point on either side of the bay. However, that path does not lead north along the ridges. To the north, each cliff becomes craggy and impassible. Back to the clock likeness, it looks impossible to walk from 9:00 to 3:00 around the ancient caldera. I doubt anyone has ever used these perimeter paths to circumnavigate the island. They only work from about 5:00 to 6:00 and 7:00 to 8:00. All in, if I had to guess, I would say the whole circumference of the island is about twenty five kilometers around.

Now, that space inside the hands, the inner reefs and the beach take up about the first third. Then you have the tree-line, the forest, the village and the farm all mixed up. On the far end of the inner island there is a steep incline where the caldera sunk at a vertical angle. The only things to grow there are vines. The cliffs look to be a hundred meters high, from the inside. It is impassable again, for even the best climber.

I move to Sunset point where I can see more of the northern section of the island. Looking through a broken piece of glass, I get a magnified view. Out of the rising crags, there seems to be a manicured path leading to a plateau. There also seems to be a couple different fruit trees surviving the harsh environment. It drives me nuts to know there is a whole area, a whole section to the north of island where the Tribe does not venture.

Something's Fishy

"Dude, she will not leave me alone," Jonah, annoyed, says to me one night at the dinner table.

"She is a hot Mermaid," I say. "You are complaining because?"

"Ok, Ok, I get it. At first it was cute, even sexy," Jonah begins. "I mean she just swims up to me one day and says, 'Jonah, you have merman hair' all giggly and shit and then swims away. I play along. Why not? We chase each other through the water, share waves, play on the reef. She goes diving and brings up little treasures for me."

Max interjects, "Yeah, Amelia can freedive like a hundred meters. More if she uses a weight. Pulls up all kinds of cool stuff from the wrecks on the reef. Pulled up a missing fin off Jonah's surfboard one day even."

"Come on Max," Jonah says, getting a little tweaked. "Lemme talk to Big Ed for like two seconds, bro."

"You know she was in the water when you two jumped, just to make sure nothing bad happened," Max continues, totally ignoring Jonah's request. "Now she is in love. Chases after Jonah totally convinced he is a merman, just missing the tail."

"Max, how would your sister say it? 'GET STUFFED!'"

"No, the proper British form is, 'stuff it, you wanker.'" Max turns back to me. "It's really stellar when they share waves." He laughs.

"Brosky, stay outta this convo!" Jonah snaps at Max. "This is big boy chat. Doubt you ever even had your sack drained."

"Wow, Jo. Little pent up there aye mate." I laugh with Max.

"Not the case, yo. I mean we have mind-bending sex, in the ocean mostly. Nut is off the chain." Jonah gets descriptive with a little smile.

"Bet it is mostly under water." Max laughs.

"It is," Jonah says. "She even helps me breathe."

"I want a Mermaid." Max laughs.

"Me too," I say.

"Guys, you don't get it, she is always there. Always. I mean EVERY time I go surfing she pops up in the lineup. It's like she never leaves the water."

"Don't look now matey, she just walked into the dining hall."

"Must have come to land just for you." I laugh.

Amelia makes her way directly to the table where we are sitting.

"Hi, my sexy merman. I hate this stinky land food. Want some oysters?" Amelia asks Jonah and completely ignores our presence at the table. "They are nature's aphrodisiac."

"No, I'm ok, Amelia. Getting full."

"I'll take some," I say to her.

"Its not for you, filthy landman. Go play with some plants!" She says scornfully then turns back to Jonah. "Anything I can get for you, my little clownfish?"

Max and I both hold back laughter.

"Hey Amelia, how long have you been a bonified mermaid?" I ask.

"Since I was born! Stupid! Mom made my first tail when I was 8."

"Hey, Amelia," Max starts in his special needling tone. "What is a Nudibrach?"

"It's a tropical sea slug, you mud pig, Duh! They are amazing! There are sixteen families in Indonesia alone. That's almost half the species in the world."

"And what are those little shrimpy guys that fish open up their mouth at but don't eat?" Max asks with a smile.

"You mean cleaner shrimp. Hello, land walker. When was the last time you had your teeth cleaned by a squirrel or chipmunk, farm boy? Mine are pearly white just like Jonah's."

We look at him. "Yes, I had my teeth cleaned by a crustacean today," he says under his breath. Max and I cannot hold back the laughter this time.

Amelia beams at us then turns back to her lover.

"Sure I can't get anything for you, my beautiful anglefish?" she asks Jonah. "There is nothing like fresh oyster under moonlight."

"No, my baby dolphin. I'm all good. Just having a little chat time with the guys."

"OK, I sea. Get it: S-E-A. I'll leave your little school alone," she says and then walks away. She looks back at Jonah once before taking her Mermaid suit and heading in the direction of the beach.

"See," Jonah says before catching himself.
"Oh, I S-E-A it." Max laughs.
Jonah glares at Max.
"Help me, Ed."
"What can I do?"
"Help me. Make her snap out of it."
"Dude, you have a hot mermaid. Live with it."

"Please help me. Please. It's a small island and we are stuck here. At first I was totally stoked on her. I mean who wouldn't want the Playboy version of Disney's Ariel chasing him. Right? Hot! But fellas this chick, this mermaid, she turns out to be bonkers."

"At least you are eating plenty a oyster." Max chuckles.

"That's enough out of you, Max. Seriously. I'm gonna smack you upside the head."

"Oh, really," Max begins. "Look Jonah, if you really want her to chill just say you rolled your ankle or something and can't go in the water for about a month. Then she will realize you are not really a merman and have to turn her attention to other sea life."

"Like you."
"Like me."

"She is making me a monofin!"
"Oh, you are screwed."

"Haha, what is that thing anyway?"

"It's how she swims so freaking fast. It's form-fitting Neoprene attached to a single elongated diving fin. It's built to be just like the fin a dolphin has. Everything from the waist down is one big swim fin when she puts on her gear."

"With lots of sparkling glitter," I add.
"Hi five," Max says to me in approval of the joke.

"Amelia ducking swam to the island from Bali with her monofin. NOTHING ELSE!" Jonah tells us. "Check it. Amelia is one hundred and one percent convinced that she is a real mermaid. In the water she is incredible guys. She can hold her breath for like five minutes. She can pop outta a wave like a dolphin and beat me back to the lineup. She always has good eats. The sex, WOW! And what an asset to this ducking Tribe she is. Shit, most of Howard's med kit and Goldie's cooking utensils were salvage she found diving the outer reef. This chick is exceptionally knowledgeable about sea life and what everything is called and does. She knows everything under the water n all about where things grow and live. She totally jives with ocean shit, waves, currents, patterns, navigation etc., etc., etc. That's all we talk about. She will play with some sea snake and tell me it is the most poisonous animal on the planet. She is like the freaking Croc Hunter of the ocean, brah. No joke. But take her out of the ocean and she is tilted. I mean totally out of her mind!"

"So in the water… amazing yeah?"
"Yup."

"Out of the water … bat shit crazy?"
"Yup."

"Well it's a good thing she is making you a fin then, merman!"

First Good Swell

"Surfing is like a safari, minus the high powered weapons and innocent animals involved. Still, there is both peace and violence in any moment one tries to hunt Mother Nature's aquatic beasts," Tess says to me as we make our way to the point.

The paddle out to the peak is really difficult. Even in the channels as the tide swings up, currents are ripping around the reef. We look up to the point. "It's big today." I say to Tess.

"About as big as the inner reef can handle," she replies.

Only a few people are out. Max has just finished a right wave, and paddles back about 50 yards behind us. He can't cut through the current as fast as we can on the bigger boards. Jonah, Howard and Tex are at the peak when we rock up. The small crowd on a big day reminds me that most on the island are not life-long surfers.

"Nice wave, Max," Tex says as he finally makes his way back.

"Watch a real pro hit the next one, 'Maxi-pad'," Jonah scoffs as he cues up for the next set wave.

"All you, merman."

Double overhead surf has arrived. The hardcore competition between Max and Jonah is put on hold. The pet names have not been surrendered however. At some points it even seems like friendly competition between the two. Tex takes the next wave. Tess shares the right with me while I go backside left. Sets are about ten minutes apart giving the group plenty of time to get back and witness my twenty second nose ride on the highline.

"Toes over the nose," Max shouts. "The big Hawaiian shows us all how to style!"

The next set comes through and we just cue up.

"Going Right!"
"Dropping Left!"
"Outside Set Wave!"

These seem to be the only words spoken for the better part of an hour. It is epic!

Max and Jonah even manage to share a wave civilly. Jonah drops left on his backside. They are very deep in the takeoff zone. Both manage a deep tube section and then get spit out nearly at the same time. The aggressive over-surfing of the prior months becomes technically impeccable. Every turn, every slash, every move is mechanically perfect and when they are done with the wave both glow with satisfaction all the way back to the peak. There is even a high five.

I am surprised to see Tex's ease in the big surf considering he grew up in northern New Zealand and then surfed off oil tanker wakes.

"Alright, everyone votes. Clearly longest time clocked on the nose goes to Big Ed. Tess gets chick surfer of the year just for being out here," Jonah begins.

"Yea yea. My sis frickin' rips all!" Max praises his sister.

"Need style and tube votes for the shredders," Jonah finishes after Max's interruption.

The competition is back.

"Tex is the fearless leader of all, let him decide." I laugh.

"Don't pull me into their petty game," Tex says.

"Tess can't vote, she is definitely biased," Jonah says.

"Which way?" She asks jokingly.

"We all know, sis," Max says to her.

"Again, which way?" She repeats.

"That leaves just me and Howey to decide it then," I say looking at Howard.

"Definitely too close to call. Ya boys gotta settle with a draw," he says.

"I vote Jonah," says a girl's voice from just above the water line.

"NO! you are an unquestionably bias, Mermaid. Go eat an oyster!" Max insists.

"Want one, my sexy merman?" she asks only Jonah.

We all laugh.

"To be determined another time, champs," Tess says to her brother.

"Come on Tex, give a deciding vote." Max is on the brink of cracking up.

"Not a chance."

"Bugger."

The issue is dropped with the arrival of the next set.

"Right."
"Left."
"Outside"

Plenty of solid and way overhead waves go completely unsurfed. Nothing but smiles and tired arms as we all end up back at the peak.

"Why does no one surf the outer reef?" Jonah asks out of the blue on the next waiting period between sets.

"Mate, you are as mental as your girlfriend … forgive me … fishfriend," Max jabs. "Even if you did make the drop-in, which is totally vert, you would have to shoot the first gap in the cliffs and then avoid getting smashed by a giant ass limestone pillar."

"Can't be done," Howard warns.

"Has anyone tried?" Jonah asks again with persistence.

"Gabe told us that one of the first survivors in the old days, a big wave surfer from Tasmania tried. He died quickly according to the story," Tex warns.

"Has anyone tried since?" Jonah is persistent.

"No dude. You try, you die!" Max says.

"This is where it's at, Jo," I say to my friend, gazing around the perfect reef wave we have had for hours. Alone. "How could you ask for more?"

Jonah nods.

"Outside!"
"Left"
"Right."

Oh Brother

The swell continues running a few days before backing off a bit. Some of the other surfers have made their way outback for the dawn patrol. The winds are strong offshore and with the low tide push the wave is spitting almond shaped barrels.

"So how does this tube thing work, ya?" Marcello asks

"Just stick your arm in and get pitted," Jonah tells him.

Both Max and Jonah paddle out back and take off the next wave. They jam their arms in and both get barreled nearly simultaneously. They are still in the green room all the way to the spot where the wave clamps shut and walls up again. In order to avoid getting smashed by the wave, they tuck tight and we see them getting spit out.

"I got this," Marcello says to me.

"It's not as easy as easy as those knuckleheads make it look." But before I can finish my sentence he is on his way to the next wave. Jonah and Max are making their way back to the peak. Marcello drops right, riding front side. It is a steep one but he manages the torque of the bottom turn and pulls up for a high line. Then, just like the boys told him, he sticks his arm into the wave to stall. As Marcello does this he loses speed and the wave throws over him. For a moment he vanishes and then by releasing his arm comes flying out of the tube.

"Well done sir," Jonah shouts from afar. Max hoops and hollers.

I take the next wave, so Marcello and I both end up in the channel together.

"That. That. That was." Marcello can barely pull words out of the adrenaline, "Awesome!"

"Atta Boy!" Max yells from the lineup.

"Nicely done, brah," Jonah congratulates Marcello as we rejoin them. "Looks like Big-E finally has some big boy competition at the peak."

"Could be, but even a blind squirrel finds a nut once in a while," I mock.

"Wooooooooooow."

"Bet he does it again E," Max encourages.

"Yeah, Big Ed, when was the last time you got shacked anyway?" Jonah taunts.

"Good point," I say while paddling wider of the lineup. "I'll say it again, Marcello, it's not as easy as it looks."

The set arrives, prompting everyone in the lineup to shout Marcello back into position. His heart is still pounding from the last wave. He drops in and squares up to the face. He has a lot of speed. At that critical moment, he jams his arm into a wave for the second time in his life. Then, just as the open tube approaches Marcello he gets as low as possible. Everyone is cheering. They stop the moment he is sucked up and barrel rolled. Hard. Three times we see his body spinning like a wild turbine through the cylindrical wave.

There is a unanimous "oooooooooooooh," noise.

"Gotta admit, dude has balls," Max nods approvingly.

"Respect."

"You are white, boy!" I remind Jonah.

We paddle toward the jumbled mass of South African and surfboard pieces.

"Guess it's not as easy as it looks." Marcello says, clinging to my board as he spews seawater out of his mouth and other orifices.

"Told you," I say.

"Can you put it back together?" Marcello looks at the pieces of fiberglass and foam that used to be his surfboard.

"Not this time, brother," I say. "But I will help you shape a new one from Balsa wood like the native Hawaiian surfers did."

"When can we start? I want another one of those tubes ya!"

Mangos & Mary Jane

"Bloody hell! I am gonna shoot them both! Dead!" Monica screams as she come tearing down the path.

"What is that all about?" I ask Svet.

"No idea," she replies as Monica goes flying past us in the direction of the village.

"Hmmm."

A moment later she comes marching back with a crossbow in hand.

"Hey Monica. Mon. Baby. You wanna tell me what you are on about." Howard is in pursuit.

"One of them found it in the night and..." she huffs at Howard who is struggling to keep up. The rest of her sentence is muffed after she passes by. Then follow up the jokers.

"Mate, she is on a rampage," Max says to me while he and Jonah walk by, keeping a safe distance from the couple.

"Is this your guys doing?" I ask of the usual suspects.

"Not this time yo."

"Yeah, have some faith."

"I have none."

"Deon." Svet points down the path to Monica's section of the farm.

"Lets go." Without hesitation all four of us follow the cloud of dust leading toward the farms.

The scene has already unfolded when we arrive. There they are, Lars and Vero, laying in a pile of peels and pits under the mango tree.

"Get up, you kraut shaiza hooligans," Monica orders as she kicks one of them swiftly in the gut.

"Can't move, too stoned," moans the first.
"Jaaaa and full," moans the other.

"That's because you ate all my mangos. The whole season's crop!" Monica jabs one of the writhing Germans again.

"Even the green mangos?" I ask.

My question goes unanswered.

 "Now show me where it is or I'll stick you both. Swear to Christ I will," Monica shouts at them through her teeth.

"Even the green mangos?" I ask.

"Yes!" Monica snaps at me as she loads the crossbow. "Even the green ones."

"Where?"

They both point to a small satchel under a fig palm.

"Tell me why I shouldn't just shoot them both. Maybe in the hand. Thieves in most tribal groups loose a hand for stealing food from their tribe."

"Honey, there must be a, well, more peachy way to fix this," Howard coos.

"No, you are right, hun, there IS a better way to solve this issue."

Before Monica stalks off to retrieve the bag of grass she turns to the Swedish girl. "Svet, be a doll and fetch me a torch from the village. Thanks love," she says coolly, a completely different tone of voice than the Monica of a moment ago.

"Sure, Monica." She takes off jogging down the path.

"Take za puff?" one of the Z Germans says from the ground as his right hand offers a crudely rolled joint.

"I'll take that mate," Max says impulsively as he grabs it and then takes a long drag.

"Puff puff pass," Jonah demands after punching his counterpart in the arm and taking the joint away.

Monica comes back to the scene and her gaze stays fixed on the two felons until Svet returns with the torch. The satchel of our marijuana crop pinned below her left foot.

"Fire is almost dead," Svet informs everyone while passing Monica the torch.

"Wonderbra, babe. Technically zis is Vero's shift," the one who must be Lars says. They both receive a kick in the gut from Monica.

"Wonderbra. Yes, Wonderbra. You two stoned morons laugh it off."

"It is kinda classic, Mon," Max laughs.

"Right, classic. Ha Ha Ha. Let's see, the island fire is nearly out. The mangos are all gone. These two are gonna have diarrhea for a week. Oh and they crushed half my herb garden looking for the grass when I planted the sticky shit half a mile away." Monica holds up two fully mature stalks of Marijauna freshly ripped from the ground. They get tossed on top of the satchel.

"De. Smokes?" Jonah asks me holding out the joint.

"Not now, dude. This is too good."

"Well then, puff puff pass back," Max insists.

"Have za puff, Monica? Vero asks. "You feel better."

"Yeah, there are totally medical uses, too, you know," Max laughs.

She walks over to Max, slaps him on the cheek and tears the joint from his lips. Then she flicks what remains of it onto the satchel and puts the flaming piece of wood to it. The weed goes up in a cloud of smoke. It's enough to give even me a contact high.

"Nooooooooooooooooooo," Z Germans scream in agony.

"How about a little wife control there, Howard?" Max instigates while rubbing his cheek.

"Good luck with that, mate."

"You best have a couple seeds tucked away my nig..." I grab Jonah by the throat and lift him an inch from the ground before he can finish the sentence.

"You must be high, Jonah."

"Yes. That, was, like, a lot, of smoke." He coughs as I release him.

"Thought so."

"But tell me you do?" he asks me quietly as Monica picks up a surviving mango from the ground and storms down the path back to the village.

I shrug.

Later that night I find Monica outside the dining hall. She has just savored every particle of the surviving mango and has relaxed a bit. I ask her, "Would you really have shot them?"

"That ever happens again, damn right I will."

Boom

There are signs of yet another new swell building during the night. Before dawn, Jonah and I make our way to Sunset Cliff. At first light we spot a small Indonesian Junkin boat making its way to the coast. From the cliff above, Jonah and I can see the surfboards stacked high and the white faces guiding it toward the bay. They aim for the same path Jonah and I took before finally breaching the current. The motor looks fully engaged as they push near to the south gap. Now about half a mile from the pillar guarding the bay, the bow of the boat strikes one of the submerged mines guarding the entrance to the bay. The boat must have had just enough weight to trigger the explosive weapon. It goes up in a mass of noise, projectiles and water. No one could have survived the blast, which launched debris some twenty or thirty feet into the air. The current quickly sweeps all that remains of it away from the island. There is nothing to salvage. I ask Jonah not to tell the group what we just witnessed. It is hard for him to shake it. Jonah has nightmares that night. His screams wake up the entire community. I'm the only one who knows why.

Moonlight Madness

A new swell arrives the next day just before sundown. Fortunately for this motley tribe, moonrise shortly follows. It's a big one and it is bright.

Max, Tess, Jonah and I already have boards under arm, ready to paddle out. Amelia, as usual, is already in the surf.

"Howie, let's make a move, bra!" Jonah yells encouragement to Howard who is halfway hiding behind his wife.

"Gonna take a pass this time, my young Padawan," he jokes.

"Not a chance, you old bogan. Get shaking," Max demands.

"Can't see a bloody thing out there, you shit. I am too old for this nonsense," Howard replies.

"So use the Force; Master," Max jokes back.

"Gonna use my fist to your jaw if you muck around any longer. Smash it up for me, boys."

Those who don't surf the bigger stuff, walk up the cliffs in pairs holding torches. Marcello and Svet stay on the beach and make a bonfire with one of Z Germans.

Tess and Tex share the first wave of the evening, an overhead peeler. Just after they take off, Max calls us over to the channel.

"OK. We only have a couple minutes till fearless leader man gets back, so, Amelia pulled these off a salvage the other day boys and girls," Jonah begins. "It is time to put on a show."

"Are those signal flares?" Max asks.

"Yeah, brah. There is one for each of us!"

"Don't you think there might be better use for them?" I inquire.

"No! Come on. What could possibly be better than crackin' one of these puppies open from inside the most perfect waves on the planet?"

"Oi. Gotta say I am with Jonah this time," Max says.

"Great minds think alike."

"They do," Amelia smiles.

"How do you reckon we get them into the wave?"

"Insert flare in teeth, like so." Jonah puts the flare in his mouth then continues in a muffled closed jaw speech. "Paddle for wave. Insert self into barrel." Jonah takes the flare from his mouth. "Place flare into hand. Pop the bitch."

"We are talking five or six second tubes today so get it on fast, aye," Max says.

"Even longer if you body surf it," Amelia says.

"They are water resistant, not water proof, so try to stay dry," Jonah gives us the last little tidbit of information.

"Let's light this place up!"

"May the Torce be with you."

We each take a flare. Max and Jonah head straight for the peak.

"Think you can keep up, Maxi–Pad?"

"Naw, I wanna watch the Jedi master first."

Jonah paddles for the very first wave of the set. It is about double overhead. He paddles, drops and pulls in. The flare goes off just as he gets barrel rolled up the tube and thrown out the front. Everyone on the cliff 'oooohs' and 'aaaaws' at the nasty wipeout. Even Amelia 'oooohs' and 'aaaaws' at his spill.

Jonah recovers his board and paddles back to where we are sitting.

"Not as easy as Skywalker made it out to be aye?" Max says tauntingly before heading to the same section of the wave.

"Get stuffed, Max."

"Oh I will," he chuckles. "Inside the wave you just boofed. 'Grumpy old kooks."

Max takes off deep on an outside set. We can barely see him under the moonlight and then he is gone altogether. He pops the cap of the flare from inside the tube and the wave comes alive. It looks like a pulsating heart in the center of a wild anaconda. Colors of red, orange and green streak from it. It moves and bends down the reef. He gets spit out of the tube, hands and flare above his head. Everyone on the beach cheers.

"Looks like he stuck it to you on that one, brah," I tease my friend.

"Duck it. Max can have night surfing."

"Guess it is my turn then," I say

"Get in there Big–E."

I pick a big right peeler so I can ride frontside, except I pop the flare mid paddle and maintain my speed with a voracious one arm stroke. Red sparks streak across the face of the building wave. During that moment of the critical drop, I use the right arm to get to my feet and turn hard off the bottom. I pull in. The flare lights up the aquatic cave from inside. There is a total loss of sound, only colors echo where I am. The red, the green, the black. As I pump down the line I can see the tunnel closing around me until the last moment when it opens to the night sky. I make it out. The flare lights up the whole bay as I run to the nose, five toes over.

Jonah smiles, "That Max, is my best friend and mentor, Obi–Wan Kenobi."

Letting Go

There is not a cloud in the sky and the midday sun swelters. Tess is just finishing her shift cleaning the Aquaponic system. There is barely a drop of water left in the basin, the rest has been pumped all the way back up to the pond.

"Deon, I want to show you something later today," she says to me.

"Yeah, what?" I ask.

"Meet me on the beach just before sunset."

"OK. I'll be there."

The air is a bit cooler when I come to the tree-line. Tess is waiting. She grabs my hand and leads the way. We come to a semi-cave carved into the cliff and mostly hidden by boulders. However, at this time of day the setting sun shines right through. We walk in together.

"It's kind of my workshop. Since I don't have a camera, I paint," Tess tells me bashfully.

"This is incredible," I gasp.

This whole time Tess has been capturing island life. There are murals on the walls. Paintings on boulders and miniatures on small rocks. The main mural shows daily life. Tex leads the group through a council meeting. Goldie cooks a mouthwatering feast. Lars and Vero stoke their fire. I carry a basket of vegetables. Monica hands herbs to Howard while they embrace. Alice mends clothing, topless. Marcello and Nely hunt monkeys. Svet radiantly works the rice patty. Tasha sits under a coconut tree rereading one of the three books that make up our island library. Jonah and Max split a wave with fishing rods in hand. Amelia dives over the shipwrecks on the reef.

They are all beautiful. They are all unique. They are spot on. I am overcome with an emotion that makes me want to cry and laugh simultaneously.

"Tess, you are incredible," I manage to say to her.

She has also taken natural reeds growing near the mangroves on the island and made parchment and canvas. The stack nearly reaches my height.

"These are my personal paintings," she says while making eye contact with me for the first time all night.

One of the paintings depicts Tex and Goldie holding hands in a moment of tenderness. Another shows Howard and Monica getting married.

"You were there for that one?" I ask Tess.

"No, but I have heard so much about it. Monica describes so vividly from memory."

Another painting shows her brother battling for waves with Jonah. In another Jonah and Amelia locked in a moment of underwater passion. Another shows Alice's initiation into the Tribe, the North Cliff lit by torchlight as they were for mine. Her paintings are not all so light-hearted. One shows Gabriel being put out to sea while the Tribe aims crossbows at him. Marcello's arrow flies just over Gabe's head. Another mysterious one depicts Tasha crawling though the dark jungle. The last painting she holds up shows the council trial held for Jonah and I.

"These paintings are a little more intimate," I say.

"This one is my favorite," she responds daringly.

From far away it looks like a Taoist Yin and Yang symbol. Moving closer, the detail sharpens into focus. Tess's white body is wrapped in my dark embrace. I look at her and smile.

"Really, your favorite of all of them?" I tease.

"Yours, too?" she answers my question with another question, anxiously again.

"Mine too," I gaze at her with a smile.

I reach to pull her in closer. Our lips meet and then stay occupied for some time. We fall out of the cave. We kiss and we touch.

Tess is not your typical Victorian knockout, yet her inner beauty glows. She is not your typical athletic type, yet she rips in the surf. She is not your typical academic or scholarly type, yet her artistic intelligence outweighs both and makes them seem trivial. She is mindful. She is funny. She laughs at life. She lives in the present. At times she even appears divine, like one born with a sense of understanding. Not learned like the rest of us. It is done. I have fallen for Tess. I am smitten.

I am not sure how long we roll around on the beach. It seems forever. It seems way too short. At one point Tess comes up for air and looks at me. I go to kiss her again and she pulls away.

"Is this our moment of awkward silence now?" I ask.
"No. I feel the same as you, just have to put a little chase into it."
"Oh, really," I say as I reach for her hand and pull her back to me.
"Just a little."

We don't make it back to the village. My kiss reaches her neck then her shoulders and then farther down. I linger for a moment and focus on that point where the curve of her breast meets her chest. A beautiful spot. Tess gives off a subtle noise to inform me that she is enjoying this moment as well. I venture a little north again and tease her pink nipple with the rough of my brown lips.

The human body is created symmetrically, with all the most important and unique vessels on the midline. From her lips down, I make my way slowly south. Again I linger near the belly button and tickle her defined abs with my fingers. I think my hands could cover her entire torso. We continue teasing and playing all the way down her midline.

Then there is the lift of the hips. That critical moment when she decides if her undergarments stay or go. The question which determines the rest of our sexual relationship: to make love or not? I have been here with dozens of women and each time it is a nerve-racking question proposed in silence. I have never been so on edge as I am now.

Simply by arching her back she noiselessly answers, "Yes, take me."

We make love on the beach. There is sand everywhere.

"Try the ocean?" I ask.
"Yeah, let's give it a go," she whispers to me.

We paddle out to the middle of the bay. We ride tandem and naked. Our clothes stay on the beach. When we are far enough into the bay we sit up. I straddle my longboard and she straddles me. It is free of inhibition. It is passionate. It is loud. It is hard to keep balance. It is fantastic. We reach climax together and fall into the ocean.

Everyone is long asleep when we make it back to the village. We sleep on the deck outside under the stars.

The next day I find Howard in the common hall stocking up his medical bag with herbs and remedies. "Are there any private huts available tonight?" I ask.

"So the real initiation ceremony is tonight then, oi mate?" he jokes.

"Could be," I smile.

"And who might be the lucky initiator?" he asks knowing full well.

"Howard, always digging and always instigating," I say under my breath to him.

"It's just another one of my part–time jobs here, Big-E. Stirring shit up around these parts aye." He laughs. "Lemme check. Tonight they look all taken, let's see … Marcello and Svet are in the Village Hut. Tex and Goldie, Jungle Hut. Jonah and Amelia, Beach Hut."

"Guess he got her to come ashore." We laugh.

"Monica and Howard, Cliff Hut," he elbows me, "Score!"

"That's all fulled up, mate. Tomorrow ok?"

"Sure."

"You got it, Big-E."

Making love to Tess in the northern Cliff Hut overlooking the bay below is divine. She lays in my arms for quite a while after as we joke and laugh casually.

"Hey Tess, when are you going to tell your bother?" I ask.
"He'll figure it out soon enough."
"How is that gonna go down?"
"Ah, he will probably work up enough courage to charge you and then in the last moment realize just how poor of an idea that is."

We laugh.

"So in other words he will get over it."
"Oi."

"That's good. I really didn't want to throw him off a cliff or something just to chill 'em out."

"Really, sometimes I fantasize about exactly that."

We laugh. A moment passes.

"Hey, Deon?" she begins hesitantly.

"Yeah Tess?"

"Can we take your longboard out for the next round?"

 I am in love.

Earning a C Note.

Tex is not only our fearless leader, he is also responsible for keeping track of time on the island. This is a normal thing for both a boat captain and a jungle chieftain. Tonight marks Nely's fifth anniversary on the island. That means she is joining the council tonight. There are no stars in the sky. Light from the half-moon barely breaks the haze above. We gather around the fire. Goldie has brewed a batch of the coconut spirits. We count aloud together and with each count she downs a massive shot.

"One," we all shout. Nely drinks.

"Two," we shout again. Nely drinks.

"Three," we cheer her on. Nely drinks.

"Four," we laugh in encouragement as she begins to sway side to side. Nely drinks.

"Five." The entire council toasts one together with her.

Tex holds a metal rod into the fire. On one end is a musical symbol for the C-Note. The improvised cattle brand is salvage from one of the wrecks on the reef. Before Amelia swam to shore, there was occasionally a day here and there when the Tribe ventured over the reef at dead low tide to look for tools and supplies amongst the wreckage. Now, every council member has the council brand on the right shoulder.

Nely is so drunk she can barely sit upright. She removes her blouse exposing her dark skin. There are scars all over her body, none of which are from surfing.

Tex pulls the red hot iron from the fire. He holds the orange wand high in the air.

"Congratulations to Nely, our newest guide in life," he speaks slowly as he plunges the searing tool to her body.

She does not scream. She does not even writhe as I do with the scent of burning flesh.

Everyone in the Tribe holds their shot of liquor high. We shout in unison, "To Nely, our newest guide!" Tex and Howard lift her from the ground, holding her high on shoulders as they swiftly carry her the entire distance to the beach. They wade out to knee deep water and lower her in. She looks to the point of passing out from pain and shock as the cool salt water softens the agony.

The rest of us stand watching at the waterline. Tess leans into me and holds my hand mid-waist. Max is just next to us.

"So, De," he begins.

"Yeah?"

"If you become my older brother, does that mean I finally get to act all ghetto and that shit, dog?"

"Not a chance, Max," I say and laugh.

The entire council swims out guiding Nely on a longboard. All hands on deck. They bring her to the inside of the reef and everyone rides a whitewater wave together back to the beach. The longboard washes up in the shallows and Monica offers Nely a hand up, which she denies. Howard offers her another coconut husk full of milky liquor. Without hesitation she downs the shot. "Sababa," is the last word we hear from her before her eyes roll back and she hits the white sand with a light thud.

Happiness in Stillness

Days pass, then weeks, then months, then seasons. Life is simple. Life is in balance. Life is amazing.

Dengue Fever

The next rainy season comes and with it an explosion of mosquitoes, followed by the first case of dengue. One of Z Germans, Lars, falls face first into the fire on his watch. The burns are not bad because he quickly comes to consciousness and rolls to the soft sand next to the fire pit. It is midday and Alice sees this from the village while working on garments. She pulls him away from the flames. Howard is called and immediately applies aloe vera to the wounds.

Tex comes to the scene next. Lars is resting on a stretcher made of bamboo and palm fronds.

"He is hot," Howard says.
"He is burned," Tex says.

"It's more. He passed out before falling into the fire and has a raging fever," Howard replies.

"Dengue?"
"That would be my first guess."

"Nobody got it last year."

"We got it now."

Monica stays up all night to brew homemade remedies. She makes just enough courses for everyone in the village before she succumbs to the fever next.

Those infected are transported to the huts on the perimeter of the island. Howard and Nely are first responders. They provide medical assistance and care for the sick. As they are in contact with the infected every night they sleep in the most distant hut from the group.

The disease is mosquito borne. Large Asian tiger mosquitoes bite during the day. Only if a mosquito bites someone infected and then shortly after someone clean is the virus passed. However, these mosquitoes don't travel too far when there is food nearby so the more distance we put between us and the infected, the more chance we have at stopping the outbreak.

Alice falls next, clothes become tattered and worn. Svet follows and then Marcello. Monica and I are left alone to care for the farm. Goldie is next. Tex cries as he carries him to the Cliff Hut. Eventually Nely catches it as well which means Howard needs new help. Tess volunteers. She becomes ill a few days later, her brother shortly after.

I volunteer next to assist with medical help. Tex says, "No."

"Deon, if you fall to bonebreaking fever at this point it could be the collapse of the food source."

"Not the case, Tex. Everyone knows how to clean the Aquaponic system and the farm is waterlogged anyway. There is nothing to do until dry season comes," I inform him.

"Yes, but could they rebuild it? Could they reorganize the farm without your expertise? It's too much of a risk. You will remain isolated," he orders.

"It's amazing that this marooned boat captain has learned nothing of farming over the past decade," I scoff.

"Watch it, Deon, remember why you are here."

"Tex, I have had dengue before, twice. I always pulled through quickly," I tell him. "If I do get it again, I promise the farm will not collapse before I recover."

"Not the case, Deon," he begins. "Every time you contract dengue the symptoms are stronger." He is correct about this. "We need you isolated."

Another few days pass and Tex joins his partner in an outer hut. When there is no one left to help care for the sick I find Howard. Sometime around mid-morning he takes a break to avoid the heat and the Asian tiger mosquitoes. We decide it is time for a surf.

"Howie, I'm gonna join you tonight to help," I inform him.

"You sure, matey?" he asks.

"Yeah, I am sure. Hey man, how come you haven't got it yet?"

"Old medicus trick, Big Ed. When we get an outbreak here I start eating a couple match heads a day," he explains. "The mozzies can't stand the sulfur in your blood. If you are going to help me out we better get you some prevention."

"Yeah, but Nely caught the bug."

"Guess sulfur was not on the Kosher menu."

"And Tess?"

"Probably already infected as she only lasted a day with me."

"Let's hope it works."

Howard and I are applying cold compress to Max and Tess who are now sharing the Jungle Hut with Nely. She is still heavily infected and showing no immediate signs of recovering. It is around midnight and we have said goodnight. Taking our leave we are out of earshot when I broach the subject.

"Howie, I am worried about Nely. She is so petite. Can her body handle such a full on attack?"

"She will pull through."

"How can you be so sure that she will pull through?"

"Cause she is the toughest person on this little island."

"Come on."

"You don't know her story yet do you?"

"Nope, but I bet you are gonna tell me." It is the first time I laugh in a few days. Howard however does not.

"As you know, Nely is Israeli. She was a spook for a special forces faction know as Shabak. Most people have heard of Mossad, but they are international spies and weak sauce compared to Shabak. These guys handle the really heavy policing, domestically and in the bordering areas, which are perpetually on brink of war, for what, the last sixty years. I mean some gnarly business, mate.

"At a stupidly young age Nely was orphaned by a Palestinian car bomb after which she spent years bouncing around the system. She has no family. Then she was recruited by the government. Started training for the job at age twelve, totally convinced she could help prevent similar attacks. Nely went underground in one of those Palestinian refugee camps at seventeen to send intelligence home.

She would still be there today except her handler sold her out for a cut of Afghan black tar. Nely barely escaped that mess thanks to a Palestinian boy who put his life on the line to protect her. Maybe they had something, maybe not. She never gives those kind of details.

"Her whole third year in the West Bank was spent subterranean. It was too dangerous to venture out in the densely crowded camp. So, she literally dug her way out though mud and shit into the Mediterranean sea and then swam the distance back to Israel -- only to find herself pronounced dead. Somehow, a few years later, she ended up on this island. Doesn't talk much as you might have noticed. Won't even tell us how she came to the island all by her lonesome. Luckily she is tough and resourceful. Marcello forced Tex to let her stay without putting it to a council vote."

"That's why she is always following Marcello around," I say. "Knows how to handle herself."

"You got it, Big Ed."

The drugs on hand help ease the pain of the dengue fever, but only to a degree. It can be fatal. There are points I think we will lose Goldie, who has also been infected before. In the end, the enitre episode lasts for about a month. It runs its course though eight of the Tribe. I mainly watched the waterlogged farm. Plus with the loss of manpower, everyone has to put in double-time time on the Aquaponics system. Even the Mermaid comes to shore occasionally to save the fish. Luckily the constant yield keeps everyone well fed during the crisis.

As the first infected start to show recovery, another swell comes through. It's almost as strong as our last good swell, but everyone is still too sick or too tired to paddle out, even Jonah.

One exceptionally rainy day, Tess loses the tiny baby she carries inside. Between the feverish hallucinations brought on by the disease and the emotion of the miscarriage, she becomes irate and caustic. Tess remains for two days after in a feverish stupor, expending the last of her energy to scream aloud when one of us walks too near the hut. Tess's legs are caked in blood and she refuses to wash herself. Howard finally insists that she must be bathed for the sanitary concerns of everyone, especially her own. We have to hold her down. She cries. Despite my deep efforts, things are never the same between us.

Running from the Dogs

The dry season swells have started to show more frequently and mid-day sessions are more regular in the cooler air. It is the first good swell of our third dry season on island. A few of us are out surfing when I recognize a sound I have not heard in a long time. Back at home it would be background noise, but here, in the utter silence of all things, it sounds like an impending clash with a dragon. Tex hears it too and sighs. A moment later the helicopter flies overhead and everyone freezes for a second, then the panic ensues.

Tex looks at Marcello, Marcello at Tasha, Tasha at Tex and then all three look up at the hovering piece of metal.

"Get back to the village, now," Tex yells.

We paddle hard in the direction of the beach. Tess, who has just finished a ride, is already on the beach and sprinting toward the jungle. The Tribe has gathered in the north end of the village. Most hold provisions or water jugs. Some hold crossbows. Everyone, including both Z Germans are present. They hold torches lit mid-day. There is still a sense of panic in the group but this is obviously a drill practiced before.

Tess, Tasha and Marcello move a large boulder. It is set on tracks made of Teak wood which hides a pit below. Stone scrapes wood. The wood beams serve as a cover and support above a long and dark path. We crawl on elbow and knees for about a hundred meters. I barely fit. At the other end there is a subterranean cave. I was not aware of it yet but the rest of the group seems to be familiar. The hatch near the north end of camp leads into another tunnel dug into the mud and then back farther into the limestone cliffs of the island. It opens to a cavern. Everyone fits inside.

It is damp but there is plenty of air. Z Germans place the torches on either end of the hall which provide enough light to see faces. At the front of the cavern I see Tex hand the Berretta to Marcello who remains in the cavern with us. Tasha and Tex then exit. At the end of the cave we can hear them close the hatch on the way back out to the village. Every other tribesman is here safely except the mermaid, who I figure chooses to remain in the ocean during such crises.

"OK. Will someone please tell me what the hell is going on?" I say after a moment of stillness.

"It's super complicated, bro," Max begins. "There is this guy, the Gentleman, and he liv ..."

"Everyone shut up ya!" Marcello says from the front of the tunnel. "Quiet ya."

I can hear that he is nervous. I make my way up the tunnel toward him. I figure it is best to be close to the guy with the gun, except he does not have it. In the dark I sense him nod to acknowledge my presence. He also implies to keep distance. Nely is in the tunnel near us as well. I can hear her soft breath. I remember the panicked scene in the square before coming to the cave. Nely held a crossbow there. Now she has my gun. I fantasize about taking it back. I decide against it. We sit in the mud entryway in total silence until the sound of stone scraping wood is heard again.

"All clear," Tex says.

No one wants to stay another minute in the dank cave or the stuffy tunnel. It is almost night time when we exit.

"Everyone get some water, we will meet in half an hour," Tex says just as Alice, the last in the chain of hideouts, emerges from the tunnel.

"Yup."
"Sure."
"Oui."

No one talks until we meet on the deck in the center of the village. It is the first seriously bad group meeting of the Tribe since Jonah and I arrived. The council is quietly sharing details among themselves. The three girls Tasha, Svet and Nely being the newest members. I pick up a few points here and there. Words like Gentleman, army, prostitutes, money, guns, people, the Tribe, sex, food, death. They are in a tight circle of discussion.

"Who is this Gentleman?" I ask. "No one ever answers me."

"OK, sorry if I am breaking Tribe protocol and all," I stand up and yell, "Will someone please explain what the hell is going on!"

I am loud, everyone stares for a moment.

Tex instantly stands and turns to me. He makes eye contact with me, "To put it simply, Tasha is willing to give up her body to a common criminal so you can stay on the island." He then speaks to the rest of the regular tribesman and says, "Fill him in, y'all." A moment later Tex and Tasha jump down from the deck and walk away. Marcello storms off in the opposite direction.

I am bombarded with information which everyone seems to have pent up.

"He is the guy who keeps this place secret," Jonah throws out first.
"He insists on be called the Gentleman," Monica snickers.
"Some Indo gangbanger," Max explains.
"Who dug his way through the shit just to become the major of it."
Nely explains in an unusually long sentence for her.

"Fleeces the gold mines in Sumbawa just across the channel," Tess says.

"He has my ski, the cunt," Max grumbles.

"Merde," Alice says in French.

"One time they come and ties us up for fun. Then stomp out the fire just to because," one of Z Germans says.

"Merde," Alice says in French again.

"His stronghold is on the other end of the island. He stays there during collection periods," Howard says.

"Nothing goes in or out of that gold mine without his say and his cut. Greedy cunt," Max says.

"His naval bombs line this island," Nely says.

"She is the Gentleman's favorite," Svet says looking in the direction of Tasha's departure.

"No matter how many Russian prostitutes he cuts through, no one pleases him quite like Tasha," Tess adds.

"Thinks he can have anything he wants," says Monica.

"And does anything he feels like," Goldie adds.

When everyone runs out of steam, Goldie asks me to take a walk with him.

"It has been the arrangement for several years," Goldie begins. "One time, before most of the Tribe came to the island, the Gentleman arrived with a small army platoon. Gabriel hid himself in the jungle but heard the shots as every other person alive on the island was killed. Two people survived. After, nobody saw the Gentleman for years. Then, about a year from the time Tex, myself, Monica and Howard came ashore he showed up again. A few of the Tribe were taken right here out of the village in the middle of the night. There were others on the island then, too. Others we do not talk about now. He told us our numbers were getting too high so he took three girls with him back to his side of the island. Those whom he thought could please him."

"What happened to the girls?" I ask.

"He raped and killed them. The bodies were dropped from the helicopter directly onto the beach. One by one."

"Holy shit. What did you do?"

"We buried them on the cliff."

"No, I mean, how did you fight back?"

"How could we, he has a helicopter and machine guns. We have a couple bow and arrows."

"So you did nothing?"

"Not true. The Gentleman probably would have killed everyone here if Tasha had not offered to go back with him, every time he comes to the island, if he stopped killing people."

"Go back?" I ask confused.

"Yes, Tasha used to work for him," Goldie begins. "A personal assistant, of sorts. She would fly in and out of the island with him on the chopper. One night she snuck off and made it to our side. There is some impassable ridge through the cliffs. Or we thought impassible. One night she just joined us," Goldie continues. "She met Marcello and decided to stay with us for good."

"Why would this Gentleman allow her to stay?" I ask in disbelief, knowing plenty of such criminal characters.

"Tasha balanced the equation for us in one simple arrangement. The Gentleman allows her to stay with the Tribe, safely, as long as she joins him when called upon. Violence never would have achieved this."

"I get it. So this thing between Marcello and Tasha is all messed up because of the Gentleman?" I ask.

I hear a breaking twig and turn around. Jonah and Max have been following us. "They used to have a thing but Marcello can't deal with the second boner," Jonah informs me.

"Yes, it seems Marcello and the Gentleman are both mad in love with Tasha, Marcello simply can't stomach sharing her," Goldie explains.

"Especially with a tyrant housing an unquenchable thirst for beautiful Russian girls," Max adds from a safe distance behind.

"Correct."

"So this Gentleman is both a blessing and a curse. He keeps this island a secret but at a heavy cost."

"Very heavy."

We return to the group about the same time as Tex and Tasha. Marcello returns from another path.

"The Gentleman is less than pleased with how large our group has grown on 'his island,'" Tex tells us first.

People turn heads at Jonah and I. It awakens me to the possibility that our arrival might have had an impact on the group's survival, which I never took seriously. It really wasn't just about food supplies. Death on either side of the island is a visceral reality.

Tasha addresses the Tribe.

"Luckily he will be occupied this trip. Has brought a few girls, but not as many as usual. The Prostitutki want more and more money for their employment each year," she says and laughs. No one else does. "I am going to stay with him until he leaves the island. I will do my best to keep him distracted."

"This is bullshit ya," Marcello says under his breath. The only other person to acknowledge it is Goldie, who shakes his head and looks away.

"You are all safe to go about your business, the Gentleman has no interest in the Tribe at the moment," Tex says to the group.

That night Marcello and Tasha are the only people missing from the common sleeping hall. In the morning the helicopter lands on the beach and Tasha goes to work. A week later the first naked body washes up on shore. The face looks Russian in features. Everything else is mangled.

We don't see Tasha again for months.

Ignorance Is Bliss

The stress of the incident a few days ago is quickly forgotten as people return to existence in the moment. Tasha seems to be forgotten, even as she performs the most important responsibility out of all thirteen of us. Forgotten by all except one.

The Marshal

Like the rest of the group, I go about my work, happy with a bountiful harvest season. I think about the flawless reef we get to enjoy every day. With the return of the dry season the wind is offshore again and the wave machine has not failed for weeks. Jonah and Max continue their wave war like two immortal titans. Neither will ever win that fight. However Jonah has finally given in to Amelia, and after a lifetime of chasing tail, he has finally found a real match. We see each other less but Jonah has never been so happy with a woman.

I think about ways to repair the relationship with Tess. When I kiss her the passion is cold. She rarely looks me in the eye. We lay together in the common hall where her sleepy head occasionally finds its way to my chest during the night. I savor those nights. I have never been a natural with women and now that I actually care about one, it is exponentially harder to understand. Monica tells me it will take time for her to heal. Luckily we have time.

More than anything, I think about my friends on the island and how unusual it feels to belong to a group, really belong. It is our third dry season here and the island finally feels like home. The ebb and flow here is so different. It is also more delicate than imaginable but people thrive in their own being, as do I. We are happy.

Then there is Marcello. Since the arrival of the Gentleman, our marshal has rarely been to the village except for food. Instead, he is seen stalking around the boundaries of our turf. He spends every day of Tasha's absence the same way. Early mornings he is in the banana trees watching for unusual movements of the cautious primates. By the time the sun is in a mid-morning position he moves to Sunrise Cliff - which has a glimpse of the Gentleman's helicopter pad on the north east side of the island. With his back to the rising sun, he can see their movements in the distance but they are blind to his. At peak sun he is on the South Cliff looking for patrol boats or reinforcements coming towards our bay. Luckily he has not yet had to raise another alarm. Sunsets he waits in the bushes along the ridge to the Gentleman's side of the island, the side no one else is thinking about.

Occasionally the tranquility of the day is pierced by a very foreign sound. Gunshots break the tranquil environment from time to time and the noise ricochets off the cliffs of our bay. I know they are not from my gun, as Tex has commandeered it for the time being. It sounds more like target practice or warning shots. Not wasteful practice of course, for bullets are just as hard to come by as guns in Indonesia.

One day in the field, Svet tries to make a move on me but I know she is only motivated by an effort to get back at Marcello for abandoning her. She cries and I do my best to comfort her. Later that same day a big group of us are in the mess hall assisting Goldie as he preps for dinner. Marcello walks in, a determined gait in his step.

"We could take them, tonight ya," he confidently states.

"What's that, bro?" Jonah asks innocently.

"The Gentleman and his people. At least half of the paramilitaries left on a speed boat yesterday. They did not come back. That means just a few guys and the personal bodyguards. I have never seen his place so unguarded."

"Why not go after him, then?" Jonah instigates. "It's our island too."

"Mate, I would love to get my ski back and be rid of this munted shithead, but reminder dude, large helicopter, small army of goons, machine guns, bombs, radios, night vision, grenades, missiles, etcetera, etcetera," Max reminds all of us.

"He has Tasha. Again," Marcello declares with anger.

"That is her choice and her sacrifice," Tex says as he enters the conversation.

"He gets more twisted every time. How long do you think this bullshit peace arrangement will really last?" Marcello questions his leader.

"Don't forget that we serve another purpose to the Gentleman. We are here year round making sure people don't come and go. If they come, we force them to stay or recognize the need for death. We handle that when he cannot. We keep the masses at bay. Both groups in the agreement keep the island a secret," Tex says.

"And what is that secret worth to you, Tex?" Marcello scoffs.

"I think you know the answer to that, Marcello."

"Then let's take the entire island this time ya," he says with a lift of encouragement. "It will be ours and ours alone."

"And what do you recommend then, Marcello?" Tex entertains the idea in order to allow Marcello to vent. "What would you have us do?"

"Throw everything we have at this feral bastard and company," Marcello begins. "Take him at night ya, we can go one by one on the pass…"

"Flawless," Tex cuts him short. "Let us assume for the moment you do succeed in gapping the pass and you make it all the way to the beast's lair. You kill every one of his henchmen and none of the Tribe gets hurt on the way. You come to the bedroom where he hides with your lover. You smash the door down and fly in like a knight from fairy tales of old. Except, when you do, the Gentleman has a gun pointed at Tasha while he uses her body as a shield. What happens then Marcello? What do you do then to save us all and take the island?"

"I shoot straight," he answers after a long pause.

"Dude is talking some crazy beef, De," Jonah whispers to me so I alone can hear it.

"We have Deon's gun," Marcello responds looking at me. "We have three highly trained agents. We have the element of surprise. This is our chance to take the island back ya."

"It's a handgun with three clips. How much damage do you really think it could inflict," I join the argument with sound military logic.

"You owe me one, Deon," Marcello looks at me with piercing daggers.

"I don't owe you this."

"You do. We could end this tonight, ya." Emotion has now fully taken over reason.

"It could all end tonight, end for all of us," Goldie steps in.

"You are a chef. Worry about the balance of sea salt and fish," Marcello loses his cool.

"ENOUGH!" Tex shouts.

"Marcello, Goldie is correct. An offensive attack could end everything. Permanently," I begin explaining in the military jargon Marcello and I have trained in. "Based on my Intel from the other side and what you have explained to me the past few days, this is the more probable outcome." I continue," The path to the other side is a narrow choke point to a walled compound. We will be easy targets on the pass, gunned down like ants marching in a line. Even if we did make it down the pass and into the courtyard, it is a textbook red zone for snipers and ordinance. If the palace is guarded by a third of the normal reserves you counted, we wouldn't make it to the front door. Once we are eliminated what do you expect to happen to the rest of the Tribe?"

"It's true, mate, the asswipe will march down here and waste every one of us in cold blood," Max finishes for me.

"You have not thought this one through, brother," I warn him calmly.

"Just the two of us then, Deon," he responds after another long pause to think. "Everyone else can hide in the tunnel."

"And that will take what, one grenade to collapse?"

"Come on, Deon."

"I won't risk that."

"Everyone dies someday."

"But not today."

"Nely?" He pleads with his sidekick.

"Balagan," Nely answers him shaking her head. "It is a fortress. It cannot be done this way."

"We can do it," Marcello begins to choke up. "Just you and I."

"Lo."

"The reward is worth the risk," in a final justification for his mad idea.

"It is not. I forbid it," Tex finalizes. "End of discussion."

Marcello turns and exits. He sighs in defeat over a battle that never occurred.

The next day I find him on his regular rounds. He is sitting on top of Sunset Cliff. The peak sun is very hot. Nely is not with him. We don't say anything for a while so I just come out and say it.

"What about going back to Svet? She misses you man and she is so sweet," I entreat him. "Don't you think things are simpler that way brother?"

"Not everyone settles for simple ya," he zaps me in that snakelike way only Marcello can.

"Simple is such a wonderful thing," I think to myself.

But Marcello and Svet end up in the Jungle Hut that night and they both smile for a few days.

House Guests

It is midday. Amelia and Jonah have been playing in the water for hours. Body surfing is not really his thing, but he is trying.

They are the first to notice it. Jonah finds Tex in the mess hall. Tex finds me.

"There is a raft approaching the island. It will most likely make the channel," Tex informs me as he hands me a loaded crossbow. He gives a second one to Jonah, who appears completely awkward with a weapon in hand. I can see Tex has my gun holstered on his hip as he moves down the path away from the Aquaponic farm.

At about fifty paces, he pauses and turns, "Coming?"
We arrive at the tree line minutes later. Just the three of us.

"What about Marcello, isn't this his job?" Jonah asks. "I have fish to catch."

"Marcello is not here," Tex replies.

"Let's find him then," Jonah suggests.

"No," Tex says with finality. "This will be handled now."

"Ok, let's go say hi."

"Not this time."

"Why not? There are just two of them, Amelia says they look harmless."

"Because Tex has other plans," I inform Jonah.

"That is correct. You two have tipped the balance once. Now you will tip it back," Tex tells me in a cold tone.

The couple on a raft are approaching the cliffs. We can see the rig in the distance. It looks to be made from hollow plastic gas cans resting high above the water line. It does not have nearly enough weight or depth to set off the naval mines. Luckily for us, they get caught in the current on their first pass.

"What are we doing here Tex?" I inquire.

"If they make it into the bay, two lives are forfeit." Tex looks out at the gap in the southern wall. The raft moves into sight, south of the pillar. They make it through with ease.

"That was a little cryptic, fearless leader man," Jonah jabs.

"I will clarify then. When they land, you and Deon will kill them."

"Like hell we will," Jonah stammers. "That is for the council to decide."

"I am the council."

"At least let us send them off. Everyone deserves a chance, we can send them away if need be," he pleads.

"So they can tell the whole world about us? About this place? About that wave you two cherish above all else?"

"It's just a wave."

"Is it?"

"Do you really understand the island?" he asks neither of us directly. "Why we are allowed to stay? There is no time for a trial now so everyone can feel better about what has to be done. This is an Executive Order and you two will carry it out," Tex says as he rests his fingers on my gun.

"Duck you, Tex."

Tex becomes irate.

"This is not the first time we have killed to protect our island and it will not be the last. You think this group here," Tex looks back in the direction of the village. "The Tribe, the one you see every day, the one you have joined, the one you love, your family, do you think that we are the first group to call this place home?" Tears form in his eyes. "We are not. Things come to pass at a cost. That psychopath living there," Tex points in the direction of the Gentleman's compound. "One day he came down and killed everyone, twenty two people to be exact. Happy survivors, beautiful people. He did it in minutes while Goldie... Oh, that bitch Tasha, she was there too, his acting secretary and translator. Gabriel, he hid in the bush. The only reason my life was spared is pure purpose." Tex pauses. "We are the population control, ironically living in fear of total extinction."

Tex looks at the raft that is nearly across the reef and into the channel. "The Tribe. They risked everything to allow you two safety." Tex looks at us. "They voted against me."

"That is how it works, right? Democracy?" Jonah can't help himself, even at a moment like this.

"Listen closely, you arrogant cunt," Tex glares at Jonah. "He has decimated the population before. He can easily do it again. I was told we were allowed no more than a dozen tribesman on the Gentleman's last friendly visit. Now we have fifteen and quite an obvious number fifteen at that." He concludes, looking at me. "They die, or we all die."

The boat is close. We can see the smiles of the excited couple on board. One time we held that same feeling.

"It's still not right," Jonah insists.

"But it is necessary to protect our home. "

As the boat nearly reaches shore, Jonah drops his weapon to the ground as a final protest. Tex picks it up and walks directly at the arriving guests. I know they are speaking because I can see their mouths moving, but it is too far away to make out the words. He approaches the young man first and fires an arrow into his bare chest. He drops the crossbow into the sand and draws the Barretta. I break into a full sprint toward the scene. The girl is screaming.

Tex turns to her and says, "It will be less painful this way." Bone and brain matter explode out the back of her skull. It takes a fraction of a second and then the gun finds its way back into the holster. The two bodies fall from the raft into the shallows. Blood flows red on the surface of the turquoise bay. Tex turns back to the tree line and walks at a brisk pace. Our paths cross halfway.

"Do you understand?"
"Yes."
"Will you interfere again?"
"No."
"Then bury the bodies."

Falsa Balsa

It has been a week now and our island marshal is back to his normal rounds with a little more perk in his step. Jonah on the other hand is still reeling from the scene on the beach. He has barely been in the water for days. A fresh thought of an old promise sends me stalking through the northern forest first thing in the morning. I never hear him coming from behind and, once again, can't believe he one-upped me.

"Still can get the drop on you, brother," he gloats. His mouth is an inch from my ear as I become lightheaded from the chokehold.

"Marcello," I gasp. "Lemme go."

"What are you doing out here this early. You should be in the water, ya?" He releases me and waits for a response to his inquiry.

"This is what I came by to chat about," I start off while rubbing my neck where he was strangling me a moment ago. "It is time for us to make that new board."

"Oh. Ok. Let's all just forget about the menace up there, ya," he starts off. "Why not just go surfing, brah?" He says, echoing Jonah.

"Exactly. There is nothing you can do now. She has been there before and she will come back. She used to work for the MoFo. Trust me, this is important right now. You gotta get back in the water and recharge some juju."

Marcello stares me down for a while and then gives in, "Maybe you are right."

"Excellent!"

There is no Balsa in Indo. Other choices are sparse at best on the island. So, we search hard for appropriate wood. We find the tree at the edge of the forest, near the spot where soil and forest recede to the rocks that make up the northern ridge of our crater. It is a giant Banyan tree and the trunk is larger than Marcello. In Bali, killing this tree would be unthinkable for any reason.

As the Bodhi tree is sacred to the Buddhist, the Banyan tree is holy to the Hindu, a divine symbol of immortality. It symbolizes both the longevity and compassion of the divine creator, Brahma. In nature, the Banyan has the ability to survive and grow for centuries and its aerial roots often form additional trunks. Luckily for Marcello's Karma, one of the major root branches of this Banyan is massive, providing more than enough surface area to shape. Still, harming the sacred tree for no reason could be considered a cardinal sin of bad Karma. However, in the case of a Tribesman needing a board to surf the most flawless wave on earth, even Ketut would understand. We apologize to the tree as the saw chisel is hammered in. It takes the whole surf crew two hours to get the branch down and even longer to carry it back to the village.

The wood is soft and will need time to cure before we can shape it. Luckily the air is hot and dry, especially in the sun but even so we don't carve for a week. Jonah gets really into it. He has never shaped a board before. So, we end up making two boards from the same log.

Most of the tools needed are already in the village tool shed. Max helps show us the little tricks of each instrument and I guide them through the soul of shaping. Once the template of each board has been drawn and sculpted, a wood planing tool carefully shaves and perfects the details. By the end of the process each stroke of the plane is guided with the utmost care. Marcello and Jonah really take their time on the last few, caressing their love and respect into their boards.

It's not until the finishing process that we need help.

"Hey, some of those wrecks out there have to have wooden hulls or decks, right?" I ask Amelia.

"Yeah, true," she responds. "Once upon a time at least. Why?"

"We need some Varnish, big tin can, says Varnish," I tease Amelia. "Can you find some for us?"

"Think I can handle that, land mammal!"

"Thanks, starfish." Jonah smiles.

"Don't look now." Amelia signals over my shoulder using her eyes. I turn to see Tess has joined us.

"Thought I might come around. Maybe I can help, too," she volunteers.

"Yes, absolutely. Don't doubt both of these guys would love a touch of your brush on their new surfboard." I grin, happy to see her. "It will have to be finished before we put the Varnish and sealant down."

"Glad to help," Tess says. The next day when she comes by to do her part, she asks, "What should I paint?"

"Girls, of course," I chuckle.

Within a couple hours there is a full length portrait of Amelia on the deck of Jonah's board. "Amazing," I jest. "Who wouldn't want an inlay of their personal mermaid?" We all laugh. Tess chooses to paint a beautiful depiction of Svet on Marcello's deck. She is holding a flower. He smiles when it is finished. The boards are sealed and ready to surf the next day. Sunset session is small but all smiles.

Anniversary

Today marks the fifteenth year of marriage between Tex and Goldie. Indonesia might have a law against it, but there are no rules about gay matrimony here. We cook for them while they spend the entire day sleeping in hammocks under the palms. Simple words spoken from the couple lead us into the celebration, "Tonight, let's get drunk."

That is exactly what happens.

Big ...Whatever Day of the Week

The swell arrives sometime in the night. It sounds like bombs going off. Jonah can't sleep all night. Neither does the rest of the Tribe. At first light he is up watching it. The beach is all but gone as walls of water break over the reef and make their way up the sand nearly to the tree line.

"It's huge, Jo," I say.

"I see."

Max pops up behind me. "All closeouts, aye boys?"

"Haven't seen it like this in years," Howard butts in as usual.

It's true. The swell is too big and the whole bay is closing out. Jonah can't take his eyes off of it. Walls of water nearly half the size of the cliffs above the bay make their way through the deep channel, reform and then fold over all at once. From where we stand it looks as if there is nothing to surf. Only enormous ranks of whitewater with nowhere to go and those are not fun at all.

"Guess we are gonna have to sit this one out, yeah bud?" I say to my friend.

"I'm not going anywhere," he says, board held in place under arm.

"Jo, there is no shape, just walls of white. Let's get some morning work done in the village," I say, turning back to the tree-line.

"Catch yas at breakfast, matey," Max says to his only competition on the island.

"Maybe," he says unmoved.

Jonah is not there for breakfast, or lunch either. Even Amelia has come to land. "The current is just too strong out there," she complains.

After midday sun, I go to check on Jonah but he has gone from the beach. The tide has shifted lower and I can see footsteps in the freshly exposed sand. They lead to Three Palm Point on the South Cliff. I follow the trail. Jonah is sitting in the shade of one of the palms.

"Brought you some agua, bro."

"Thanks Big Ed." He downs it quickly. There are also a few coconut husks next to him. It is hot.

"How was breakfast?" he asks.

"Delicious as usual," I answer. "How are the waves?"

"Tide is still high, no ducking chance at a paddle out."

We sit for a while. "Watch," he says, "The medium size sets, they are useless. The swell hits the North Cliff too hard and doesn't have a damn chance to wrap the outer reef before closing out the freakin' pillar. But the big ones Eddie, you gotta see the big ones, bro."

About fifteen minutes pass in idle chat and then a corduroy of swell appears way out over the Indian Ocean. Jonah stands to his feet and shouts, "Here it comes." The breaking wave must be nine or ten meters high. It jacks up on the reef in front of the opposing cliff and wraps the reef with incredible speed. It holds a surfable line but doesn't quite clear the pillar guarding the bay.

"It still smashes into the pillar dude," I say to Jonah in a consoling tone.

"I know, but check this out. What time is it? About two o'clock?" he asks me.

"Yeah, probably."

"Tide's not bottomed-out yet. It's gonna work, you'll see. At dead low. I know it, brah. It's ducking gotta work!"

I look again at the waves. It looks like death to me.

"It's hot up here, Jo."

"Wait," he pleads. "Just watch with me, man."

"There is no way in hell we are surfing out there, dude," I begin reasoning with him. "The wave itself is scary enough, but all those hulled-out boats from the mines. They get exposed at dead low tide. Come on, Jo. We're not talking wiping out at the wedge. That, out there, that's jagged reef with skeleton monsters waiting to eat you."

"I gotta see it, De."

"You gonna stay up here till sundown?"

"Yup."

"You want some real food?"

"I'd love some."

"Cool, be back in a while."

A couple hours pass. Before I can make it back up to the lookout point Jonah comes screaming down the path.

"De, Max, Howard. You boys gotta see this."

"See what?" Max asks.

"The wave!"

"The wave is closing, been too big all day."

"Not the outer reef."

"Out where?"

"Com. Wa." Jonah can barely speak he is so excited. He goes racing off and we can hardly keep up.

"Look." He points.

Just as the sun is starting to set over our left shoulder, a group of waves appear on our right. The set is rolling through and we have a perfect vantage point. It is a big one. With the water sucked completely out, the outer reef is far more exposed. Jonah is correct in his prediction, kind of. There are about a dozen waves in the set and each is breaking farther back on the reef. It builds in the same fashion as before, starting to build on the other cliff and wrapping over the reef toward the pillar. However, about one in three waves clear the pillar and continue to peel across to the second gap in the cliff.

"See," Jonah says.

"Dude, you are absolutely munted. Deeply, deeply depraved. Is your brain even turned on? Cause you better flip that switch and check your noodle if you think we are gonna paddle that," Max lays into Jonah.

The tide is so low and the swell so big, as the water sucks back to form the massive waves, you can actually see the hull of the yacht Tex and Goldie arrived in.

"Scared?"

"Not scared, just not munted like you."

"You are scared."

"Mate, it's all fun and games till someone gets killed, you mental asswipe."

Max turns and walks down the cliff. Howard puts his hand on Jonah's shoulder and then follows Max. I stay with my friend until the sun sets.

The swell holds through the night. Thunderous booms and walls of whitewater backlit by moonlight. The surge, assisted by the high tide, makes it all the way to the jungle line. No one can sleep. Just after midnight or so the whole dormitory empties. We all go down to the beach to listen. Everyone writes it off as too big to surf. Everyone except Jonah.

Before dawn he is in the water. Amelia spots him first and wakes us all up. Everyone quits the village to come out and watch. About the time we reach South Cliff, Jonah has defeated the currents. He times it just right and is sitting way out back. The set arrives shortly after.

Jonah paddles for the first set wave, makes the drop and comes firing back up the face with full momentum. Then, with a huge air, he launches off the top of the lip and literally hurtles over the rock pillar. By this incredible feat, he connects both sections of the wave and kicks out the back before the wave sucks dry. He looks up at us on the cliff with both hands in the air. His body screams, "I told you I could do it!" But, instead of coming back into the bay he back-paddles for a second wave. It is bigger than the first. The entire thing engulfs him in a giant stand up tube and he comes screaming out just five meters short of the wrecked yacht.

The entire Tribe goes wild with excitement. You can sense Jonah feeding off the energy. It is ten minutes before the next set of waves corduroy the horizon. He is waiting and watching. Jonah cues for the fourth wave in the group. It is huge, by far the biggest wave I have ever witnessed. Jonah paddles with all his might. He makes the drop well behind Sunset Cliff and appears to fall from a skyscraper. As crazy fast as he is falling, he is no match for the speed of the wave. Jonah does not get enough momentum off the bottom turn and the heaving beast closes out on him. We see his surfboard shatter against the pillar.

Amelia dives off the cliff. She gets there quickly with her monofin and knife. She cuts the leash from his ankle just as Jonah has swallowed enough water to drown. Howard and I paddle out to save him. We hug the cliff as close as possible to avoid the vicious current. We stroke the water as if our own lives hang in the balance. Jonah is unconscious but with Amelia's help we get him onto the bigger longboard. Howard jumps up and straddles Jonah's body. He pumps on his chest and performs CPR using the longboard as a stretcher in the surge of the deepwater channel. I have to ditch my own board so Amelia and I can stabilize doctor and patient while pulling them back toward the sanctuary of the North Cliff. We find a protected area of the cove and after a few minutes Howard manages to resuscitate my best friend.

He coughs up water. We get him to the beach. Jonah's arms are mangled from the razor sharp coral reef. His right thumb hangs by a thread of ligaments. I touch the scars on my face from the wounds repaired in Bali an age ago. They were nothing compared to Jonah's now. His face is wide open across the left side and blood spills from an open gash. His right eye hangs out of the socket. Amelia is hysterical.

"Can you patch him up?" I ask Howard through tears. "Please."

"I will do my best."

I spend the next weeks in Jonah's hut assisting Howard at every turn of health. Tess spends as much time with me as she can handle. She sleeps with me at night in the bed next to Jonah and Amelia.

All Good Things.

I stand in the middle of the village, my gun pointed at my head. Two more from behind.

Let me catch you up to speed.

A body was dropped on the beach yesterday morning. She was badly beaten but alive. It was Tasha. She tells us that the Gentleman is getting anxious again. He says it is a warning that the group is growing too large and it could mean the end of our arrangement.

Sometime in the night Marcello secretly takes my gun. He scales the pass through the western ridge which leads to the Gentleman's stronghold. It was a feeble but heroic attempt to end the conflict by his own means. He is captured and beaten near to death. He never made it to the front door.

On the island, Hayarti is known only by a new nickname of his choice, 'The Gentleman.' Of course he recognizes the pistol given to me as severance pay for our past endeavors together. He has come down to the village with the two Pygmy guards. They are armed with assault rifles. Hayarti carries my Beretta in hand and a personal pistol is holstered on his hip.

Marcello's body is thrown upon the square platform in the center of the village. Tasha lies next to him. They are still breathing. Barely. Just so there is no question about the severity of the situation, The Gentleman points my gun at Tasha and pulls the trigger in front of us. Blood leaks from her chest. He orders the Tribe to come out in full.

He calls me by my last name.

"Mister Montgomery!"

The entire tribe has been rounded up. They are forced to kneel in the sand. Like I said before, there are three guns pointed at me.

"Mr. Montgomery." Hayarti spits on Marcello's near lifeless body. "You betray me, after all we have accomplished together and you send a simple assassin, a nigger like yourself, to kill me. I discerned your plot and I do not approve."

"What is he talking about, Deon?" Jonah stands next to me.

"Jo. There is a lot you don't know about me. I have kept many of the details about my past from you. I have had to do bad things for bad people in the past so good things can happen for good people. I always thought the ends justified the means, especially when no one else was willing to help."

"So it is true! And now you plot against your former employer," Hayarti shouts.

"No, with politeness I say you are mistaken, Mr. Hayarti. Your presence here on the island was unknown to me. I travelled in ignorance with my friend. We came to surf--- nothing more."

"Then why did you ask for a gun, specifically your gun, when you came to me on Gili Trawangan?"

"Protection, simple protection from simple bandits."

"I am NOT a simple bandit!"

"Your logic is sound, Pa Hayarti. If I had known this island was yours I would not have come. I was ignorant. I am learning all of this right now in the moment. I meant no harm."

"You are ignorant."

"Yes."

"You are only here to surf, not like in Sumatra?"

"This is true."

He hands me my gun, grip down, safety on. The weight seems heavy after so much time without handling it. Hayarti immediately points his own gun at me.

"Prove yourself," he says.

"How?" I ask.

He extends the three clips of bullets to me. His gun and the two automatic rifles remain targeted.

"Pa Montgomery, I believe you," he begins. "You have never left me any doubt or tried to betray me in the past."

"Thank you, Mr. Hayarti."

"However, that broken beast there killed my pilot in an attempt to kill me. For that there will be retribution," he begins after a quick glance at Tex and then walks toward our leader. "Our previous arrangement has ended," Hayarti exclaims as he kicks Tex's head down into the sand. "You see, Mr. Montgomery," Hayarti turns his dark eyes back to me, "Tex and Goldie, they were given a simple choice once, the same choice I am about to offer you." A smile creeps up his face. "When I discovered you were here, on my island, well I just had to come myself and see you. See your face after all those years without. See your mind process all this information in that way it does. In the way you like to choose the lesser of two evils. The way that you like to pretend your actions are preordained and out of your control. Thus, I will make it simple for you. There is only one choice this time, Mr. Montgomery. You and your blonde friend may stay. From now on you, you two alone, will guard this side of the island from pests. The rest must be exterminated," Hayarti tells me. His orders are clear.

"What?" Jonah shouts. "Go FUCK yourself."

"Quiet, Jo." I look back at my friend.

"Dude is crazy if he thinks you are gonna kill all these people," Jonah stammers. "Our Tribe."

"He is not crazy Jonah, he is totally insane."

"I don't suffer from insanity, I enjoy every minute of it." Hayarti smiles wider like an aged maniac.

"You have until the count of five, Deon. It will be a slow count because I wish to savor every moment. If you do not begin cleansing these parasites off my island, I will kill you along with them. Personally, I prefer to save my ammunition." With Hayarti's orders our conversation ends. He gives a command to the two pygmies in Indonesian. Then he begins counting.

"One."

I turn the gun in my hand and load the first clip into it.

"Two."

I chamber the round.

"OK, De, it's time to get ghetto on these Indo fools," Jonah says discretely to me.

"Three."

I look back at my friend. I look at the guns pointed at me. They could kill me and then every remaining member of the Tribe in five seconds. I look back at my friend. My eyes show my sorrow.

"No, Deon, you can't!" Jonah shouts.

One of the Pygmy guards hits Jonah in the face with his riffle, despite the bandages.

"Four."

I walk to the platform. Marcello is barely breathing. He has been tortured. There is blood flowing from several open wounds. He has been castrated. His hand clings to Tasha's corpse.

"You always got the drop on me partner," I tell him with the tone of honest respect as a friend and a brother. He raises his right arm. Our hands grasp and hold tight. It is the closest thing to an embrace we can have. I click the safety off.

"Five."

The gun kicks upward from the recoil. It is more of a mercy killing than a murder.

I wipe the blood and sweat from my face. The entire group is looking at me. I turn to Tex on the ground. I aim.

"I am sorry, Tex," I mouth to him.

"I understand, Deon. It is the same choice I accepted all those years ago," he confesses.

They are his last words. Tex is executed with two bullets in the head. I take a deep breath.

Time is now moving very slowly again. Like the first time I killed and every time between, I cannot choke down the emotions or silence my inner voice.

"I will miss your cooking. You are one hell of a chef," I tell Goldie as his green eyes look up at me.

He turns to the lifeless body of his partner and then back to me with tears filling those green eyes. "I couldn't live without him anyway," he says, offering permission of sorts through his sorrow. I squeeze off two more shots.

I take a deep breath.
I turn to the Svet.
She receives a pair.
Someone cries out.
I remind myself of Tex's lecture. His dire actions to conserve our way of life here on the island. His words from the beach ring in my ear, "They die, or we all die."

I start to weep.

I put a new clip in the chamber and empty three shots for Z Germans. The French girl starts to run and I gun her down in the back. Everyone else remains seated, frozen, staring at me. They are waiting to die. I take another deep breath. When my gun targets Nely I make hard eye contact with her. Her eyes say, "I understand." I look right, then left. The message is clear. I double check my peripheral vision. She nods her head to the left and then right, accepting her fate.

It happens fast.

The Pygmies have started to relax and watch the show unfold. I spin around as quickly as I can putting several bullets into the Pygmy closest to me. Then I throw the pistol in Nely's direction.

The second Pygmy does not notice the toss and instinctively turns toward me. Remembering my days of basic training and how to duck and roll I hit the ground with speed putting as much distance between us as can be managed in the short time. The Pygmy is up and on the run. He reshoulders his rifle to take aim at me but before he can even fire his weapon, the little girl from the West Bank empties the rest of the clip into him. She then tosses the gun back in my direction. I crawl across the sand and reach for it. Once in hand, I pop out the empty clip and slide in the last full one. I manage this just in time to witness Nely being gunned down by Hayarti's six-shooter.

At the same moment Hayarti realizes he has shot down the unarmed Israeli girl, he pauses and turns his gun and gaze back to me. We shoot each other. In all this commotion we are very close in proximity. Hayarti is hit in the head twice, point blank. He folds and falls to the ground but before he makes it to the dirt he manages to squeeze off his last shots. I take three Indonesian bullets in the leg.

The three of us lay in a mixed pool of blood. Nely has just a few breaths of life remaining.

"Is he dead?" She asks me.
"He is dead," I say.
"Todah Raba."
"Bevakasha."

It is over.

The Last Chapter

The survivors of the event move me to Cliff Hut where infection is less likely. Two of the bullets have passed through my leg. Howard removes the third bullet from my calf and sows up the wounds. I lay in the hut listening to the waves outside for a short eternity. I have only this pen, this journal and a tremulous history to keep my mind occupied. Monica and Howard visit every day to check on me. They bring food from the farm. They inform me that once I heal they will return to Australia. Max and Tess recovered their jet ski and have long since left the island.

It takes time but I recover. However, my left leg is rendered useless. Any weight on it causes spasm and eventually the muscle atrophies and dies. I will spend the rest of my days in Paradise watching the perfect wave, handicapped. I cannot surf.

Dug into the limestone vantage point above the South Cliff, there are now eight new unmarked gravesites facing the wave. I sit with Jonah under the shade of the palm trees for a long time. It is the same spot where we watched the swell build nearly a year ago. It is the same spot we always watch the wave from above. We sit in silence for some time. We are alone.

"Without Hayarti and Tex guarding the island, people will show up like crazy," Jonah says to me while concentrating on the wave below with his eye.

"Let them come."

LAST THOUGHTS

"Surfing equates to living in the very moment of 'now'. When you ride a wave you leave behind all things important and unimportant, the purity of the moment is upon you."

— Billy Hamilton (surfer/shaper)

The Author

Tyler Trafas is the author of Tropical Depression and several short stories about life as a foreigner in Japan and Indonesia. He is a life long surfer and grew up in the waves near Los Angeles during the 80s and 90s. He graduated from Occidental college in 2004, where he studied East Asian Religions and Sociology.

Shortly after graduating, Tyler left Los Angeles to live in Japan. At first he worked as a private teacher and then later a professor of English at Meiji University. During this period he also found work in the entertainment districts of Osaka and Tokyo. After leaving Japan, Tyler spent the next few years traveling and chasing surf through Asia, primarily Indonesia, where he lived amongst surfers from a multitude of nationalities.

Tyler now lives with his dog River back in California, where he teaches a course on proper surf technique, surfer etiquette and the benefits of Yoga practice for new surfers. He also works on surfboards for fun, when he is not seeking that perfect wave.

www.ingramcontent.com/pod-product-compliance
Lightning Source LLC
Chambersburg PA
CBHW071301250626
47159CB00004B/1260